A TOXIC

Inheritance

BOOK EIGHT OF THE SYDNEY LEGAL SERIES

CHRIS TAYLOR

LCT Productions Pty Ltd
18364 Kamilaroi Highway, Narrabri NSW 2390

ISBN. 978-1-925119-60-2 (Paperback)

A Toxic Inheritance is a work of fiction. Names, characters, places, brands, media and incidents either are the product of the author's imagination or are used fictitiously. Any resemblance to actual persons, living or dead, events, or locales, is entirely coincidental.

Published in the United States of America.

BOOKS BY CHRIS TAYLOR

THE MUNRO FAMILY SERIES
The Profiler
The Investigator
The Predator
The Betrayal
The Deception
The Negotiator
The Christmas Vigil
The Ransom
The Defendant
The Shooting
The Maker
(Available in Audio)

THE SYDNEY HARBOUR HOSPITAL SERIES
The Perfect Husband
The Body Thief
The Baby Snatchers
The Final Bullet
The Debt Collector
The Lab Test
The Stolen Identity
The Cliff-top Killer
The Likeable Fraudster

THE SYDNEY LEGAL SERIES
An Accidental Murderer
At the Hand of Her Father
A Woman Scorned
Lies and Deception
Ordinary Evil
The Ties That Bind
The Perfect Crime
A Toxic Inheritance
Malicious Love

THIS IS WHERE IT ENDS SERIES
Jessie's story
Ryan's story

Holly's story
Sarah's story
Veronica's story

THE CRAIGDON FAMILY SERIES
Callum
Joel
Isabella
Nicholas
Sophia
Flynn
Noah
Logan
Elizabeth

THE BARRINGTON FAMILY SERIES
Broken Lives
Broken Promises
Broken Bonds
Broken Spirits
Broken Vows
Broken Minds
Broken Dreams
Broken Hearts
Broken Homes

Get a FREE book when you sign up for Chris Taylor's
newsletter at: www.christaylorauthor.com.au

Love Audiobooks? Check out Chris Taylor Books on audio
on Audible.com, Amazon.com and Apple Books.

Join Chris Taylor's Facebook reader group/fan page and be
among the first to receive news of book releases, read and
review books prior to release and other amazing offers. Join
Now at: www.facebook.com/groups/1758023621144744/

Find out more about all of Chris Taylor's books, by visiting her
website at: www.christaylorauthor.com.au/about/books

DEDICATION

This book is dedicated to my extended family and to all the families around the world. Though we might not always say it, we love you through the good, the bad and the downright ugly! Family are forever. Amen

And as always, to my husband, Linden. My best friend, my soul mate. I love you to the moon and back.

Acknowledgments

As usual, no book comes into being without a lot of help and support by my friends and family. A world of thanks must go to my wonderful editor, Pat Thomas. Thank you for everything that you do to make my stories even more amazing than I could ever dare to dream. To former Detective Superintendent Michael Kilfoyle, thank you for lending my story credibility. Any mistakes are wholly my own.

To Damon Freeman, Alisha Moore and all of the staff at damonza.com, thank you for yet another fantastic book cover. To my sister, Nicole Guihot and to my friend, Ally Thomson, thank you for your excellent editorial comments, proof reading skills and suggestions. I hope you like the final result.

To Amy Atwell and her dedicated staff at Author E.M.S. who are so much more than book formatters. Amy, once again, thank you for your magic.

To the fantastic writer organizations such as Romance Writers of Australia, Romance Writers of

America and Romance Writers of New Zealand for all the help, support and encouragement they offer new and aspiring writers, including me.

To my readers, thank you for your support and love for my stories. Your encouragement and enjoyment make this journey all worthwhile.

And lastly, to my friends and family, especially my husband and children. Thank you for putting up with late dinners and even later conversations as I've emerged day after day from the sometimes scary but always enthralling world I've created on my computer.

PROLOGUE

Sweat poured down Meghan Chifley's face. Her breath came fast and her forearms burned. Still, she didn't let up on the driving punches that connected with satisfying *thwacks* against the solid boxing bag that hung from the iron beam above her head. This was the kind of night she hated most.

Unable to sleep, her head filled with the familiar torment and distress caused by her family, she found herself in the basement gym of her building, taking her frustration and anger out on the boxing bag. Sometimes the punishment lasted for hours. More often than not, she collapsed, exhausted, on the cold concrete floor where she would finally find peace. At least for a little while.

One good thing—the only good thing—to come of such extreme physical exertion was the effect on her body. Slim and toned and muscled, without an ounce of fat, every time she caught a glimpse of herself naked in the mirror, she was reminded of the way Angelina Jolie looked in a number of the action films she'd starred in. Not that Meghan had set out to become a warrior queen. If her family hadn't been so dysfunctional, so unable to get along, it wouldn't have come to this. She couldn't help but wonder if other families went through the regular turmoil hers did. *Surely not.*

The sound of her phone ringing interrupted her dismal thoughts. She blinked in surprise. It was past one in the morning. *Who would be calling so late?* Tearing off her boxing gloves, she strode over to where she'd left her phone on the workbench and checked the screen.

Cody.

Her heart sank. There could be no good reason her twin brother was calling at this hour. She wondered what it was this time. She was determined not to give him any more money. She refused to support his drug habit, no matter how much she loved him.

Steeling herself for a difficult conversation, she answered the phone with a brusque "hello."

"Meggieeee, *thhhansk* goodness you *anshered*!"

She grimaced at the way he slurred his words. He was either drunk or high—or both. The speed at which her high-flying stock broker brother's life had spiraled down and out of control was frightening.

"What is it, Cody?"

"I-I know izzz's late and I shouldn't have called yyyou. No doubt you have some high profile court case to show up to in the morning. It's just that..."

His voice broke. A moment later, she heard him sob. Her heart clenched in an agony of indecision. *This was her brother!* Crying in such despair. He sounded…broken. She drew in a deep breath and let her impatience and irritation with him slide away.

"What is it, Cody?" she asked more gently this time.

"Meggie! I… I'm sorry! I'm so fucked up! I didn't mean to do it! He forced me! I didn't have a choice! Please, Meggie! *Please!* You've gotta believe me! I'm so sorry…"

Once again, he was overcome by a tumultuous bout of sobbing that tore at her heart. She forced herself to concentrate on what he'd said. Foreboding, in a cold trickle, slugged its way through her veins.

"What are you talking about, Cody? Who forced you to do what? You're not making sense!"

The call was abruptly terminated. In the dimness of the basement, she stared down at the phone in her hand, filled with a mixture of confusion, fear and disbelief.

"Oh, Cody," she whispered, her raspy voice loud in the silence. "For the love of God, what have you *done?*"

CHAPTER 1

The bright Monday morning sunshine that poured through her office window should have lifted Meghan Chifley's mood. Instead, she resisted the urge to scrub her fingers through her hair in frustration. The man who sat opposite her had tested her patience to the limit and she'd had just about enough. With a supreme effort, she gritted her teeth, drew in a calming breath and tried again.

"Mr Collins, you just don't seem to understand what I'm saying. Your father left his entire estate to be shared equally between you and your three siblings. Unless you can bring evidence to show cause as to why your siblings shouldn't get an equal share, I'm afraid there's nothing I can do."

"But they had nothing to do with my father! They didn't even live in the same city! Wesley lives in New York, for Pete's sake! He hasn't been back to Sydney for years! Marion only ever came around when she needed money. And as for Victoria, don't get me started on her. I'm the only one who ever visited our father! Helped him… Why should they get the same as me? It isn't fair!"

Once again, Meghan called on her patience. "I'm not disputing your dedication to your father," she said as calmly as she could manage. "From what you've told me, you were wonderful to him, especially during the last few months of his life. But the thing is, your father left his estate equally to his four children, as is his right. No court will overrule that without good reason to do so and unfortunately, your siblings' neglect and the selfishness you're referring to… Well that doesn't count."

The man continued to look belligerent and Meghan suppressed a sigh. Sometimes her job as an estate and probate attorney was like pushing a barrow of concrete uphill. When the phone on her desk buzzed, she breathed a silent sigh of relief.

"Excuse me," she murmured and picked up the receiver.

"Meghan, I have a man by the name of Arjun Patel on line three. He says it's urgent."

Meghan frowned at her secretary's announcement. *Why would her father's gardener be calling her and why would it be urgent?* A shiver of apprehension trickled down her spine.

"Meghan? Are you still there?"

Meghan blinked. "Yes, ah… Sure, Dorothy. I'm still here."

"Would you like me to take a message?"

"No, it's fine. I'll take the call."

She shot the man who sat across from her an apologetic smile. "I'm sorry, Mr Collins. I need to take this call. It's a family emergency. I think we're just about done here anyway, aren't we?"

Looking none too happy, her disgruntled client pushed back his chair and stood. "Are you sure there's nothing I can do to challenge the will?" he asked.

"Other than the fact you spent more time with your father than your siblings, do you have any reason the court would move to overrule your father's last wishes with regard to his estate?"

The man's shoulders slumped on a dejected sigh. "No. But it isn't fair."

She looked at him sympathetically. "You're right. It's not. But that's the way it goes. Of course, you can always bring a challenge, but I can't give you any guarantee of success. Now, if you don't mind, I really need to take this call. I'll be in touch as soon as the final paperwork is ready for your signature."

Collins nodded and turned toward the exit. As soon as he'd left the room, she picked up the phone. Concern over the reason for Arjun's call continued to swirl in her belly.

"Hi Arjun, it's Meghan. What can I do for you?"

"Meghan! I'm so glad I caught you. Have you spoken to your father recently?"

She frowned. "I called him last week. He was buying herbs at his local market. Said he was going to cook spaghetti sauce. Why?"

"It's just that I haven't seen him for a few days. Normally he takes his breakfast out by the pool. He's as regular as clockwork. Scrambled eggs, two pieces of toast, juice and coffee. He eats his breakfast and then reads the paper. Occasionally he'll call out to me and ask me about my day, but for the past three days he hasn't turned up. I wondered if he could be away."

Meghan's frown deepened. "No, not that I know of. He would have told me if he was going away. Are you sure he's not home?"

"He might be home, but I haven't seen him. I checked the gardens, the pool and the boathouse. I even checked the garage. All four of his cars are there."

"Have you been up to the house?"

"No."

"Have you spoken to Mrs Abbott?" Meghan asked, referring to her father's housekeeper.

"No. Mrs Abbott's mother died so Mrs Abbott's been away for a week. Your father's been there on his own."

"You're right. I remember he told me about that. The funeral's in the country. He told Mrs Abbott to take all the time she needed."

"Yes, he's always good to his staff," Arjun replied. "I offered to get my cousin to come in and cover for Mrs Abbott while she was away, but he assured me he was quite capable of looking after himself, for a short while at least."

"I wonder where he could be?" she murmured. "Have you tried calling him?"

"Yes. Several times. The calls went through to his voicemail."

"I see. Well, I'll try him, too. If I don't get an answer, I'll come over and see what's going on. Is that all right?"

Arjun's voice flooded with relief. "Yes! Thank you, Meghan! I knew you were the best one to call."

She pondered that comment for a moment and then shrugged. It was true. Out of the three of her father's children, she was probably the closest to him and she definitely spent the most time with him. She knew the staff better than her brother and half-sister did, too. No doubt that was why Arjun chose to call her.

"I'll let you know how I get on, okay?" she added.

Once again, the gardener's thanks were profuse and filled with relief. Meghan ended the call and then immediately fished her cell phone from her handbag, stowed under her desk. Quickly, she dialed her father's number. The call rang out and eventually went through to voicemail, just like Arjun had described.

"Hi, Daddy, it's Meghan. Call me, okay?" With a sigh she tossed the phone down on her desk, perplexed.

Could he have gone away without telling her? And where would he go? All of his motor vehicles were still in his garage, so if he went anywhere, it had been by cab. There was no way he'd hop on a bus or even the train. *Could he have caught a plane somewhere? Surely he wouldn't take a trip out of town without telling her.*

She sighed again. There was no help for it. She'd have to call at his home and check on him. A stirring of misgiving filled her belly. *What if he'd tripped and fallen down the stairs? What if he were hurt?* Even now, he could be lying injured, bleeding, in pain with no one the wiser.

Trying hard to tamp down her panic, she collected her handbag and picked up her phone. Tossing it into her bag, she strode across her office and opened the door.

"Dorothy, I need to go out for a while."

Her secretary acknowledged her comment with a nod. "Of course. How long will you be gone?"

"An hour or so."

"So you'll be back in time for your eleven o'clock?"

"Yes, I expect so."

"Good. Because they're new clients and I know for a fact the partners will be impressed if you manage to land them. They're the executors of a multimillion-dollar estate. It will mean significant fees for the firm and would go some way to supporting your quest for promotion." Her secretary shot her a quick sideways glance. "I take it you're still angling for a partnership?"

"Of course. Isn't that the goal of every junior attorney?"

"I'm just looking out for you, Meghan."

"Yes, and I appreciate it, Dorothy. You, above anyone, know how these hallowed halls work. I just have to duck out for a moment. It's a family emergency. I promise I won't be long."

"No problem. In case anyone asks, I'll cover for you while you're gone."

Meghan shot her a grateful look. The woman had been at Sydney Legal almost as long as the founding partners. There wasn't anything that happened in the place that Dorothy didn't know about.

Turning on her heel, Meghan headed toward the bank of elevators and pressed the button. It arrived a few minutes later and as the doors slid open, she was thankful it was empty. There could be several legitimate reasons why she might be leaving the office at just after nine in the morning, but she preferred not to have to explain her departure so soon after her arrival.

Striding from the building, she made her way to the parking spot where she'd left her car. Often it was quicker and more convenient to catch a bus into the city from her condo in Bondi, but today she'd taken her car and now she was grateful. Her father lived in an exclusive and ultra-expensive part of the eastern suburbs. Though there was a public bus that serviced the area, it would be much faster to get there by car.

It was the same place where Meghan and her brother and half-sister had grown up. She'd had a privileged childhood, but despite her father's wealth, she liked to think she was a well-rounded individual, prepared to work hard and do her bit to contribute to society. Just like Cody.

At the thought of her brother, she frowned. It had been three days since his bizarre late-night phone call. Though she'd called him back the next morning and several times after that, the calls had gone straight to voicemail. She was almost certain he'd gone on a bender—heroin was now his drug of choice—and she wouldn't hear from him again until he'd come out from under his drug-induced fog and decided to rejoin society. Sadly, this wasn't the first time.

Everyone suffered from his absence. Well, maybe not everyone...

Meghan had called her brother's estranged wife, Tanya, yesterday to ask if she'd heard from him. Tanya's response was brief and concise. She didn't give a fig where Meghan's brother was. The sooner he overdosed and removed his sorry ass from this world, the better, as far as she was concerned. She had two kids to raise and she didn't need him and his drug-addicted presence in their lives. Period.

Though Tanya's bitter spray saddened Meghan, it was well-deserved. Cody had gone from being a highly respected, incredibly talented stockbroker with a six figure annual income to a man who could hardly get out of bed in the morning, a man who had turned to illegal drugs. It had affected his career, his marriage, his relationships. She couldn't deny it had changed the way she felt about him. Even so he *was* her brother, her *twin*. For all his flaws, she could never abandon him. She'd been worried about him ever since that strange phone call. And now there was something up with their dad. Maybe.

Her late model white Mazda CX-3 stood where she'd left it, squeezed in between a large SUV and a pickup. Reversing out of the parking spot, she joined the stream of traffic headed south-east away from the city. Fortunately, rush hour was almost at an end and she made good time up New South Head Road.

Less than thirty minutes after she left the office, she pulled up at the high wrought iron gates outside her father's harborside mansion in the exclusive suburb of Point Piper. She punched in the security code and waited impatiently for the gates to swing open. Accelerating up the paved driveway, she drove past the manicured lawns and symmetrical flower beds brimming with color and finally came to a halt outside the grand entryway that led into the house. Climbing out of her Mazda, she walked up the wide stone steps to the front door. As usual, the handle turned beneath her fingers. Her father never locked the front door when he was home.

"Daddy? It's me. Where are you?"

Her voice echoed in the silence. She made her way across the glossy parquetry floor that lined the wide entryway and beyond and headed toward her father's study. The door was open so she entered.

The smell of his cologne immediately assailed her senses. Strong and pungent, smelling like alpine forests, it reminded her of all the times she'd sat in there reading or doing homework or texting her friends while he worked behind his cedar desk. He'd made his money from real estate and even at the age of sixty-two, he continued to oversee the business, mostly from this very room. It held so many fond memories, but right now it was devoid of life.

"Daddy?" she called again as she crossed the wide hall and into the kitchen. "Where are you?" Once again, the house was silent.

The kitchen was also empty. With a sound of frustration, she left the room and headed toward the staircase that was reminiscent of the resplendent staircase in *Gone with the Wind*. As a dreamy-eyed teenager, she'd found the whole idea of it so romantic. Now she barely noticed its grandeur.

Hurrying now, she reached the top and turned left toward the wing where her father had his suite. It had been years since she'd been in his rooms. There had been countless nights after the death of her mother when she'd taken refuge in her father's bed, but that had been sixteen years ago. She couldn't remember the last time she'd been there.

"Daddy? Are you up here?"

No answer.

She frowned. *Surely he must be somewhere close by?* The front door had been unlocked, after all. If he'd gone away for more than a few hours, he would have secured it, like he did when he traveled.

The door to his bedroom was closed. A sudden surge of foreboding sent an icy shiver down her spine. Goosebumps rose on her skin.

"Daddy?"

Turning the knob, she eased the door open and stepped into the room. A faint odor, not immediately recognizable, filled her nostrils. With dread weighing down her every step, she moved further into the room.

The king-sized bed with its huge carved wooden headboard was neatly made and empty. The room was spotless. Not a single item of clothing was on the floor. She crossed over to the master bath. The smell got stronger. With her heart pounding, she forced herself to open the door.

Her piercing scream rent the silence. Shock held her immobile. Her father lay stretched out, naked, in the bathtub. Stab wounds, too many to count, pierced his chest. His face was covered with a wash cloth. He could have been asleep except that his skin was completely bloodless and his body was grotesquely swollen. This close up, the smell of decomposition was nauseating.

She held her hand up to her face as a rush of acrid vomit filled her mouth. Bending over, she emptied the contents of her stomach on the pale gray marble tiles. Tears streamed from her eyes. When the retching stopped, she stood up shakily and tried to pull herself together.

"Daddy," she whimpered. "Oh, Daddy!"

Forcing herself closer, she reached out and took his hand. It was pale and cold and bloated. The underside that had been resting against the bathtub was a mottled dark purple where the blood had gathered and come to rest. And then she forced herself to look at the awful pattern that had been played out against his chest.

The stab wounds were dotted across his chest and abdomen in a pattern of unrestrained havoc. A fresh wave of nausea rolled in her stomach and she braced herself against the unavoidable. To her relief, it was only dry retching. She'd already emptied everything there was.

She needed to call the police because she was

standing in the middle of a crime scene. She shouldn't have touched anything. What if she'd messed up vital evidence? Oh, God. Her father was dead.

The thoughts rushed through her mind in a kaleidoscope of increasing anxiousness. She was still deep in shock. *Who could have done this?*

Hatred permeated every corner of the room.

This couldn't be happening. It was a nightmare from which she'd wake up. It had to be. The alternative was unthinkable.

Chapter 2

Detective Sergeant Zane Sullivan drove through a set of high security gates and continued along an impressive paved driveway that led up to the main house. He climbed out of the unmarked police car. His partner, Willie Whitehouse, followed suit. The brightness of the sunlight hurt Zane's eyes. It didn't help that he was nursing the mother of a hangover. His head thumped in time with his heartbeat. He fought off a wave of nausea.

Willie shot him a look of concern. "Are you all right?"

Zane nodded carefully. "I'm fine."

With gritted teeth, he took a moment to survey the architecturally designed house that stood before them. Three stories of sandstone and glass, the home of the late Grant Edward James Chifley was something to behold. Spread out on nearly an acre of manicured lawns, it perched on the very tip of Sydney's most exclusive peninsula and boasted uninterrupted north-easterly views of the harbor. Zane had never seen such a grand place.

"Wow!" Willie murmured, his voice low and filled with awe. "My whole apartment wouldn't even fill half the garage."

Zane knew exactly how he felt. "Yeah, mine too. I wonder what it's like to live in a place like this."

"Too bad he didn't live long enough to fully enjoy it," Willie replied.

Zane compressed his lips and nodded. "Yeah. It just goes to show you, all the money in the world can't keep you safe. Sixty-two is too young to die."

"You've got that right. Shall we go in?"

"Yeah."

They made their way across the paved path that led from the driveway up to some wide stone steps.

"What do we know about our vic?" Willie asked.

Zane frowned and did his best to recall the details provided to him by dispatch. "The bare essentials," he replied. "His name is Grant Edward James Chifley. A grand name to go along with his grand house. He's the founder and CEO of Chifley Real Estate. Made his name out here, selling extremely pricey eastern suburb waterfront property."

"Looks like he saved the best for himself."

Zane shot him a wry look. "Wouldn't you?"

"Do we have any leads?"

"Not at this stage. It was called in by his daughter. She was the one who found him."

They reached the top of the steps. A uniformed officer guarded the entry to the double front doors. Zane reached into his pocket for his credentials.

"Detectives Sullivan and Whitehouse. We're here about the homicide."

The young cop glanced at their IDs and then stepped aside to let them enter. The impressive entrance opened up into a grand foyer. A magnificent staircase stood off to the left. Beyond that, Zane could see a wide expanse of living area that backed up to a wall of floor-to-ceiling glass that took full advantage of the breathtaking water views.

"The Intel we have is that he was found in the master bath," Zane murmured.

Willie nodded and the two of them made their way up the stairs. Priceless artworks positioned among family portraits lined the sandstone-colored walls as they made their way up to the master bedroom. Zane paused at the top of the staircase and swiped his hand across his forehead. His head continued to pound.

The murmur of low voices from a room to his left caught his attention. He and Willie headed toward the voices.

The modest entryway opened up into the largest master suite Zane had ever seen. Thick plush carpet muffled their footsteps. The room was dominated by a super king-sized bed. Zane crossed to another open door that he guessed led to the master bath.

The murmur of voices got louder. Stepping into the bathroom, his gaze was immediately drawn to the enormous freestanding white porcelain bath that took pride of place before a wall of glass that looked out onto the magnificent expanse of the harbor. A nanosecond later, he registered the naked dead body of a middle-aged white male lying sprawled out in the tub. The familiar odor of death and decay assailed his nostrils, along with the acrid stench of fresh vomit.

A uniformed officer stepped forward.

"Detective Sullivan, I'm Sergeant Paul Foster. Constable Nash and I were the first on the scene."

Zane eyed the sergeant and introduced Willie.

"Was there any sign of forced entry?"

"No. The deceased's daughter was the one who called it in. Meghan Chifley. She said the door was unlocked, but that wasn't unusual when her father was home. They have plenty of security around the perimeter of the place. You might have noticed the gates on your way in. We left them open in anticipation of your arrival, but Meghan told us they're normally closed. The only entry to the place is through those gates and unless you know the code, someone needs to buzz you in."

Zane's gaze flicked over to where a woman stood in the far corner of the room. Small and petite, but at the same time she was lean and muscular, with a head full of curly blond hair. Even the devastation grief had wrought on her pale face couldn't conceal her beauty. His heart skipped a beat.

As if sensing his perusal, she lifted wide, red-rimmed blue eyes to his. Zane's gut clenched reflexively at the sadness and vulnerability he saw there. He didn't even know the woman and already he felt her pain.

"I take it that's Meghan?" he murmured.

"Yes. She told us she came looking for her father about an hour ago."

Zane's gaze once again went to the daughter. She wore a cream-colored, sleeveless linen dress that fit her body like a glove and no doubt cost a fortune. Her arms were now crossed tightly over her chest. She stared out the window at the sparkling water below her, but seemed oblivious to its beauty.

He dragged his gaze back to the man in the bath.

Large and overbearing, even in death, Grant Chifley looked like he weighed more than two hundred and fifty pounds. It was a good job the bath was so generous, otherwise it would have been a struggle for the man to fit in. Thick, gray, curly hair peeked out from beneath a wash cloth that covered his face. Multiple stab wounds were peppered across the wide expanse of abdomen and chest with at least a dozen concentrated on the area around the man's heart. It didn't take a genius to work out the cause of death.

Zane pulled out a pair of gloves from his jacket pocket and tugged them on. Ignoring his headache and the nausea that threatened, he moved closer to the body, taking care to sidestep the puddle of vomit that decorated the marble tiles. Drawing in a shallow breath, he bent over the late Grant Edward James Chifley. Willie did the same.

Zane's gaze centered more closely on the stab wounds. Given their number, the place should have been awash with blood, but there was nothing. Not a single speck. Not on the floor, on the wall, on the glass, in the bathtub. And not on the body, either.

Every inch of Chifley's skin had been washed clean. The deep gashes across his chest stood out in stark contrast to the paleness of his skin. If he'd been murdered in the bathtub, someone had done a meticulous job of cleaning away the evidence.

"This is weird," Willie muttered, looking uncomfortable.

"Yeah. I've never seen anything like it. Someone spent a whole lot of time and went to a lot of trouble to clean up, which tells us they weren't in a hurry. Whoever did this knew they weren't about to be disturbed."

"Does he live alone?" Willie asked.

Standing only a few feet away, Sergeant Foster glanced quickly toward Meghan and then answered. "According to the deceased's daughter, yes. Apart from the housekeeper and the gardener who live in the staff quarters at the bottom of the garden."

"Has anyone spoken to them, yet?"

"No," the sergeant answered. "Mrs Abbott, the housekeeper, has been away at least a week. The gardener is here somewhere. I'll have someone locate him."

"Do you think our vic was killed here?" Willie directed his question to Zane.

"It's hard to tell. If he was, someone's cleaned up all the blood. We'll take a look around. If you ask me, this looks personal. Take a look at those wounds. Overkill." Zane shook his head grimly and straightened. It was time to talk to the daughter.

Steeling himself against her breathtaking beauty, he went over to where she stood and held out his hand.

"I'm Detective Sergeant Zane Sullivan. I understand the deceased is your father."

The woman turned slowly to face him. After a slight hesitation, she shook his hand.

"Yes, I'm Meghan Chifley. I'm his youngest daughter."

Zane hated that he noticed that her skin was smooth and soft and supple. Expensive perfume mingled with the other less pleasant smells in the room. Giving her another quick once-over, along with the designer dress, he catalogued expensive high heels. Heavy gold jewelry. Diamonds that sparkled at her ears. She was beautiful in every way... He shook himself. She was old money from head to toe—way out of his league. Her kind never offered a second glance to men like him.

Where had that come from? He thought he was done with that insecurity shit. He'd come a long way since high school and he'd done it on his own. He was proud of the man he'd become. Women like Meghan Chifley could take their high-born attitude and shove it. With an effort, he did his best to focus on the job at hand.

"Ms Chifley, I know this must be difficult, but I need to ask you a few questions. The sooner we get this over with, the sooner you can leave."

She compressed her lips and tears glimmered in her eyes, but Zane also noted the determination that straightened her spine. "Of course, Detective. Do what you have to do. I'll help you in any way I can."

"Was there a particular reason you came over here this morning?"

"Yes. I had a call from Arjun Patel. He's Daddy's gardener. He said he hadn't seen Daddy around for a few days. He was worried. I called Daddy on the phone and he didn't answer. I wasn't aware he was going away, so I offered to come over and take a look."

"And what time was this?" Zane asked, taking out a notepad and pen.

"Arjun called me just after nine. I left work almost immediately. I guess I arrived here about half an hour later."

"Where do you work?"

"I'm an estate attorney at Sydney Legal."

Zane hid his surprise and jotted the information down in his notebook. Beauty and brains. It was a heady combination. It was also interesting the daughter of such a wealthy man chose to pursue any kind of profession, let alone such a challenging one.

"Do you work full time?" he asked.

"Yes."

"And where do you live?"

She gave him an address in Bondi. It was another eastern Sydney suburb where the average house or condo came with a hefty price tag. Not quite as exclusive as a Point Piper address, but still, far from shabby. No surprise there.

"When did you last see your father?"

The woman frowned. "Four days ago. We had breakfast together."

"Here, or somewhere else?"

"No, not here. At my apartment."

"Was anyone else with you?"

"No, it was just Daddy and me."

"Did he seem worried to you? Did he express any concerns?"

She shook her head and looked bewildered. "No, he was fine."

Her voice choked and Zane could see she was struggling to hold back tears. He made another note and then continued. "The sergeant you spoke to earlier told me you said there was no sign of forced entry. Can you tell me a bit more about that?"

She sighed quietly. "Daddy has—had an extensive security system. There are all kinds of cameras and alarms surrounding the perimeter. No one can come in or leave without him knowing. As a result, whenever he was home, he left the front door unlocked. It was convenient for everyone."

"And it was unlocked when you arrived?"

"Yes."

"Can you think of anyone who would want your father dead? Jealous business rivals, disgruntled clients?"

The woman shook her head. "No, I can't think of anyone."

"Did he get into an argument with anyone recently?"

The woman appeared to think for a moment. "There was an argument with Arjun last week. Daddy accused him of stealing some money he'd left out on a dresser in his bedroom. It was only a few hundred dollars."

She shook her head. "I'm not sure why Daddy would think it was Arjun. He's been with us for years. He looks after the pool and the gardens. He never comes into the house. Even when he was concerned about Daddy, he didn't come inside. Instead, he called me."

"Have you spoken to Arjun since your discovery?"

"No. I called out to him and phoned him, but he didn't answer. I assume he's around here somewhere. He knew I was coming over to check on Daddy."

"What happened about the missing money? Was it found?"

"No, not as far as I know. Arjun denied taking it. Daddy refused to believe him, but I did. Like I said, Arjun's been with our family for years. He practically helped raise me. I honestly don't know what Daddy was thinking, accusing him. Besides, it could have been anyone. There were workmen here all that week. They were repairing a leak in the upstairs bathroom. Come to think of it, Daddy told me he'd argued with them over the bill."

"Do you have any names?" Zane asked.

The woman frowned. "Yes, it was Dorrington Plumbing Services. I don't have their number, but I'm sure you'll find them on the Internet."

Zane made a note of the information. "Thank you. Is there anyone else close to your father who needs to be notified?"

"My mother died when I was ten. There's only my brother and half-sister."

"I'm sorry. We'll contact them and let them know what happened. Do you have their details?"

"If you don't mind, Detective, I'd like to be the one to tell them. It's going to come as an awful shock and I think it might be better coming from me."

Zane nodded in agreement. "Okay. But I'll need to talk to them anyway."

Frown lines marred the smooth skin of the woman's forehead. "Why? Surely you don't think this had anything to do with them?"

"At the moment, we don't know what to think. We're covering all bases. I'll need to talk to the gardener and the tradesmen, too."

Somewhat reluctantly, she checked her phone and gave Zane the information he sought. He wondered about her strange reaction and shelved it for further consideration. Closing his notebook, he slid it back into the pocket of his jacket. He stuck out his hand and once again had the pleasure of her touch, albeit briefly.

"Thank you for your cooperation, Ms Chifley. We appreciate you talking to us."

She inclined her head slightly in acknowledgment. "Please, call me Meghan."

Her invitation to dispense with formalities surprised him. *Perhaps there was more to Meghan Chifley than met the eye?* Before he could contemplate that possibility any further, she spoke again.

"What happens now?" Her tone had turned distant.

"There'll be an autopsy. You'll be notified when the body is ready for release."

Her eyes flashed in sudden anger. "That's my father! Don't refer to him as a body—

As if he's nothing."

Zane held his hands up in a sign of surrender. "I'm sorry. I didn't mean to offend."

She didn't look mollified by his apology. Instead, fresh tears formed in her eyes. Zane watched her swallow. It was obvious she found it difficult to hold back her pain. Despite himself, he felt an instinctive urge to offer her comfort and almost took a step forward before pulling himself up short. To his relief, Willie appeared beside them.

"Forensics have arrived, along with the people from the morgue. We need to clear the room."

A fresh wave of sadness and resignation flooded Meghan's face. With her gaze averted and her fists clenched, she left.

Zane eased out his breath on a quiet sigh of relief. Reaching into his pocket, he pulled out a packet of paracetamol and emptied three into his hand. He swallowed them dry and prayed they wouldn't take too long to work. It was going to be a long day.

Chapter 3

Meghan stumbled down the wide stone steps that led away from her father's house and did her best to get her shock under control. She rubbed her arms to ward off the chill that had invaded her bones the moment she'd spotted her father's body. For as long as she lived the image of him lying dead in the bath tub would haunt her.

A cool breeze blew in from the harbor and ruffled her short curls and sent another shiver rippling down her spine. The warm spring morning had started out with such promise, but now she couldn't see through the thick fog that weighed her down like concrete. There were things she had to do, calls she had to make, but for the life of her, she couldn't bring herself to do anything. Even breathing was a struggle.

She tripped on the last stone step and her ankle twisted. With a cry of pain and surprise, she fell heavily to the ground. One elbow scraped across the hard surface. A knee took the brunt of her fall.

Sobs of desperation, disbelief and anguish bubbled up inside her and spilled out of her mouth. With her head in her hands and her knees pulled up tightly to her chest, she sobbed her heart out.

Her father was dead. Murdered by a vicious killer. She had no choice but to confront the horrible truth of what had happened and she was left wondering how on earth she was ever going to accept that he was gone. And not just gone, but murdered in such a brutal way.

She'd overheard the detectives murmuring amongst themselves from across the room. Words like "overkill" and "personal" and "no forced entry." They hammered inside her brain and she couldn't help but think of Cody.

The night her brother called her, he'd sounded desperate, panicked, frantic with fear. Now he'd disappeared. She didn't want to think he might be responsible. Her mind automatically rebelled against the idea. There was no way her brother was capable of such violence, and especially not against their father. Okay, so the two of them didn't always see eye to eye, but Cody loved their father as much as she did. There was no way he'd murder him.

She was filled with a flood of urgency. She needed to find him before the police did. They'd be looking for him and if they couldn't find him, they'd draw their own conclusions. *Dear, God.*

When the good-looking detective with the tailored suit, broad shoulders and bloodshot eyes had asked for Cody's address and phone number, she'd immediately gone into panic mode. His late-night phone call had filled her head and with it, all her unanswered questions. She refused to believe he had anything to do with this, but she needed to speak with him, seek reassurance, an explanation—before the police arrived.

So, she'd given the detective a wrong number and had supplied him with the address of Cody's wife. It would buy her some time. Not a lot, but something.

When the detective found out she'd given him the wrong information, no doubt he'd be annoyed, but that was an issue she was prepared to deal with and she'd already formulated an excuse. She'd blame her mistake on the shock of her recent discovery. Finding the body of your murdered father wasn't something anyone got over in a hurry. She'd apologize profusely for any inconvenience... Say she forgot her brother no longer lived there. After all, it had only been a few months... Somehow in her shock and panic, she'd given them the wrong phone number. She'd forgotten that he'd also recently changed it. All fully understandable under the circumstances and it meant she had a few extra hours up her sleeve to find her brother and demand answers. She hoped it was enough.

Slowly her sobs subsided and with an effort, she pulled herself together. Still on the pavement, she hunted around in her handbag for a tissue, wiped her eyes and blew her nose then drew in a few deep breaths. Finally, she regained a semblance of control. Pulling out her phone, she dialed

Cody's number and waited. And waited. Like all the other times she'd phoned him since the night of his unsettling call, once again, it went through to his voicemail.

A stab of pain went through her and she cried out on another gasp of alarm. "Cody! Where are you? I need to speak with you! I need to know you're all right. I need to know you had nothing to do with this…"

Fresh tears burned behind her eyes and her chest went tight. She was on the brink of falling apart. Again. She still had to tell Sarah. Her half-sister's relationship with their dad had been volatile in recent years, but the two of them still loved each other. They were family. Of *course* they loved each other.

With trembling hands, Meghan dialed Sarah's number. She didn't want to break the awful news over the phone, but her half-sister lived in Macquarie Fields. It would take Meghan more than an hour to get there. Any minute the media could get wind of what had happened. Grant Chifley was a high-profile figure in Sydney society. His murder would be big news. It wasn't fair to anyone who loved her father to find out that way. There was nothing she could do about reaching Cody, but she prayed silently that Sarah would answer her call.

"Hello?"

Meghan's heart skipped a beat. "S-Sarah," she stammered.

"Yes?" The woman's voice held a touch of impatience.

Meghan resisted the urge to snap back. Sarah was thirteen years her senior, but Meghan was no longer a small child to be pushed around and treated with disdain. Still, now wasn't the time to bring up old hurts. She drew in a deep breath.

"It's...Meghan. I... I'm afraid I have bad news."

A lump of emotion lodged itself in Meghan's throat, making it hard to breathe. The steel band around her chest tightened. She tried to fight through the fog in her head to find the words to soften the blow, but there was nothing. "Sarah, I'm sorry... I'm so sorry..."

"What the hell are you talking about, Meghan?" Sarah's voice now held a note of panic.

Fresh tears filled Meghan's eyes. She drew in a shaky breath and prayed for the courage to see this through.

"I-I'm at Daddy's place. The police are here. He's been...murdered."

Her voice broke on a gasp of pain.

Sarah's howl of disbelief and anguish filled Meghan's ears.

She winced and closed her eyes tightly in an effort to block it, but that was useless. Shock and pain surrounded her, inside and out. The tears she'd tried so hard to hold back resurfaced and once again coursed down her cheeks.

Sarah's grief continued to ring in Meghan's ears. With a shaky hand, she withdrew the phone and slowly ended the call. Slipping from her grasp, the phone fell to the pavement. The screen cracked.

On another desperate gasp, she crumpled back into a heap of misery. Heartfelt sobs of anguish overwhelmed her once again. Her father was dead. Brutally murdered. She was twenty-six and life as she'd known it was over.

What on earth would she do?

Zane took off his jacket and stepped into the loose green cotton pants provided to him by the morgue assistant. Pulling on a matching, short-sleeved shirt, he slipped flimsy booties over his shoes and headed toward the room where the autopsies were conducted. The protective clothing was required by all visitors, including law enforcement. He wasn't complaining. The last thing he wanted to do was have body fluids splashed on his suit, or any other part of him for that matter.

He grimaced at the thought and swallowed a sigh. No matter how many autopsies he witnessed, he never got used to the sight of a dead body stretched out on a stainless steel table and being attended to by a forensic pathologist brandishing a saw. He'd learned long ago to distance his mind from the reality of what was happening, and this time with Grant Chifley would be no different.

Pushing open the door with his shoulder, he walked into the main room and was pleased to see a masked Doctor Samantha Wolfe garbed in surgical scrubs already leaning over the body.

Three other pathologists were busy with other bodies further down the line of gurneys.

Samantha was the chief forensic pathologist at the Glebe Morgue and was the finest forensic pathologist the state had to offer. It reassured Zane to know Grant Chifley was in the hands of the best.

As if privy to his thoughts, Samantha looked up from what she was doing and greeted Zane with a nod. "Detective Sullivan, it's good to see you again."

Thankfully, Zane's headache had receded, but his response felt more like a grimace than a smile. Samantha didn't seem to notice.

"So, what do we know about this guy?" she asked, and picked up a scalpel from the tray beside her.

"His name is Grant Edward James Chifley. Sixty-two years old. He was found naked in the bath tub earlier this morning."

Sam looked at him questioningly above her surgical mask. "He doesn't appear to have been submerged in water," she murmured.

"You're right," Zane replied. "The bath was empty."

"What else do we know about him?"

Zane cleared his throat. "He was found by his daughter. She says she saw him alive, four days ago. Apparently they had breakfast together."

Samantha nodded. "Okay, so if she's telling the truth, we know he was alive four days ago. Let's see if we can confirm that and see what else we can find."

With that, she made a Y incision and slowly opened him up. Zane swallowed and looked away. In silence, Samantha catalogued the man's organs and recorded her findings into a Dictaphone as she went. She stared down at the stab wounds and slowly shook her head.

"Someone sure wanted this guy dead," she murmured. In silence, she counted the stab wounds, resting her gloved finger lightly on each one. When she was finished, she lifted her gaze to Zane.

"Forty-seven stab wounds altogether. He also has a large contusion on the back of his head. He was hit with a heavy flat object."

"Before or after he was dead?" Zane asked.

"Before. See the blood congealed here in his hair? That wouldn't have happened if his heart wasn't beating."

Zane stared down at the body. "What kind of weapon do you think he was hit with?"

Samantha shrugged. "I can't say for sure. It could have been anything. Something that was heavy enough to knock him off his feet. You can see here from the angle of the stab wounds, it's clear the killer was standing over him when the victim first came into contact with the knife. He was already on the ground."

Reluctantly, Zane inched closer. "So he was struck on the back of the head first. That means he was probably taken by surprise. What else can you tell me?"

Samantha reached for a steel ruler and measured several of the stab wounds. "The killer used a four-inch, non-serrated blade. Each of the wounds are angled left to right. It's my guess our killer is right-handed."

Zane nodded, impressed as he always was with the skill and expertise of the forensic pathologists who showed up every day to do their bit to provide grieving relatives with answers and help solve crimes in their city. Samantha bent over the body, spreading open the walls of Chifley's chest.

"Ten of these stab wounds went through his heart," she continued. She looked up at Zane. The expression in her eyes was somber. "One would have been enough."

Zane nodded. "Overkill."

Samantha nodded once. "You have that right."

Zane stared down at the body, his gaze taking in the mountain of stab wounds. He'd already come to the same conclusion back at Chifley's house.

"There's a lot of hate here," he murmured.

"You're right. This looks personal."

Zane recalled how Chifley's face had been covered with a washcloth. It was almost as if the killer had been ashamed of what he'd done. Like he couldn't bear the victim looking at him, accusing him, judging him.

"You mentioned a daughter. Does he have any other family?" Samantha asked.

Zane nodded. "Yeah. Two other adult kids. His wife is deceased. I checked the records. Motor vehicle accident. There is an ex-wife, but they've been divorced for more than twenty years. I can't see her being involved in this."

"What about disgruntled business partners?"

"No. As far as we know, Grant Chifley was a one-man show."

"You said he was found in the bath tub. Was there any damage done to the porcelain?"

"No. The bath tub was clean. Not even a nick out of it."

"So he was killed elsewhere and then brought in and lifted into the tub," Sam murmured. "That would take a fair degree of strength. Our victim weighs in at two hundred and sixty-five pounds. Whoever did this was strong."

"Either that, or there was more than one of them."

Samantha conceded his point with a nod. "True, but the evidence seems to indicate all the stab wounds were done by the same person. Did you work out whether he was even killed in the house?"

Zane regarded her steadily. "We checked the house, but we didn't find anything suspicious. As far as we could tell, there was nothing out of place. Every room was clean and tidy. It was like somebody had just come in with the body and placed it in the bath tub and then left again. Bizarre."

"Yep," Sam replied. "We get all types in here. That's the way we like it. You should know that by now, Detective." She chuckled behind her mask.

Zane tried to return her smile, but failed miserably. Somehow he couldn't find it within himself to joke. Not in there. It was just too...weird.

"Is there anything else you can tell me?" he asked.

"From what I can tell, he's been dead about seventy-two hours. He died shortly after eating dinner. His stomach contents show partially digested food. By the looks of it, it could be pizza. You might like to check the pizza shops in the area, see if they have a record of his purchase. That will help narrow down your timeline. I'll open up his skull and get a look at his brain, but I don't think there's any doubt about the cause or manner of death. The blow to the head would have stunned him, but it didn't do enough damage to kill him. No, this man died from multiple stab wounds. Manner of death: homicide. One other thing, Grant Chifley had a large tumor pressing on the left side of his brain. It was only a matter of time before it killed him."

Zane stared at her. "You mean he was already dying of cancer?"

Samantha nodded. "Yes. From the size of the tumor, I'd say he had a matter of weeks to live. Ironic, isn't it?"

———

Meghan rode the lift to the penthouse suite and sighed quietly in relief when the doors opened and she let herself into her multimillion-dollar apartment overlooking Bondi Beach. It had been a gift from her father on her graduation from law school. She'd protested over the lavishness of his present and hadn't wanted to accept it, but she'd taken one look at it and had fallen in love.

It was close to her dad and close to work. She was a stone's throw from some of Sydney's finest beaches. Her dad told her how happy it would make him for her to take it. He gained pleasure from giving her things. In the end, she'd accepted his generous gift with graciousness and love and invited him to spend time with her there whenever he could.

Now he was gone and she'd never have breakfast with him again. Never have him there to confide in, listen to her problems, offer his advice, his love.

A fresh wave of sadness overwhelmed her. Pushing a hand against her mouth, she held back a sob. Despite the damage to her phone, she'd managed to call Dorothy and cancel her appointments and had then cried all the way home from her dad's place.

She had to get a grip. She still hadn't been able to contact Cody and her anxiety increased with every second. Sooner or later the police would come calling again, asking for his updated details. She needed to find him. Fast.

Ignoring the pain in her ankle and knee, she hobbled to the couch.

"Where are you, Cody?" she whispered. "Please don't be involved in this. Please, God. Please..."

The Cody she knew and loved could never be responsible for such a heinous act, but he was a different person under the influence of drugs. And now he'd switched from heroin to crystal meth. When she asked him about it, he told her meth was cheaper than powder and since losing his job, money was tight. That was no excuse and it pained her deeply to know how reliant he'd become on drugs and how far he'd fallen from his once oh-so-glamorous life.

Their father had flatly refused to fund his drug habit, and so had she. Now she felt weighed down by guilt. Had he been forced to find a cheaper way to get high because he'd run out of cash? If she'd given him more money, would it have made a difference? Had she inadvertently forced him to into using crystal meth, or ice as it was often called? And had he done something horrific while he was high? Is that what he was talking about the last time he called?

Ice users were known for their unpredictability and violent tendencies. She'd seen an example of that only a month earlier when a heated argument between her brother and father had turned physical. Cody had punched their father in the face and bloodied his nose. It was only when she put herself between them that her brother had walked away. His violent and unrestrained behavior had frightened her. She'd never seen him like that before.

Had he argued with their father again over money and this time, had he gone too far? Is that what had happened? It didn't bear thinking about.

Once again, her faith in her brother resurfaced. It surged up inside her, fierce and strong. No, she refused to accept her brother could be responsible for their father's death, despite how far his life had spiraled out of control.

She spared a thought for his wife and children and knew they'd been suffering too. When someone's life took such a drastic turn, it effected everyone around them. The Chifleys might have more money than they could spend in a lifetime, but that didn't insulate them from grief or other torments. She just prayed the police would find someone else was responsible for her father's murder—and fast.

She thought about the handsome detective who'd plied her with questions. Even in the midst of her horror and grief, she'd noticed him. Perhaps because he hadn't been quick enough to conceal the frank interest when she'd caught him giving her a quick onceover. With his bloodshot eyes, his tie askew, longish, ruffled hair and beard he'd looked a little worse for wear, but in a sexy way. Like a model on the cover of a magazine.

She wondered if he was merely sleep deprived from keeping their streets safe or if there was something else going on in his life. Whatever it was, she hoped he had the wherewithal to resolve this nightmare. The only thing worse than knowing her father had been brutally murdered was not knowing who was responsible.

Chapter 4

Zane tilted the bottle of water to his lips and drank greedily. The day had barely begun and already he'd had enough. He was dehydrated and tired and achy and he only had himself to blame. For the second night in a row, he'd gone to bed far too late and had suffered through torturous dreams soaked in Jack Daniels. The alcohol helped him deal with his demons, but still, it was no excuse. The last thing he wanted was for the grog to interfere with his work. One thing he'd always been able to rely on was his expertise on the job. He had a sixth sense for knowing what had gone down at a murder scene. He didn't know how he'd come to have that, but it was there nonetheless.

Perhaps he'd been born with it? Who knew? It wasn't like either of his parents had hung around long enough to discuss it. His father hadn't even bothered to wait until he was born. His mother had put him up for adoption the minute she was able. So much for a mother's love.

"How're you doing, Zane?"

With considerable effort Zane lowered the water bottle and turned to acknowledge Willie's arrival. His partner had a wide grin on his face. It annoyed Zane that the man was always so cheerful, especially this early in the morning in the middle of yet another complicated homicide investigation. It just wasn't right.

"What's put you in such a good mood?" he grumbled sourly.

"I'm alive and well; the sun is shining. What more could a man want?"

Zane made a disgruntled sound and headed toward the tea room. Pouring himself a cup of black coffee, he took his first hit of caffeine for the day. The strong, hot brew hit the spot. A few sips and a couple of Tylenol later and he was beginning to feel almost human again. With a refill in hand, he made his way to his desk.

"Any luck finding the gardener?" he asked Willie as he sat down and pulled his keyboard toward him.

"Yes. He finally answered his phone."

"Where is he?"

"Strangely, in Queensland, of all places. Visiting a sister. Apparently he took some leave."

Zane frowned. "That seems awfully suspicious. Yesterday Meghan Chifley seemed convinced he was still on the grounds."

"You're right. It took me by surprise when Patel admitted he was interstate. He also admitted he was aware his boss was dead. Definitely peculiar. Right now, he's on the top of our list. By the way,

I tried to call Cody Chifley. The number Meghan gave us has been disconnected."

Zane's frown deepened. "Disconnected? Are you sure you keyed it in right?"

Willie stared at him, one dark bushy eyebrow raised in silent query. Zane blushed with embarrassment.

"Okay, I'm sorry. Of course you did. I just don't get it. Why would Meghan give us a disconnected number?"

Willie shrugged. "Maybe it only happened recently. As in, yesterday or the day before? I haven't checked with the phone company. Besides, we didn't ask her how often she's in contact with him. Perhaps they aren't close."

Zane compressed his lips and nodded slowly. "Yes, except she wanted to be the one to give him the bad news. That implies a degree of closeness."

"I guess. We can always go around to his place and see if he's home."

"Yes. Let's do that. Meghan's had enough time to tell him about their father's untimely death. It's time for us to ask some questions."

"What about the gardener?" Willie asked.

"Do we have an address in Queensland?"

"Yes, but it doesn't matter. He's agreed to fly back to Sydney to talk to us."

Zane frowned in surprise. "Okay... He's been gone less than a day and he's agreed to do that?" he said slowly. "That's awfully accommodating of him."

"Yeah, that's what I thought. I guess we'll have to wait and see if he shows."

Zane grinned. "I won't be disappointed if he doesn't. The weather in Queensland this time of year is more than pleasant. I wouldn't mind spending a day up north in the sunshine. All in the name of the job, of course."

Willie chuckled. "Of course. Especially on the Gold Coast; apparently that's where he is." Willie's grin faded. "How did you do at the morgue?"

"Good. Samantha Wolfe did the autopsy."

"That was lucky."

"Yeah. In her opinion, the vic had been dead approximately seventy-two hours when he was found. He had partially digested food in his stomach. It looked like pizza. We need to call the pizza shops in his area and see if he put in an order on the night of his death."

Willie nodded. "I'll get on it. If we get a hit it will help narrow down the timeline, maybe even point to someone else..."

"Exactly." Zane took another mouthful of coffee, relishing the strong brew. "What time do we expect the gardener's plane to land?"

"He said he'd catch the first flight back this morning." Willie glanced at his watch. "I checked the airlines. There was a Virgin flight departing at six."

"It should be landing soon then." Zane pushed back from his desk and stood and reached for his jacket.

"See what you can find out about the pizza shops. I'll try to catch Patel at the airport. I'll call you when I finish and we can meet at Cody Chifley's place."

Willie nodded. "Sounds like a plan."

"Good. Do you have the brother's address?"

"Yes. I took it down when Meghan Chifley gave it to us yesterday."

Zane grimaced. "Let's hope it's current."

Willie shrugged. "People change their phone numbers. Not many of them change addresses at short notice. Surely she knows where her brother lives."

"You'd think so," Zane replied dryly, irritated anew at the memory of his body's reaction to Grant Chifley's beautiful daughter.

"What about the other daughter? The half-sister?"

"Yeah, Sarah. We'll put her on our list. She lives in Macquarie Fields. It's at least a three-hour round trip to speak with her."

"We'll see what happens with the brother first, then regroup. He lives closer to the city."

"Right. I'll see you there, then."

Willie waved in acknowledgment and reached for his phone. Zane pulled on his jacket and after letting one of his colleagues know where he was going, he left.

The morning traffic heading out to the airport was lighter than usual and Zane made good time. He arrived at Mascot forty-five minutes after leaving headquarters and parked the squad car in a loading zone. He'd taken a few minutes to pull up Patel's driving license and had a reasonable idea of what the gardener looked like, at least insofar as what the small license photo revealed.

Striding into the arrivals lounge, he scanned the crowd of recently disembarked. Sunburned kids carrying boogie boards, and bedraggled parents hefting suitcases dominated the throng of people streaming in.

Waiting off to one side, he canvassed and discarded several possibilities before he spied a man he thought might be Arjun Patel. Short and slight with graying hair and weathered brown skin that implied many hours in the sun, the man looked nervous as he carried a small backpack through the lounge. He kept looking around, as if searching for someone, but no one came forward to greet him. Making up his mind, Zane approached him.

"Arjun Patel?"

The man halted with a visible start. "Yes?"

Zane flashed his credentials. "I'm Detective Sergeant Zane Sullivan. I'm investigating the murder of your former employer, Grant Chifley."

Tears glinted in Patel's eyes. He swiped at them with the back of a wrinkled old hand, as if embarrassed by his display of emotion. His grief appeared genuine, but cold-hearted killers had been known to tear up when the occasion demanded it. Zane tamped down the instinctive surge of compassion that rose inside him and leveled Patel with a look.

"I need to ask you some questions. We can do it here or back at the station. Where would you prefer?"

The gardener glanced around at the crowds of people streaming through the airport lounge. He looked less than impressed with the idea of being questioned by the police in such a public place. Zane understood the man's reticence, but he wasn't about to cut him any slack.

"Such a shock it is... I-I'm on my way back to the Chifley place now," the old man stammered. "Would it... Would it be possible for us to speak there?"

Zane held his gaze and assessed the man's sincerity. Satisfied with what he saw, he gave a brief nod.

"Do you have a car here?"

"N-no." The man lowered his gaze. "I caught the bus."

"You can ride with me."

The man accepted Zane's announcement without comment. Zane glanced at Patel's backpack.

"Is that all your luggage?"

Patel looked uncomfortable. "Yes. I... I left in a bit of a hurry. I didn't have time to pack more."

As they strode outside the airport toward Zane's unmarked squad car, he shot Patel another look.

"Why were you in such a hurry?"

Color flooded the old man's face. He stared down at the ground. "It's not what you think! I had nothing to do with Mr Chifley's death! I swear!"

Zane merely shrugged and indicated the squad car in front of them. "Get in."

In silence, Patel took the backseat. Zane climbed in behind the wheel and pulled on his seatbelt and asked his passenger to do the same. He checked over his shoulder before heading out into the traffic. They made good time across the city and pulled up outside the Chifley residence in just under an hour. The high gates were closed this time. Zane turned to the gardener.

"Do you have the security code?"

Patel nodded. "Yes, of course."

He recited some numbers and Zane punched them in on the pad. A moment later, the gates swung inward on well-oiled hinges. The manicured lawns looked much the same as they had the day before. Once again, Zane brought the car to a halt outside the front entrance to the house.

"I live in a cabin at the bottom of the garden," Patel murmured, collecting his backpack from under his feet and climbing out. "You're welcome to speak with me there. It will be cooler than out here in the sun."

Zane followed the gardener down a wide stone path that bordered the northern end of the main house. It came out beside a pool surrounded by loungers and large umbrellas. The crystal clear water sparkled like diamonds in the sun, the light bouncing off the royal-blue colored Italian tiles that lined the walls and floor of the pool. Zane wondered what it would be like to swim there.

Patel continued past the pool and down a set of steps that led to a lower level of verdant tropical gardens. Palm trees, frangipani, tree ferns, bougainvillea, birds of paradise and a passion fruit vine all flourished under the morning sun. Zane could only imagine the humidity while working in the gardens in the heat of summer. Still, it was an impressive display and was testament to Patel's ability as a gardener.

"Are you responsible for all this?" Zane asked, spreading his arm wide.

Patel blushed and lowered his gaze. "Yes. I've worked here for nearly twenty years. There was nothing but grass and a few trees when I first started. It grows well."

Zane gave him his due. "It looks like a lot of hard work and dedication."

Pride glinted in the old man's eyes before he once again lowered his gaze. He came to another wrought iron fence, this one about five feet high, and opened a gate. More steps led down to another lower level. The lawns were wide and green and in one corner stood a rose garden. Laden with blooms of all colors, the air around them was heavily perfumed.

"It's just through here," Patel murmured and led the way along a narrow gravel path that finished outside a small outbuilding.

"This is where you live?" Zane asked.

"Yes. There is an identical one on the other side where Mrs Abbott resides."

"The housekeeper, right?"

"Yes."

"I understand she's been away?"

"Yes. She's been gone for a week. Her mother died."

"So she wasn't here when your employer died?"

"Right."

"Does she know about what happened?"

Misery filled Patel's expression. He nodded sadly. "Yes, I called her last night. She's as devastated about it as I am."

Turning away, the man fitted a key into a lock on the front door and turned the knob. Zane followed him inside. The cabin was small but comfortable. It housed an open concept kitchen, dining and living room. There was a short hallway with two doors leading off it where Zane assumed a bedroom and bathroom were located. The place was neat and tidy. There was no indication its occupant left in a panic.

"I understand you called Mr Chifley's daughter yesterday and asked her about her father. Is that correct?"

Patel's expression turned wary. "Mr Chifley has two daughters. Sarah and Meghan. I called Meghan."

"Right. And what was the purpose of your call?"

Patel sighed heavily and moved to stand by the window. He stared out into the garden, seemingly lost in his thoughts. A few moments later, he turned back to Zane.

"I was worried about Mr Chifley. I hadn't seen him for a few days and that didn't sit right. Normally he's as regular as clockwork. He has breakfast by the pool around seven. By eight, he's reading the paper. By nine he's back inside, in his study. He hadn't told me he was going away, so I was concerned. Mrs Abbott was away and though Meghan is his most frequent visitor, none of his children visit every day. So I called Meghan. She agreed to come over and check on him."

"So you hadn't gone inside the house yourself to take a look?"

A look of shock came over Patel's face. "Of course not! It's not my place to go inside Mr Chifley's house. The closest I come to it is the back patio, off the pool."

"What did Meghan say when you called her? Was she concerned?"

"Yes. Meghan's a sweetie. She loves her daddy so much. If she wasn't so busy with her law practice, I'm sure she'd spend more time with him."

How did she react to your phone call?"

Patel sighed. "She told me she'd call him and if she couldn't reach him by phone, she'd come over and take a look around."

"Were you here when she arrived?"

"Yes. I was in the garden."

"Did you see her go inside?"

"No, but I saw her car come up the driveway."

"The forensic pathologist estimates Mr Chifley died three days before he was found. That puts his death on the night of October fifteenth. Were you here that night?"

"Yes, of course. I only have one day off a week and that's usually on Sunday. And even then, most times I'm here."

"Did you hear anything suspicious? Anything to indicate what was happening?"

"No, of course not! I would have called the police if I thought Mr Chifley was in trouble. I heard nothing. Then again, I'm a heavy sleeper. I always go to bed at eight. If it happened after that, I wouldn't have heard a thing. You'd be best to check the CCTV footage and see what it shows. "

Zane came alert. He should have realized a place like this would have security cameras. In fact, Meghan Chifley had mentioned it during their conversation about why the front door was unlocked. He cursed under his breath. *Had he slipped up?*

"When did you discover your employer had been murdered?" he asked, putting the troubling thought aside.

Patel's gaze fell. "I saw all the police cars arrive. I knew something had gone wrong. I was too scared to ask anyone directly, but I overheard one of the officers speaking into their radio. I realized my boss was dead."

Zane stared at the man. "Why did you run?"

Embarrassment lit up Patel's features. He continued to avert his gaze. "I don't know," he admitted. "I panicked. I was here alone with Mr Chifley. I didn't want the police to turn their suspicions on me."

Zane frowned. "Why would they do that?"

Patel continued to look uncomfortable. "It doesn't make sense, I know. But I've been wrongly accused once before in my life. I was only ten at the time, but I never forgot it or the feeling of not being believed. I was terrified it would happen again. In the end, my sister convinced me I was being paranoid and by staying away, I was only making myself look guilty." He shrugged. "That's why I immediately purchased a return ticket and agreed to fly home when I received the police call."

Zane regarded the man steadily. He appeared to be telling the truth. The man's gaze remained shadowed with distress. His short-sleeved shirt and long cotton pants hung off his slight frame. Zane had a sudden picture of Grant Chifley.

Samantha had weighed him at two hundred and sixty-five pounds. Arjun Patel was lean and wiry and probably stronger than he looked, but still...

Zane was almost convinced the gardener wasn't their man. As a final precaution, he asked to see the man's hands.

Patel frowned in confusion, but obediently held his hands out, palm up, for Zane to see. Zane examined them closely. Old and wrinkled, the pale skin was in stark contrast to the darker weathered skin on the opposite side. They were unmarked by any sign of trauma.

There was no way the person who attacked Grant Chifley so viciously could have walked away from that scene without a mark. The handle of the knife would have been slippery with the victim's blood. It was highly likely the perpetrator would also have received cuts from the blade as it slipped in his hands.

Zane nodded briefly. "Thank you, Mr Patel. You've been more than cooperative. If I have any further questions, I'll be in touch. In the meantime, here's my card. Call me if you remember anything else."

Relief flooded the gardener's face. He reached out and took Zane's card. "Are we done?" he asked.

"Yes." Zane turned away. He'd taken a few steps before he turned back once again.

"Did Mr Chifley accuse you of stealing from him a short time ago?"

The gardener looked resigned. "Yes. I'm not sure where he got that idea from. It was strange. He'd never accused me like that before and it's not like I'm ever inside the house. I still can't explain his accusation."

"So, it's twice you've felt like that. Accused of something you didn't do? Where will you live now that your employer has died?" Zane asked quietly.

Sorrow filled Patel's expression. "Yes, twice. And living... I don't know. I've lived here for nearly twenty years. I have nowhere else."

Zane compressed his lips on a surge of sympathy. It wasn't up to him to find housing for the gardener. Hopefully old man Chifley had been generous to his help in his will.

Patel showed him to the door. He made as if to follow Zane up the path, but instead Zane shook his head. "I'll find my own way out, thank you. If you don't mind, I might take a look around."

"Of course, Detective. Let me know if you need anything. For now, I'm not going anywhere."

CHAPTER 5

Zane headed away from the gardener's cabin and turned down a path that led to the water. He could hear the crashing of waves against the shore... A soothing sound. He couldn't imagine what it would be like to live there, with your own private beach just a stone's throw away. Another perk of being super rich, he supposed.

A boathouse and jetty came into view. He made his way along the stone path and stepped onto the dock. The door to the boathouse was padlocked, but the windows fronting two sides of the building were clean enough that he could peer through.

A top-of-the-line luxury motorboat filled most of the space. Zane recognized it as a Fairline Targa 52, worth almost half a million dollars. No doubt it was small change for someone with the net worth of Grant Chifley. Zane had seen one just like it at a boat show he'd attended a few months back. It had been way out of his price range, but he'd always loved being on the water—and a man could dream, couldn't he? A fat lot of good all that money had done Chifley. Somewhere along the way, the man had made a deadly enemy who had brought his life to a sudden and violent end.

Zane moved back to the door and examined the padlock. It was old and rusted and looked like it hadn't been used in a while. No doubt, Chifley didn't have much time to cruise around the harbor. He'd been too busy getting rich.

Zane made his way back up through the garden, branching off to take the same path he and Patel had taken earlier. Finally, he reached the pool gate and followed the stone path between the buildings that led to the front where he'd parked.

Climbing into the driver seat, Zane pulled out his phone and brought Willie up to date on his interview with the gardener.

"It sounds like we can cross the gardener off the list," Willie responded.

"Yeah, that's what my gut's telling me, too."

"I guess we go talk to Cody Chifley and see if he can shine any more light on the matter."

"See you soon," Zane replied and ended the call. He punched Cody's address into his GPS and headed back down the driveway. The gates swung open automatically upon his approach.

Interesting. They must be on a sensor. If so, was it possible the killer had lain in wait nearby, seeking the right moment when the gates were opening...? The killer wouldn't necessarily know when a vehicle would be exiting, but perhaps that hadn't mattered. The killer had likely been on a deadly mission to destroy Grant Chifley—and could afford to wait.

Or else it hadn't happened that way at all and the killer was someone who knew the code and had simply let themselves in. Zane didn't know enough about what happened to make a guess either way.

He sighed as he waited for a passing car. From across the road, a woman waved and hurried toward him. She teetered on the uneven pavement in her extremely high heels. A tight, hot-pink skirt that finished well above her knees was teamed up with a white sleeveless blouse, its neckline filled with plump flesh that jiggled as she moved. Zane's gaze drifted higher. The woman's brassy blond hair and bright white teeth defied the age lines visible beneath the heavy makeup on her face.

"You sir! I need to speak with you!"

Zane opened his window and waited for the woman to come closer. A wave of cloying perfume filled his nostrils as she bent down and leaned in close.

"What can I do for you, ma'am?" he asked politely.

She frowned at him. "You're a police officer, aren't you?"

"Yes, ma'am. Detective Sergeant Zane Sullivan. And you are?"

The woman held out a slim, well-manicured hand. Zane shook it.

"Mary-Beth Moore, at your service," she replied and gave him a saucy wink.

Zane tried to hide his discomfort. "It's nice to meet you, Mary-Beth. What can I do for you?"

She leaned forward, even closer, and Zane tried not to gag on her perfume. Her voice lowered to a conspiratorial whisper.

"I heard Grant Chifley was murdered yesterday."

Zane wondered briefly how the news had leaked out. He purposefully avoided the question. "Are you a neighbor of his?"

"Yes. I live right across the street." She stood and pointed to an impressive mansion, directly opposite the Chifley residence. "Of course, I don't have the ocean views Chifley has because my husband, Gerald, was too tight to spend the extra couple of million. But it's nice enough."

Zane tried not to show his impatience. "Ms Moore, I'll ask you again. Is there anything I can do for you?"

"Well, as a matter of fact, it's what *I* can do for *you*, Detective." She chuckled knowingly. Once again, Zane fought to hide his impatience.

"Oh?" he asked in a bored tone.

"Yes! You see, I know something you might find interesting." Her smile widened as she waited for him to respond.

Zane bit back a groan. "And what would that be?"

Seeming to be disappointed by his lack of enthusiasm, the woman once again moved closer, almost putting her head through the open window.

"Yes! You see, a few nights ago I was out in my front garden. I saw one of the twins drive up. It looked like Meghan, but I can't be sure. She and her brother are so alike. Of course, Cody's a little taller, but in the dark and from a distance it's easy to mistake them and Cody drives a white Mazda, too, just like his sister. Anyway, a little while after she disappeared into the house, I heard shouting."

Zane came alert. As if oblivious to his sudden interest, Mary-Beth's forehead creased in a frown. "Come to think of it, Meghan isn't usually one to start an argument, so perhaps it was her brother, after all. Of course, I didn't think too much of it at the time—Grant Chifley was always shouting at someone. You'd think with all that money, he'd be happy." She shook her head and pursed her lips. "No way. He's just as irritable as Gerald." She chuckled again and looked at Zane. "Grant and his oldest daughter, Sarah, were the worst. You put those two together and there were always fireworks."

Zane's heart rate picked up its pace. He stared at the woman and realized she might very well have information that was helpful to his investigation.

"What day and time was this exactly?" he asked.

"It was the night of October fifteenth. I remember because I was watching my favorite TV show before coming outside. I'm not sure of the time, but it was after eight because my show finished at eight. In fact, it was probably closer to nine, come to think of it. Maybe even later."

Zane suppressed a groan of frustration, At least he knew that the argument had occurred sometime after eight. After the time when Arjun Patel told him he went to bed.

"You said you weren't sure which one of the twins it was," Zane said. "How do you know it wasn't Sarah?"

The woman laughed. "Oh no, Detective! I would have known if it was Sarah."

"I take it she doesn't look like her siblings?"

"You're right. She looks exactly like her father. The twins, Meghan and Cody are Grant's children, but they have a different mother. Sarah's mother and her father divorced when she was young. I'm not sure what happened to Eleanor, his ex. I haven't seen her for years. There was talk, she was put into an asylum..."

The woman waved the words away with a chuckle. "Of course, that was just a rumor. I don't think people are put away in asylums these days, are they?"

"Do you know where I can reach Eleanor?" Zane asked, ignoring the question.

Mary-Beth laughed. "Oh, Detective! I wouldn't have a clue. It might be best to ask Sarah, or Meghan. Of course, the divorce happened before Meghan was born, but she's the glue that keeps that family together. She was always the peacemaker, even when she was a little girl. It's probably why she got so good at negotiating her way through conflict. She's a hotshot city lawyer, you know."

Zane nodded. "Yes, I've met Meghan."

A sly expression filled the woman's face. "Oh, so you know she looks like a million-dollar beauty queen, then, don't you? And set to inherit millions too..."

Despite himself, heat suffused Zane's cheeks. He clenched his jaw. "I recall she has blond curly hair and blue eyes. As to her father's will, I have no idea," he managed.

Mary-Beth looked at him knowingly but didn't comment. "Well, Sarah Chifley looks nothing like her half-sister, but I guess you'll find that out for yourself. For a start, she's at least a decade older than her siblings and boy, does she look it."

Zane nodded, suddenly anxious to get on his way. Tearing a piece of paper out of his notebook, he handed it to the woman, along with a pen. "Write down your name, address and phone number, in case I need to get in touch. And take my card. If you remember anything else, please call me." He watched as she scribbled her contact information.

Then the woman took the card from Zane's fingers and slid it inside the deep crevice between her breasts. One long, hot pink-coated fingernail scraped lightly along his arm.

Her voice turned breathy. "Oh, I will, Detective. You can be assured of that. If I remember anything, anything at all, I'll be in touch."

With that, she gave Zane back the piece of paper, folded in half, and smiled.

Tossing it on the seat beside him, he offered her a tight smile then, with the briefest of waves, he left. It was going on for noon and many people were out and about, on their way to lunch appointments.

It was more than forty minutes later that Zane pulled up outside a California-style bungalow on a quiet street in Maroubra. It wasn't quite on the scale of the Point Piper address, but it was far from shabby and only a few blocks from the beach. As Zane climbed out of the squad car, Willie pulled up behind him and got out.

"Good timing," Zane murmured with a grin.

Willie nodded. "You ready?"

Zane unlatched the low gate that provided entry to the property. A cement path directed them to the stone steps leading to the house. Zane lifted the heavy iron knocker and rapped twice against the front door. A few moments later, the door opened. A woman with long straight brown hair, dressed in gym clothes and bare feet stood in the entryway, a quizzical expression on her face.

"Can I help you?"

Zane fished for his ID. "I'm Detective Sergeant Sullivan and this is my partner, Detective Whitehouse. We were wondering if we could speak to Cody Chifley."

A look of distaste twisted the woman's attractive features. Zane put her age somewhere in her mid-twenties. Her brown eyes were wide and clear, though anger glittered in their depths.

"What's he done now, or should I even bother to ask?" she said caustically.

"Are you Tanya Chifley?" Zane asked, ignoring her question.

"Yes."

"Is your husband home?"

She glared at Zane. "No. And please don't refer to him as my husband. He lost the right to call himself that a long time ago."

Zane started in surprise. Meghan Chifley had told them nothing of this. *What the hell was going on?*

"I'm sorry. I didn't realize you were...estranged."

The woman's answering laughter was filled with bitterness. "Estranged. That's a nice way of putting it. I tossed Cody out on his sorry ass four months ago. He hasn't been game enough to show his face around here since. Good riddance, is what I say. The kids and I don't need the likes of him."

Zane half-turned to face Willie. His partner's expression reflected the surprise and confusion that flooded Zane. *Why had Meghan sent them there?* It didn't make sense.

"Do you know where Cody is?" Zane asked, turning back to face Tanya.

"No. Why don't you ask Meghan? They talk every day. Sometimes several times a day. It used to drive me nuts. I mean, I understand they're twins and they need to stay in touch, but three or four phone calls a day?" She shook her head, her expression filled with disgust. "He spoke to his precious sister more than he spoke to me. And that was before his life spiraled out of control." She made a sound of disgust in the back of her throat. "As if things couldn't get worse."

Once again, Zane flicked a look of surprise in

Willie's direction. His partner merely shrugged. Zane returned his attention to the woman.

"We spoke to Meghan yesterday. She gave us this address."

It was Tanya's turn to frown in confusion. "I'm not sure why she did that. Meghan was the first person I called when I tossed her brother out. It didn't come as any surprise to her. He'd been taking heroin on and off for the past year. Then he turned to ice."

She shook her head. "It was the worst thing he could have done. It changed him. Turned him into a monster. He was angry and aggressive and violent. I was scared for me and my kids. I had no choice. I threw him out."

"And you're certain Meghan knew all this?" Zane pressed.

"Of course. Cody doesn't call me as often, but he calls her with some pity story every time he sobers up enough to realize his life has turned to crap. I've had numerous conversations with her about it. I even feel a bit sorry for her. She's caught in the middle, between wanting to love her brother, but unwilling to support or condone his drug habit and the way it makes him behave."

Zane frowned in thought. *Why hadn't Meghan told them any of this and why had she given them this address instead of where he lived now?* According to Tanya, Cody had moved out four months ago. Meghan must have known that. *Why had she deliberately given them the wrong information? What was she trying to hide?*

Zane eyed the woman in front of him. "Do you

have Cody's phone number? I'm afraid the one we have has been disconnected."

Tanya compressed her lips and nodded. She rattled off a number. Zane took note of it and then checked it against the one supplied by Cody's sister.

"Do you know how long he's had this number?" Zane asked.

Tanya frowned. "What do you mean? He's always had this number."

Of course he has, Zane thought grimly. *What the hell game was Meghan Chifley playing?*

He thought back to his conversation with Mary-Beth Moore. The obliging neighbor had plenty to say about the goings on in the house across the road. *Which twin had she seen that night?* Who was Meghan Chifley trying to protect by handing off misleading information? Her brother...or herself?

Zane brought his attention back to Tanya. He reached into his jacket pocket and pulled out his card and gave it to her.

"Thank you for your time, Mrs Chifley. If you hear from your husband—Cody—let him know we're looking for him."

Her expression slowly filled with resignation. "He's in trouble, isn't he?"

"We're not sure. His father was found murdered yesterday. We need to speak with him. If you hear from him, tell him to give me a call."

Ignoring the woman's quiet gasp of shock, Zane turned away and made his way down the steps and along the path to the front gate. Willie followed him. The woman remained standing in her doorway, staring off into space.

"What do you make of that? Talk about strange," Willie murmured when they were out of hearing distance.

Zane compressed his lips and nodded grimly. "In my experience the only reason people lie is because they've got something to hide." He filled Willie in on the information volunteered by Mary-Beth Moore.

"You think Meghan might have more to do with her father's murder than we first thought?"

"Who knows? What we do know is that she's a hell of a liar and perhaps a lot less innocent than we pegged her for. My guess is she knows far more about what happened than she's told us. It's time we pay another visit to little Miss Meghan and this time we're not leaving without satisfactory answers."

Meghan sipped from her mug of herbal tea from her position on one of the loungers that decorated her wide balcony. The sun was high overhead, but she was still in her pajamas. She'd spent most of the night crying and every time she thought of her father, the tears welled up again. It was the day after she'd discovered his lifeless body and she still hadn't gotten over the shock of it. Neither had she heard from Cody.

Someone had walked into her father's house

and murdered him—brutally stabbed him over and over, too many times to count. The level of hate and anger and passion that seemed to fill every corner of that bathroom terrified her. It was like the detective had said: This was personal. This was someone with hate in their heart, hell-bent on seeking revenge. This was more than a random break and enter where her father just happened to get killed. There was nothing random about this. She was sure of it.

But that didn't get her any closer to knowing who murdered her father. She didn't want to contemplate that it could have been Cody, but she was forced to accept it wasn't beyond the realm of reason. Not that she'd tell the police that. There was no way she'd point them in the direction of her beloved brother. Not ever, no matter if he did it or how much he might deserve to be punished.

The truth was, Cody was suffering from an illness. He'd become addicted to dangerous illegal drugs. They turned him into something he wasn't, something unrecognizable... Something terrifying. If he'd been under the influence of ice the night of her father's murder, it was quite possible he could have inflicted the shocking violence on a man they both loved.

She'd tried several more times to call him, but to no avail. The not knowing where he was and what he'd done, ate away at her, churning in her stomach until she could barely keep anything down. She'd turned to herbal tea out of desperation, but even the usually soothing peppermint and ginger concoction didn't ease the tension she felt deep inside.

By now she was sure the murder had hit the papers. The possibility that Cody had found out about their father's death that way filled her with sadness. If he was innocent of any wrongdoing, he'd be devastated.

"Where are you, Cody? Why don't you call?" she whispered.

She'd lost count of the number of messages she'd left for him, each one more desperate than the last. She'd even thought about calling Tanya again. And then she remembered their last phone call and her shoulders slumped on a heavy sigh. Tanya didn't give a fig about Cody. There was no way he'd taken shelter with his young family.

The sound of her front door buzzer interrupted her thoughts. In bare feet, she padded back inside, across the vast expanse of marble tile until she reached the screen affixed to the wall in the kitchen. The familiar figure of Detective Sullivan filled the space. Her heart skipped a beat and a rush of heat flooded her veins.

He might have been investigating the murder of her father, but her body responded to him as if there was a real possibility of something between them.

As if. They barely knew each other. She was merely reacting to an attractive man who just happened to have the ability to send her pulse skyrocketing. With an effort, she slowed her heartbeat and depressed the intercom button.

"Yes?"

"It's Detectives Sullivan and Whitehouse. Can we come up? We'd like to speak with you."

Nerves of a different kind immediately took hold. Her fingers clenched involuntarily over the phone. She'd already told them everything she knew. *What else would they want to speak with her about?*

Had they already discovered she'd given them a false number? She hoped not. She needed more time to find Cody, to beg him to tell her the truth. She didn't know what she'd do if he confessed to killing their father, but she needed to know if he was responsible.

"Ms Chifley? Are you still there?"

She bit her lip and tried to quell her frantic thoughts. The last thing she wanted to do was face another interrogation from two detectives. She wasn't sure if she was more wary of their probing questions or the inexplicable pull of attraction she felt between her and Detective Sullivan. Even in the midst of the horror in her father's bathroom, she hadn't failed to notice how handsome he was. Tall and dark and brooding, with a body sculpted to perfection, even under the well-fitting suit.

"Ms Chifley?" The voice came again, this time with an edge of impatience.

She swallowed a sigh. There was nothing for it. Now that they knew she was home, she had to let them in.

CHAPTER 6

The buzzer, allowing them entry to the swish apartment complex, sounded above Zane's head and the ornate iron gate swung inward. According to the numbers on the security box near the gate, the complex was comprised of ten units, all perched on the hill above Bondi Beach.

In the bright sunshine, the white rendered walls of the building hurt his eyes. The complex looked like it was built in the last five years. There was nothing between the building and the vast expanse of golden beach and deep blue of the Pacific Ocean. Zane could only imagine what kind of view each of them was afforded. It was amazing what a few million dollars could buy.

The wide entryway was faced with pale gray marble tile. The walls were lined with a gold-and-white embossed wallpaper. An elevator stood beside an antique hall table decorated artfully with an arrangement of fresh flowers. The whole place screamed of money and privilege. He wondered if Meghan Chifley enjoyed living there.

Of course she did, you idiot. Did you see the way she was dressed? The jewelry that adorned her neck? The unmistakable air of elegance and refinement that rich people wore like a second skin? She was old money all the way through to her bones. She wasn't born for the likes of him. He'd best get any ideas about her right out of his head. Pronto.

On the way over, Willie had tried Cody Chifley's number. The call had gone straight to voicemail. Willie had left a message before ending the call. Now he reached over and pressed the button for the penthouse. Moments later, the silver doors slid open and both men walked inside. The elevator was every bit as impressive as the foyer. The walls were lined with beveled glass. The floor was shiny black marble. The buttons were edged with gold.

Ding! In no time at all, the elevator arrived at their destination and once again the doors slid open. Directly across from the elevator was a white-painted, wooden double door. Discretely off to one side was the number ten in gold numerals. Zane knocked on the door.

A moment later, it opened and Meghan stood on the other side.

"At least we have the right address this time," he muttered irritably and tried not to notice how good she looked.

Gone was the expensive linen dress and in its place was a plain white designer T-shirt and loose charcoal-gray sweatpants. Her curls were mussed, like she hadn't bothered to brush them yet that morning. Her face was clear of makeup and her eyes were red, like she'd been crying. Her feet were bare.

Somehow, the whole combination served to make her look younger, more vulnerable. Zane clenched his jaw against the instinctive need to comfort and protect this woman and steeled himself to demand the answers he was owed.

"Can we come in?" he asked, his voice rougher than he intended.

She stared at him. For a moment, he thought she might refuse. Then slowly and with obvious reluctance, she nodded and stepped back, allowing them to enter.

The inside of the condominium was even more impressive than the outside. More pale gray marble shone underfoot from the overhead lights above them. The walls were painted a soft blue that contrasted perfectly with the gray. Colorful artworks and a collection of framed black-and-white family photographs filled most of the living room wall above a white leather couch that faced a wall of glass that looked out onto the Pacific Ocean. The view took his breath away. He thought of his modest apartment in the inner west suburb of Newtown and wondered what it would be like to live in such grandeur.

"What can I do for you, Detectives?"

Meghan's quietly voiced question penetrated Zane's thoughts. He blinked and focused his full attention on her.

"Why did you give us the wrong address and phone number for your brother?"

Zane's tone was terse, but he made no apology for it. The fact was, Meghan Chifley had deliberately given them the wrong information and Zane was there to find out why.

He watched her closely. A flush of embarrassment or guilt—he couldn't tell which—crept up her neck and colored her pale cheeks. He noticed she kept her gaze averted from them when she replied.

"I-I-I didn't realize I'd given you the wrong details, Detective. Are you sure?"

Zane's temper rose. She was playing games with him. He narrowed his eyes at her.

"Yes, Ms Chifley, I'm very sure. The phone number you provided has been disconnected. That's if it was ever connected at all. And he's used another number for years… One thing's for certain, the number you gave doesn't belong to your brother. We visited with his wife. Or should I say, his *estranged* wife. Another little detail you managed to keep to yourself. Why didn't you tell us your brother was no longer living at that address? You were well aware he hasn't lived there for the past four months. You sent us on a wild goose chase and I want to know why."

Zane's voice had lowered to a threatening growl by the time he finished. Fear flashed across her face, but was quickly concealed behind a blank mask of indifference. For the first time since their arrival in her condo, she looked at Zane directly, challenging him with her gaze.

"Detective, you seem to have forgotten I was suffering under extreme duress when I provided you with that information. My father had been brutally murdered, lying not more than a few feet away, covered with stab wounds, and naked in his bath tub. I was in shock. I wasn't thinking straight. Surely I'm not the first person in that situation to provide you with incorrect information?"

She glared at him and Zane had to admire her spirit. He accepted that the crime scene she'd witnessed would rattle anyone, but he didn't believe for an instant she'd mistakenly given him the wrong information—and yet, even with him breathing down her neck, she wasn't prepared to concede her duplicity.

"I don't believe you."

Zane's low response elicited a gasp of surprise from the woman. She stood so close he could see the darker flecks of blue in her wide cobalt eyes. A whiff of her expensive perfume wafted toward him, teasing his nostrils. Her hand came up to her mouth and she turned her back to him. With hands clenched into fists, her body visibly trembled from the effort it took to maintain her self-control.

Without conscious thought, Zane's gaze roved over her. Even the simple T-shirt and sweatpants couldn't disguise her attractive figure. He reflexively catalogued the sweet curves and valleys of her petite frame. Toned, muscular shoulders and narrow hips atop slender thighs. Without the benefit of her high heels, she barely came up to his shoulder. The thought gave him pause.

Grant Chifley had been a sizeable man. They'd already established it would take a great deal of strength to move his dead body into the bath tub. Even though Meghan Chifley looked fit and strong, unless she'd acted with a much stronger co-assailant, there was no way she could have accomplished the deed on her own.

Of course, there were numerous stories where people had been capable of extreme strength in extraordinary circumstances and perhaps the level of rage that had been present in the room during Chifley's death would give rise to such supernatural abilities, but Zane had his doubts someone Meghan's size could have accomplished the deed, angry or not.

And then his mind snagged on another thought. It was well known that drug addicts under the influence of methamphetamine had proved they had a supernatural strength. Zane had seen it for himself. He'd once come face to face with an addict high on ice who had torn a huge chunk of metal off the side of a car with his bare hands and had tossed it at the police officers who were trying to subdue him.

It had been a frightening situation, something Zane didn't want to repeat. It was one thing to deal with drunks, or even addicts under the influence of drugs such as cocaine or heroin. It was quite another to deal with someone with ice flowing through their veins. *Someone like Cody Chifley...*

In two long strides, Zane placed himself directly in front of Meghan. The distraught expression on her pale face gave him pause, but he irritably thrust the surge of compassion aside. This woman had withheld evidence. She knew far more than she'd said and in his gut he knew it had something to do with her brother.

"Where's Cody?" he demanded harshly. "And don't even *think* about lying this time."

Her eyes flared with outrage, but they were also shadowed with fear. Zane's heart pounded. So, his initial instincts were right: She knew more than she was willing to admit.

"I... I don't know where he is." Her voice was low and hesitant. Her gaze remained directed toward the floor. Once again, Zane's anger stirred. Beautiful or not, he'd had just about enough.

"Bullshit."

She blinked in surprise and took a step back, almost colliding with Willie who stood his ground. Flustered, her hands came up to her face.

"It's the truth," she cried. "Cody called me five nights ago. I haven't seen or heard from him since."

Zane stared at her, trying to determine if she was telling the truth this time. "Why should I believe you? It's not like you've been forthcoming to date." His tone was laced with sarcasm. A blush stained her pale cheeks.

Pressing home the advantage, Zane took a step toward her, his gaze narrowed on hers.

"Your father was murdered five days ago. I'd say it's way too much of a coincidence that your brother calls you the very night your father was murdered. You think it was him, don't you? That's why you sent us on a wild goose chase. You're giving him more time to hide," he taunted.

Meghan's eyes opened wide in anger and alarm. "*No!* The murder had nothing to do with my brother! There's no way he's capable of doing something like that!"

Zane glared at her. "I don't believe you," he replied, his voice low and threatening. He flicked a gaze at his partner. "What about you, Detective Whitehouse? Do you think the lady's telling the truth?"

Willie's expression remained somber. "Nope. And I don't think she believes it, either. She's covering for him."

Fear once again chased itself across Meghan's expressive face. Zane's glare intensified.

"Yeah, that's what I think, too. Listen here, Ms Chifley, and listen well. If you hear from your brother, you tell him we need to talk. It's in his best interests to show his face sooner, rather than later, because we'll find him—and when we do, we might not be as patient as we normally are."

She nodded jerkily and clenched her hands into fists. The rapid rise and fall of her chest was in time with the pulse Zane spied beating frantically in the side of her neck. She was worried or scared or both.

Good. Scared people made mistakes, acted without thinking. He indicated with a movement of his head toward Willie and with a final searching look in Meghan's direction, he headed toward the door.

"What do you think?" Willie asked as they waited for the arrival of the elevator.

Zane's lips compressed into a tight line. "She's lying about something and I bet it has to do with her brother. She's covering for him. Why else would she give us incorrect information?"

"What are we going to do?"

"We're going to apply for a telephone intercept warrant and see what we can find out. It's my guess she'll continue to try and contact her brother. Now that we have the right number, we'll be able to listen in on any conversations they have. You never know what we might learn."

Willie grinned and gave Zane a wink. "Sounds like a plan, boss. Now, can we go and get lunch? I'm starving."

"Speaking of lunch, did you have any luck with the pizza shops?"

"Yes, as a matter of fact, I did. Jerry's Place on New South Head Road delivered a super supreme thin crust pizza without anchovies to Chifley's Point Piper address a little before eight on the night of his death."

Zane nodded. "That's great. That narrows our timeline down. Samantha Wolfe found partially digested food in his stomach. It's her guess he was killed shortly after eating."

"What time did your witness say she heard shouting from the house?"

Zane frowned, recalling his conversation with Mary-Beth Moore. "It was sometime after eight but before nine. She was a little unspecific."

"Still, the timeline could fit. If Chifley tucked into

his pizza shortly after it was delivered, he could have been murdered before nine."

Zane compressed his lips, feeling grim. Mary-Beth was sure she'd seen one of the twins arrive at Chifley's house right before she heard shouting.

Had she inadvertently caught sight of the murderer right before their deadly deed? And if so, which twin had it been? He was determined to find out.

"I forgot to mention the gardener told me the house was protected by security cameras. We need to get hold of that CCTV footage," he added.

Willie nodded and climbed into the passenger seat of the squad car. "I'll get on it. But first, can you stop by KFC?" He grinned. "You can't expect me to work on an empty stomach."

Meghan picked at a loose cuticle on one of her perfectly manicured nails, still anxious even though the detectives had departed. Even now, they were probably on the hunt for her brother and unless Cody had stumbled across the daily newspapers or happened past a news screening, he mightn't even know of their father's death.

She had to find him. And she had to do it before the way-too-clever detective did. Just the way he'd looked at her, she could tell he knew she was hiding something. Today his eyes were clear and bright. His sharp-eyed gaze missed nothing and from the determined look in his eyes when he glared at her, she knew he wouldn't stop until he discovered just what it was she was keeping from him. In an effort to buy herself some time, all she'd managed to do was turn the detective's suspicions on her.

"Oh, Dear Lord! What am I going to do?" she wailed into the silence.

Ordinarily, the sight of the wide blue expanse of ocean soothed her. It had the opposite effect now. The stunning, serene beauty outside the glass wall seemed to mock her. With a cry of despair, she reached for her phone and for the hundredth time, dialed Cody's number. She gasped in shock when he answered.

"Meghan! What's wrong? You've left a thousand messages and now there's a detective chasing my tail. What the hell's going on? Is everything all right?"

Her relief at finally being able to talk to him overwhelmed her. "No, Cody!" she wailed. "Everything's *not* all right!"

"What happened?" he asked, his tone far more cautious, almost afraid.

With gasping cries, she told him. When she was finished, she was met with shocked silence.

"C-Cody?" she hiccupped. "A-are you still there?"

He sighed heavily. "I'm still here, Meggie. I... I can't believe it." His voice was clogged with tears.

Meghan collapsed back against the couch. *Surely he wouldn't sound so shocked if he'd had prior knowledge of their father's murder?* She clung to that thought.

"Cody, where are you?"

"I'm nowhere," he muttered.

"You must be somewhere," she persisted. "Please tell me and I'll come and get you. You can stay with me for a while."

"I don't think that's a good idea, Meggie. I'm… I'm not in a good place."

Her heart sank. "Do you mean you're using again?"

"You don't understand what it's like, Meghan!" he cried. "You think I'm weak because I can't get my shit together, but it's not as easy as that. I wish I'd never started on the stuff. It's ruined my life. Now I can't stop."

Meghan closed her eyes and fought back a wave of tears. It pained her to hear the despair in her brother's voice. The lure of getting high had been too much for him to resist. She'd known when he'd called her that night that he was high. She heard it in his voice.

Still, she refused to judge him any longer. He was her brother, her family. She loved him—for better or worse. Right now, he needed her. And she needed him, too.

"Please, Cody, let me help you. Together we'll sort this thing out. I'll go with you to the police. The sooner they interview you and dismiss you as a suspect, the better. Then they can go about finding out who did this. Putting Daddy's killer behind bars is the most important thing right now. We can deal with the rest later."

"I don't think I can deal with *any* of it!" Cody's voice broke on a tortured sob. "I can't believe Dad's dead! Murdered! Who would *do* such a thing?"

His anguish sounded so genuine, her heart was put to rest. There was no way Cody had killed their father. She swallowed a sigh of relief.

"We don't know," she replied softly. "But we owe it to Daddy to find out."

"Does Sarah know?"

"Yes. I called her. She's just as upset as the two of us."

"Oh, God. I can imagine. She must be devastated. She spent so much time fighting with him these past few months. Like I did."

His voice caught on a cry of despair. "Oh, Meggie! He's dead! What am I going to do? Now I'll never get the chance to say I'm sorry. I'm never going to see him again!"

Loud sobs filled her ear. "Please, Cody, tell me where you are! You'll be safe here, I promise."

It seemed to take forever for him to reply. When he did, she had to strain to hear it.

"Okay. I'll come. But don't worry about collecting me. I'll get there myself. Where are you?"

"I'm at home."

"Not at work today?"

"No. I... I took some time off."

Cody fell silent. Meghan bit her lip against another surge of tears. She swiped at her eyes with the back of her hand and forced herself to speak again.

"How far away are you?"
"I'm downtown. I'll see you in an hour."
With that, he was gone.

Chapter 7

After leaving Willie to satisfy his cravings for fried chicken and a promise his partner would head straight back to the station and get to work on the telephone intercepts, Zane put Sarah Chifley's address into his GPS. Unlike her younger siblings, Sarah Chifley chose to reside far outside the city limits in a much less desirable part of town. Macquarie Fields was about twenty-four miles south-west of downtown Sydney and a world away from the gloss and grandeur of the eastern suburbs.

Zane checked the house numbers and pulled up beside a place that had seen better days. The dark red brick was faded and cracked. Trash littered the front yard. The meager scattering of grass was yellow and looked like it hadn't seen water in a long time. Climbing out of the squad car, Zane made his way along the uneven concrete path and up three wooden steps. As he crossed the porch, he noticed it was missing a number of boards. The cracked white paint came away under his fingers as he knocked on the door.

He'd already tried the phone number Meghan had given him for her half-sister and was only slightly surprised when Sarah answered. *So it was only Cody she'd felt the need to protect by giving the wrong information… Interesting.*

A woman with gray-flecked, straggly short brown hair met him in the doorway. She looked to be in her late thirties, maybe even a little older. She was taller than Meghan and heavier, too. Her face was pockmarked. It must have been difficult growing up so homely next to someone as beautiful as her half-sister.

Zane tugged out his credentials and flashed them at the woman. "Detective Sergeant Zane Sullivan. Are you Sarah Chifley?"

The woman nodded. "Yes, that's me." Her voice was subdued. Up close, Zane could see her pale blue eyes were red and swollen.

"Are you here about my father?" she asked without enthusiasm.

Zane nodded. "Yes, ma'am. I'm sorry for your loss."

Tears welled up in the woman's eyes and her face crumpled. Huge sobs shook her fleshy shoulders. She cried noisily. Zane stood to one side and waited for her sobbing to subside. When it finally lessened, he tugged out a handkerchief and offered it to her. She accepted it gratefully and dabbed at the moisture in her eyes.

"Th-thank you," she stammered. "You're very kind."

"Do you mind if I come in?" Zane asked quietly.

The woman nodded and backed away, allowing Zane to enter. He squeezed past her through the narrow opening and headed into the nearest room. An overstuffed couch with one cushion missing dominated the small space. Empty takeout food cartons littered a worn and marked coffee table. A flat screen TV stood on a newish-looking cabinet. It was tuned to a daytime soap, the sound turned low.

Sarah entered the room behind him. "Please, Detective. Take a seat."

Zane looked around him. The only available place to sit was the sofa. He perched gingerly on one end, taking care to avoid the stains, and pulled out his notebook and pen.

"Ms Chifley, would you mind if I ask you a few questions about your father?"

She nodded and a fresh wave of tears filled her eyes. He pushed through.

"I understand you're the oldest child from an earlier marriage, is that correct?"

Sarah nodded again. Her double chin jiggled. "Yes. I was ten when my parents divorced. My father remarried two years later. The twins came along a year after that."

"How did you feel about that?" Zane asked.

Sarah shrugged. "I don't know. Okay, I guess."

"It must've been hard to share your father with a new wife and two new babies."

Sarah lifted a shoulder as if it was of no consequence. "They were good kids. Besides, I'm thirteen years older than they are. I wasn't at home very long while they were growing up."

"How do you get on with them now?"

Sarah regarded him steadily. "Fine. Like I said, I didn't have a lot to do with them when they were younger. I left home by the time they were eight."

Zane looked around at the shabby apartment. It was so different from Meghan's posh pad. Even Cody lived at a far more illustrious address. Zane couldn't help but wonder whether Sarah's father had favored the twins and left his oldest daughter out in the cold. It would be interesting to know what the man's will revealed...

He sat up straighter in his seat. If he was on the right track, favoritism toward the twins would surely harbor some deep-seated resentment against her father. Zane couldn't imagine having a couple of his siblings treated like a king and queen while the other was left to fend for herself.

"How well did you get on with your father?" he asked.

Sarah blinked rapidly. A moment later, her eyes filled with tears once again and she let out a cry of pain.

"I loved my father with all my heart! Don't ever let anyone tell you different! We may have had our differences, but we loved each other just the same. No one could come between us. Not even the twins."

Zane eyed her curiously. He hadn't even suggested there had been any different treatment between the children and yet her words seemed to indicate something had been awry. *Interesting.*

Sarah swiped the back of her hand across her eyes and blew her nose noisily into his handkerchief. It was then that he noticed the bandage on her right hand.

"What did you do to your hand?"

She looked down at it and started in surprise, as if she'd forgotten the bandage was there.

"The knife slipped while I was cutting vegetables. It's only a scratch."

Zane made a note in his notebook and then looked back up at her. "What can you tell me about your mother?"

A gentle smile came over Sarah's face. It transformed her from someone plain and homely to a woman who was passably attractive.

"My mother was an angel," she whispered. "For certain my father didn't deserve her. I was glad when they divorced."

Zane blinked in surprise. It wasn't the response he expected. "I thought you said you got on well with your father?"

Sarah shrugged. "I do. I did. That doesn't mean I didn't think my mother deserved much better."

"And yet you stayed behind, with your father."

Sarah's eyes flashed with anger. "My father took my mother to court. He won custody. I stayed with him because I had no choice."

"Interesting," Zane murmured. It was far less common back in those days for a father to get custody of a female child. "Your father must've fought very hard."

Once again, anger darkened Sarah's features. "Of course he did! He had more money than she did. He could afford the best lawyers, the best barristers. He probably even paid off the judge. He fought until my mother had nothing left."

Sarah's breath came fast. Gone was the sad apathy and in its place was a bitterness she didn't bother to conceal.

"Where's your mother now?"

The woman bit her lip and looked away. The anger eased from her face. When she finally replied, her tone was sad and distant.

"She died a year ago. Cirrhosis of the liver. She drank herself to death. I think she died of a broken heart."

"Did you see her much over the ensuing years?"

Sarah shook her head and anger once again lit up the depths of her eyes. "No. My father saw to that. By the time he finished dragging her through the Family Court, he'd convinced anyone who mattered that she was insane. I was told she'd been taken to a health farm."

Her lips twisted into a grimace. "I might only have been ten, but even I knew that was polite talk for the loony bin."

She shook her head slowly back and forth. "I still can't believe he did it. My mother. My beautiful mother. Within two years, he'd replaced her with a new wife."

"And yet, you loved your father with all your heart, right?"

Sarah nodded sadly. "Yes. I did. We didn't always see eye to eye, but I loved him just the same. He was the only father I had."

"So you didn't blame him for sending your

mother away? Removing her from your life? You were ten years old. A time when any little girl needs her mother. Surely you were upset with him for doing that?"

Instead of the anger Zane expected, there was only sad resignation. "Of course I was upset, but that was a long time ago, Detective. I learned to forgive him. To let the past go. Besides, it wasn't all bad. I had my brother and sister for company. They were two cute little peas in a pod. They were very easy to love."

"When did you last see your father?" Zane asked quietly.

Sarah's bottom lip trembled and once again tears glinted in her eyes. "A little over a week ago. We had dinner."

"At your place or his?" Zane asked."

"His."

Zane looked around the modest room. "Are you married, Ms Chifley?"

"No."

"What about kids?"

"No."

"Your father has plenty of room in his house. Why not live with him?"

Sarah grimaced. "He wouldn't let me. When I first moved out of home, I shared a place with some friends. We pooled our resources. We didn't have much, but we made it work. Over the years my friends drifted away. I'm here now by myself."

"Where do you work?"

"I'm between jobs at the moment."

"What do you normally do?"

For the first time, Sarah looked uncomfortable. "This and that. Nothing in particular."

"When was the last time you held down a job?"

She frowned. "I worked as a waitress in high school. For a couple of weeks. I quit. They only wanted me at night and it was always on weekends. I had better things to do with my time. I did have a life, you know."

Zane nodded. He remembered how he held down three jobs all through high school just to make ends meet. He wasn't lucky enough to have a rich daddy picking up the tab.

"If you're between jobs, how do you pay the rent?" he asked. "Does your father help out?"

She scoffed. "Not likely. Dad didn't approve of my inability to get a job. He cut off my allowance. Forced me to live like this. Do you think I'd live here if I didn't have to? It's been three years. Let me tell you, I'm well and truly over it."

"So, why not get a job?" Zane asked. "It works for most of us."

Sarah's eyes narrowed in a glare. "Spoken by someone who's never known what it's like to be handed everything on a silver platter," she snarled. "It's hard when all that comfort, all that luxury is suddenly switched off. Just ask Cody. He didn't take it so well when Dad threatened to write him out of the will."

Zane sat up straighter. "What do you mean?"

Sarah waved his question away. "I'm sorry, Detective. I spoke out of school. You should talk to Cody about that."

"How did you feel about having your allowance cut off? That must have been upsetting."

"Of course it was, but I didn't hold it against Dad," she continued. "I understood where he was coming from. Some would say he did it for all the right reasons. That it was for my own good. He forced me to grow up, take responsibility for myself. I guess that's not a bad thing. For anyone."

"So, have you? Grown up?" Zane asked, looking around him.

Sarah's expression turned sly. "No. But I'm working on it."

There was a pause while the two of them sat in thought. Zane jotted down a few more notes and then glanced up at the woman again. He purposefully kept his voice low and conversational.

"Where were you five nights ago, Sarah? The night of October fifteenth?"

"I was here," she replied. "I had a microwave dinner. Watched some TV. Then I went to bed."

"Can anyone back that up?"

Sarah shook her head. "No, Detective. I live alone. I didn't realize I'd need an alibi."

"What did you watch on TV?"

"I don't remember."

"What time did you go to bed?"

"Ten, maybe eleven. I don't remember."

"How did the twins get on with your father?"

Sarah blinked at his abrupt change of topic. "Okay, I guess. Of course Meghan was his favorite.

She could do no wrong. It was always that way. She's the golden child."

Zane watched her closely. Try as he might, he couldn't detect any bitterness in Sarah's tone. Either she was exceptionally good at forgiving or she was a far better actress than he'd given her credit for.

"How did your father deal with Cody's drug addiction?"

Surprise flared in her eyes, but she quickly recovered and answered. "He wasn't happy about it. Like I said, the last time he and Cody were together, Dad threatened to cut Cody out of his will. He refused to fund Cody's drug habit. Meghan felt the same."

This time it was Zane who felt surprise. "What does Cody do for a living?"

"He's a stockbroker in the city. At least, he used to be. He lost his job when the drugs took over. That's one of the things he and Dad argued about. Dad couldn't understand why Cody couldn't give up the drugs and get his shit together. Dad thought an addiction was a sign of weakness and if there was one thing my father couldn't stand, it was weakness."

"How's Cody supporting himself if he's no longer working?"

Sarah shrugged. "Same way I am, I guess. On benefits. Going from week to week." Her bark of laughter was utterly devoid of humor. "It's ironic isn't it? Dad's richer than Croesus and two out of three of his kids are destitute."

Once again, Zane watched Sarah closely, but

only the faintest hint of bitterness was visible on her face. She had every reason to be resentful, but it appeared she wasn't.

Satisfied, he tucked his notebook back in his jacket pocket and stood. He held out his hand to Sarah. "Thank you for speaking with me, Ms Chifley. I want you to know we're doing all we can to find your father's killer." He reached into his pocket and pulled out a business card and handed it to her. "If you think of anything else, call me."

She nodded and tucked the card into her bra. He was reminded of Mary-Beth, the deceased's neighbor. Sarah slowly got to her feet and showed him to the door.

With a murmured farewell, he left. Once back in the squad car, he called Willie and brought him up to date.

"So what's your take on the sister?" Willie asked when Zane was done.

"It's an interesting one, that's for sure."

"In what way?"

"Well, it's hard to get a reading on her. She has plenty of reasons to be angry and resentful toward her father, but she doesn't seem to feel that way at all. She's probably physically capable of lifting two-hundred-and-sixty-five pounds of dead weight, but does she have enough motive? We don't know yet what the will says."

"Her rich daddy cut off her allowance and refused to let her come back home. That would be enough to piss me off," Willie replied dryly.

"Yes, but that was three years ago. If she was

that aggrieved, surely it would have come to a head by now?"

"Yeah, I guess. Although what do they say about revenge being a dish best served cold?"

Zane laughed. "You've been reading too many Agatha Christie's, Willie."

"Agatha who?"

Zane rolled his eyes. "Forget it. Listen, have you had any luck with the telephone intercepts? I'd really like to track down the brother. I have a feeling he has a lot more to do with this than we know."

"You're in luck. Judge Harrow was on call. He approved the intercept with barely a discussion. We're good to go. The techies should have it up and running within the hour."

"Great. Grant Chifley's neighbor said she saw one of the twins arriving at his house the night he died. That sounds suspicious to me. My money's on one of them being our guy."

"Don't forget we still have to interview the plumbers," Willie said.

"You're right. Chifley had some kind of dispute with them not long before he died. We'll definitely talk to them, but my gut's telling me this is personal. Still, I'm not ruling anyone out. Everyone's a suspect until we prove otherwise, and that includes the gardener and the oldest Chifley sibling. No one can be *that* forgiving."

CHAPTER 8

Meghan glanced up from where she was seated at the breakfast table and managed a wan smile in Cody's direction. He stumbled down the hallway toward her in a borrowed T-shirt and sweatpants that were a few inches short. With his overlong hair askew and dark whiskers shadowing his normally clean-shaven cheeks, he looked almost as bad as he had when he'd arrived the night before.

His blue eyes remained sunken and bloodshot. The scratches on his arms were still angry and red. Worried he'd hurt himself, she'd asked him about them and had been taken aback when he'd reacted angrily, telling her it was none of her business. Besides, he'd added, they were nothing. He couldn't even remember getting them.

"Would you like some coffee? I just made a fresh pot."

He nodded gratefully and helped himself to a mug. Adding sugar and cream, he took a sip and sighed heavily.

"Ahh, that's good. Thanks." He took a seat opposite her at the table.

She regarded him steadily and tried hard to conceal the concern that hadn't gone away since his arrival.

"Stop looking at me like that, Meg," he grumbled.

"Like what?"

"Like you're trying to work out what the hell happened to me," he snapped.

Embarrassment heated her cheeks, along with a stirring of anger. The last time she'd seen him had been at their birthday party a month earlier and apart from the occasional sporadic phone call, like the one he'd made the night their father had been murdered, she hadn't heard from him. He looked like he'd been living rough all that time. Not so long ago, he'd been flying high, a successful stockbroker who wore thousand-dollar suits and had a six figure income. *Surely she was within her rights to feel worried?*

With an effort, she swallowed her irritation and replied with a degree of calmness.

"I'm just concerned for you, Cody. Is that so bad? The last time I saw you was when you threw a punch at Daddy. It shocked me to the core. Now he's been murdered. Is it bad to care that my brother looks like he's hit rock bottom and my family's falling apart?"

Her voice cracked with the force of her emotions and she tried desperately to hold back sobs. She'd cried enough already.

Cody remained silent. He stared down at the table. A muscle moved in his jaw and then a silent tear rolled down his cheek. Meghan was overwhelmed with sympathy. Forgetting about her own distress, she pushed back her seat and ran to his side, holding his head close against her.

"Oh, Cody! I'm sorry! I didn't mean it! I love you! It kills me to see you like this! I know it's not my fault, but somehow I feel responsible! I hated that you and Daddy were fighting—and now he's dead and you're never going to be able to say you're sorry! I only want to help you! I wish I could turn back time to when we all were happy. I wish Daddy were still alive and could reassure us things would work out all right, no matter how dark and gray they seem. But that's never going to happen. We're never going to see him, hear him, hug him again."

Her tears began to fall in earnest. Cody cried along with her. It seemed they were both powerless against the outpouring of their grief. From some distant point in her mind, she registered the sound of her phone ringing, but was depleted of what was required to answer it. After what seemed like an eternity, their sobs quieted and gradually, they pulled themselves together. Meghan hunted for a tissue and after finding a box on the kitchen counter, handed it to her brother.

"Look at us. We're a mess," he joked, remnants of tears still glistening in his eyes.

She managed a weak smile and blew out her breath on a sigh. "Yep. But I'm pretty certain we have a good excuse, right?"

Cody nodded sadly. "Yeah. It doesn't get any easier every time I think about it. Poor Dad."

Silence fell between them as they each became lost in their thoughts. Cody was the first one to break it.

"Do the police have any idea who murdered him?"

Meghan squirmed uncomfortably and averted her gaze. Cody's voice sharpened.

"What is it, Meg? What aren't you telling me?"

She closed her eyes and compressed her lips and searched for the courage to tell him. "The police have you on their list of suspects," she blurted out.

Shock flooded Cody's face. "*What?*"

Meghan eyed him steadily. "It's true. They interviewed a whole bunch of people, including me. I think we're all suspects."

"That's ridiculous!" He pushed away from the table and began to pace, as if he were unable to sit still another moment.

"Is it?" Her quietly voiced question had him rounding on her, his eyes wide with shock.

"What are you talking about? Don't tell me *you* think *I* had something to do with Dad's murder?"

She bit her lip and looked away. Her hesitation seemed to infuriate him.

"Meghan Chifley! Look at me!" he demanded.

Slowly she lifted her gaze to his and steeled herself against the anger she saw there. "I'm sorry, Cody. I had to ask."

"Why the hell would you ever think *I* was the one responsible?"

She compressed her lips and shrugged,

reluctant to answer. Cody's lip curled upwards in disgust.

"I don't believe it! My own sister! My twin! She thinks I brutally murdered our father!" He shook his head slowly back and forth in disbelief.

"No, Cody! It isn't like that!" she protested. "I don't *want* to believe you did it. But..."

He shot her a dark look. "But what?"

She sighed heavily. There was nothing to do but to lay her suspicions at his feet. It would be a relief to unburden herself. She clenched her hands into fists and hoped like hell he had the right answers.

"You called me late one night. The same night we now know Daddy was killed. Do you remember?"

Cody's forehead scrunched up in thought. "Not really. I've... I've been doing a lot of bad shit lately. It messes with my head. I can't keep things straight. What did I call you about?"

"You sounded terribly distressed. You kept telling me you were sorry. That you'd messed up. That someone forced you to do something." She paused and looked at him, her breath coming fast. "Do you remember any of that?"

Cody slowly walked back to the breakfast table and threw himself down in a chair. With his elbows on the table, he dropped his head into his hands.

"I was in a bad way, Meggie. I didn't know what to do."

Her heart leaped into her throat. She tensed, unsure if she was ready to hear what he had to say. "So, you remember making the call?"

"Yes."

Dread settled like a cold hard weight in her belly. "What were you talking about, Cody?" she whispered.

It was a long moment before he spoke. "I owed my dealer some money. That night, I was downtown in a seedy bar, looking to get high. Gordo found me there. He'd come to collect his money. It wasn't a lot. A few hundred dollars, but I didn't have it. He roughed me up a bit, pulled a knife. He cut me." He held up his left hand and she saw the slash across the back of it.

"Gordo's a real piece of work. He told me if I didn't show up with the money the next day, it would be my last."

She held her breath, hardly daring to breathe. "What did you do?" she managed.

"I told him I knew where he could get his hands on some stuff he could sell for way more than I owed. I... I gave him your address and the security code to your condo. I told him to break in during office hours. You wouldn't be home then."

His voice was thick with shame and fresh tears escaped his eyes. He sobbed quietly into his hands. Still, her mind clung to every word he'd uttered and though she was shocked by his confession, she was also overwhelmed with relief.

Her brother hadn't called her that night to confess to killing their father! He'd merely been trying to warn her that he'd given some low-life drug dealer the tools to break into her place.

What he'd done was unbelievably awful and she was shocked to her core, but it wasn't murder. Thank God it wasn't that. She eased out her breath and the tension inside her lessened, even as she made mental preparations to change her locks and the security code.

She put her hand on Cody's shoulder. With comforting strokes, she rubbed his back until his distress eased. Finally he lifted his head and regarded her with swollen, red-rimmed eyes.

"I'm sorry, Meggie. I'm sorry for everything. I'm such a fuck up."

"You've made some poor decisions lately, Cody. That's for sure," she said softly. "But none of us are perfect and it's not too late to turn your life around. I love you, Cody and I want to help you in any way that I can. But first we need to deal with Daddy's murder. We need to help the police find his killer and we can do that by making sure they stop looking in our direction. We both know they're wasting their time. We need to make certain they believe that, too."

Cody's expression filled with resignation. "There was a message on my phone asking me to call a Detective Sullivan. Is that the officer you've been dealing with?"

At the mention of the detective's name, Meghan was flooded with heat. Memories of his physical presence, his unspoken authority coupled with a mocking arrogance she hated to admit she found attractive... She squirmed with embarrassment and averted her gaze.

"Yes. And his partner. Detective Whitehouse. They're in charge of the murder investigation."

"Whitehouse. Yes, he's the one who left the message." Cody shook his head slowly back and forth. "I still can't believe Dad's dead. That he was murdered. I can't think of anyone who might have done it."

Meghan nodded. "Me, neither."

Cody's shoulders slumped on a heavy sigh. "God, what a mess."

Meghan compressed her lips, feeling grim. "You can say that again."

"Let's just hope the cops find who's really responsible," Cody murmured.

"Yes," Meghan agreed. "Just out of interest, when did you see Daddy last?"

Cody hesitated. He drew in a long breath and blew it out between his lips. His seeming reluctance to answer her question brought her alarm once again to the fore.

"Cody? When was the last time you saw Daddy?" This time, her tone brooked no argument.

Cody glanced up at her and then returned his attention to the cuts and scabs on his arms. He began picking at them with his fingers.

"Cody?" Her voice was thick with warning.

He sighed. "I saw him the same night I called you."

She gasped in shock. "*What?*"

His gaze remained fixed on the table. "I needed money, Meggie. I went to see Dad."

Coldness gripped her insides. "Oh, Cody. Please don't tell me you had an argument?"

He nodded, his expression bleak. "Oh, yeah. We argued, all right."

Her belly sank. Now knowing the reason for his late night call, she was certain her brother hadn't murdered their father, but this bit of information? It didn't look good for him. She had to make certain the police would never find out.

"What happened?" she asked dully.

"I went over there, hoping to find him home. I was desperate. Gordo wanted his money. I knew he'd find me that night and demand it. I didn't have it. I went over to Dad's house hoping he'd give it to me."

"Was he home?"

"Yes."

"What time was this?"

"I don't know. Maybe eight or nine."

"What happened?"

"I let myself in through the front door. The house was dark and quiet. I found him in his study. When I asked him where Mrs Abbott was, he told me she was visiting her sister in the country."

"Did he know you were coming?"

"No. I put in the security code down at the entrance gates. He wouldn't have heard me drive in."

"Was he happy to see you?" she asked hopefully.

Cody's lips twisted on a grimace. He shot her a look. "What do you think?"

She compressed her lips and remained silent. The last time Cody and her father had been in the same room, Cody had punched him in the face. She could only imagine what took place the night her father died...

"Anyway, like I said, I found him in his study. He was already dressed for bed. I tried to make small talk, but he shut me down and asked me point blank what I was doing there. Like I was a stranger come in from the street."

Anger colored Cody's voice. Meghan's hands curled into fists. She didn't know if she wanted to hear what was coming, but she had no choice.

"What happened then?"

"I told him I needed money. That I was desperate," Cody continued quietly, his voice gruff with emotion.

Meghan barely dared to voice the next question. "What did he say?"

Cody's answering bark of laughter was filled with bitterness. "He said no, of course! Not in quite that way. Let's just say he didn't hold back pointing out my deficiencies and stating there was no way in hell I was getting a dime. He reminded me about his threat to cut me out of his will and then proceeded to gloat about how he'd already given instructions to his lawyer to that effect. He laughed at me, Meggie. He called me a loser. A drug addict. He called me pathetic."

Cody's breath came faster and anger flushed his face. Meghan prayed silently that the argument hadn't turned violent. With her heart in her throat, she forced herself to ask the next question. "What did you do, Cody?"

He was silent for so long she thought she'd scream. She was about to ask him again when he answered.

"We shouted and yelled at each other. He pushed me and I pushed him back. He told me to get the hell out of his house and never come back."

Cody was breathing heavily, as if he were back there in that moment. Meghan held her breath and waited for him to finish.

"I wanted to plead my case again, but I could see it was no use. Any love he might have had for me was gone. It was all my fault. I was the one to blame. If I hadn't gotten hooked on drugs, I would never have found myself in this position in the first place. Dad was right to turn me away...and so were you."

He looked up at her and the pain in his eyes made her heart clench.

"Oh, Cody! I didn't want to! You have to believe me! I'd do anything for you! I love you! But you were breaking my heart! I couldn't give you money, knowing you were going to shoot it up your arm. I offered to pay for rehab, remember? The best facility in the state. I'm still willing to do that, if you'll let me." She softened her tone. "What do you think?"

He stared up at her and his eyes filled with tears. "I don't deserve you, Meggie," he choked. "After I left Dad's, I went to Gordo and gave him your security code. I'm such an asshole. A selfish prick of an asshole."

"You did what you had to do, Cody. I understand. You were desperate. If you'd been in your right mind, you'd never have done it. At the end of the day, we're family. Family sticks together, no matter what." She paused and then added, "So, does this mean you're willing to give rehab a shot?" She couldn't keep the hope from her voice.

Cody nodded slowly. "Yes. I want to get clean more than anything. For you, for me, for Tanya and the kids. I've let so many people down."

Meghan squeezed his shoulder. "Don't be too hard on yourself, Cody. Your life went off course for a while, but it's time to get back on track. I just wish.

Daddy was around to see it."

This time, it was she who choked on her tears and it was Cody who offered her comfort. He stood and gathered her in his arms. She laid her head on his shoulder and allowed a few tears to escape. After a while, she pulled back and looked up at him.

"You didn't finish telling me about what happened while you were at Daddy's."

Cody grimaced and dropped his arms to his side. "Things ended the way I expected. Dad continued to refuse to give me money and I eventually walked out."

"Where was he when you left?"

"Still in his study. He told me to get out and leave him alone so he could take himself off to bed."

"He was found in his bathroom," she said quietly.

Cody acknowledged her comment with a brief nod. A long moment of silence passed between them.

"We need to go to the police, Cody," she finally said.

His expression turned grim, but he nodded again. "Yes."

CHAPTER 9

Zane pulled on his seatbelt and glanced across at Willie. "Do you have the address for Dorrington Plumbing Services?"

"Yep. Ten fifty-six Maddox Street, Alexandria," his partner replied.

After entering the address into the GPS, Zane put the squad car into gear and pulled away from the station. His belly grumbled and he was reminded he hadn't eaten. He'd been busy all morning at the station and hadn't had time for lunch. And still he was no closer to solving the Chifley murder, despite the hours he was putting in. The knowledge churned in his gut.

The two-story, red-brick industrial building that housed the offices of Dorrington Plumbing had seen better days. Zane pulled up beside the curb and he and Willie climbed out. A laneway ran down the side of the building to a large steel shed. Zane guessed it contained tools and plumbing supplies and other paraphernalia a plumber might need.

He opened the door that led inside the building and walked up to the reception desk. An elderly woman with snow-white hair and bright green eyes greeted him.

"Hello, there. What can I do for you?" she asked.

Zane pulled out his credentials and showed her. "I'm Detective Sergeant Sullivan. This is Detective Whitehouse. We'd like to ask you a few questions about Grant Chifley. Did you do some work for Mr Chifley a week or so ago?"

She nodded. "Sure. The boys couldn't stop talking about that mansion out at Point Piper. I wish I could have gotten a peek." She chuckled.

Zane acknowledged her comment with a brief smile. "It's some place, that's for sure."

The woman's smile faded, as if she suddenly wondered about why the police would be there asking questions about one of their jobs. "Why are you asking, Detective? Is something the matter?"

"Grant Chifley was found murdered in his bathroom the day before yesterday. We believe he'd been murdered about three days prior. Your men were there in his house in the days before. We'd like to talk to them."

A look of fear crossed her face. "Surely you can't think my boys had anything to do with this? They're good boys. They wouldn't have been involved in something like this. Murder?" She shuddered. "No way."

"I appreciate you saying so, Ms...?"

"Mrs Dorrington. Clara Dorrington. My husband started this business forty-eight years ago.

Unfortunately he died of lung cancer last year. My sons, Harry and Riley, took over the business. It was lucky for us they'd both learned the trade. They've done a good job of it, too. I'm so proud of them. There's no way they could have been involved in something like this."

Willie stepped forward. "Thank you, Mrs Dorrington. We're sure your boys are good and decent, just like you say, but we'd like to speak to them. Are they around?"

"Harry's out back. Riley's gone to another job."

"Do you mind calling Harry into the office?" Zane asked.

The woman nodded warily and picked up the phone. She spoke quietly into the receiver. A moment later, she ended the call.

"Harry's on his way."

A few minutes later, a door behind the reception desk opened and a tall burly man who looked to be in his mid-thirties filled the small space. He stepped forward with his hand out. His muscles bunched under his work shirt.

"I'm Harry Dorrington."

Zane shook his hand and made the introductions. Then he cleared his throat. "Your mother told us you had a job over at the Chifley house recently?"

"That's right," Harry replied.

"Are you aware Grant Chifley was found murdered a couple of days ago?"

Zane watched the man closely. What looked like genuine shock filled his face.

"We've been told there was a dispute between

you and Grant Chifley over the bill," Willie said. "Do you know anything about that?"

Harry nodded. "Yes. For some reason, Mr Chifley disputed our hours. Our rates are fair and we charge only for the time we're on a job. I met with him and showed him the timesheets we always keep on every job. In the end, he paid the bill in full."

Zane's gaze roved over the man, from his wide shoulders to his broad chest. He certainly looked strong enough to carry the dead weight of Grant Chifley.

"Where were you on the night of October fifteenth?" Zane asked.

"I went to a bar with my brother after work and then I went home."

"Was anyone else there?" Willie asked.

"Yeah, my wife Annabelle and our two kids. We watched TV and went to bed about nine."

"Do you mind showing me your hands?" Zane asked.

Harry shrugged then held out his hands. Zane's heart skipped a beat. A mess of small nicks and cuts were visible across the man's fingers. Zane glanced at Willie. His partner nodded. He didn't need to be told about the significance of the wounds.

"What did you do to your hands?" Zane asked, keeping his tone casual.

Harry looked down at his hands in confusion. "What do you mean?"

"Those cuts," Willie said. "Where did you get them?"

"Oh, those. I was gutting fish on the weekend. We went out on the Parramatta River. Caught some good ones, too."

"Anyone else with you?" Zane asked, making notes in his notebook.

"Yeah. Mom was there and so was Riley and a couple of other mates. Oh, our wives were there, too. There's no one who can make beer-battered fish fillets like my wife does."

Zane nodded. "Are you left- or right-handed, Mr Dorrington?"

"I'm right-handed."

"What about your brother?" Willie asked.

"He's right-handed, too."

"Did he work on the Chifley house?" Zane asked.

"Yes. We were both there together."

Zane acknowledged the comment with another nod and after taking down a few more details, closed his notebook and returned it to his pocket. From Harry's account of what had happened, the dispute over the bill seemed to have quickly been sorted out. It didn't seem like the sort of thing that would engender the kind of passion and hate that had overwhelmed the crime scene. Still, until they had a clearer idea of their killer, no one was getting ruled out yet. *And there were those injuries to his hands…*

Zane handed Harry a business card. "When your brother returns, ask him to call me. If you think of anything else that might help the investigation, let me know."

The man nodded and tucked the card away in

a pocket of his shirt. With a nod of farewell toward Clara, Zane and Willie let themselves out.

"What do you think?" Zane asked as they headed away from the building.

"He looks strong enough to have done the deed and he does have some suspicious looking cuts on his hands. He's definitely a possibility."

"What about the fishing story?"

"Well, he nominated a list of witnesses. Too bad for him they're all related to him. Not exactly impartial."

"Yeah, but he offered an alibi for the night in question and to tell you the truth, I'm just not feeling it," Zane replied. "The level of hate in that bathroom... That was personal. I just don't see a plumber, even one who had a minor beef with the guy over a bill, could work himself up to such a state. But you never know. I guess we'll see what the brother has to say."

"What now?" Willie asked.

"Back to the station, I guess. Let's check on the progress of those telephone intercepts." Halfway to the squad car, Zane's phone rang. He pulled it out and glanced at the screen.

His heart skipped a beat. It was Meghan.

———

Meghan glanced nervously around the metal-gray walls of the police station and made a conscious effort to stop tapping her nails against her handbag. Cody sat beside her in one of the hard plastic chairs that lined the back wall of the room, looking just as nervous. The usual posters denouncing drunk driving, speeding and other illegal behavior decorated the otherwise bland walls.

As a lawyer, Meghan should have been used to being inside a police station, but she was an estate lawyer and generally had no reason to visit the cells. Her clients didn't call at all hours, desperate for legal advice and for her to arrange bail. In fact, the only time she'd even been inside a police station in her career was while she'd been in college. One of her compulsory courses had been criminal law and her lecturer had included a tour of their local police station as part of the coursework for them to cover.

That had been years ago, and even though this wasn't the same station she'd toured in college, the smell of the place was reminiscent. Sweat and unwashed bodies and most of all: fear. She could never have been a career criminal. Just the thought of being locked up in a jail cell had her on the edge of panic.

Gripping the leather straps of her handbag, she forced herself to calm down. She risked a glance at her brother and her alarm ratcheted up another notch. If she was on the verge of a panic attack, he was on the brink of a full-on breakdown.

Pale and sweating, his hand trembled violently as he ran his fingers through his hair, leaving it all askew. She'd insisted he clean himself up a bit before they left and had washed and dried his clothes. He'd showered and shaved and now looked halfway decent, but nothing could conceal the abject fear that shadowed the depths of his blue eyes.

She reached over and squeezed one of his hands. "It's going to be all right, Cody. You'll see. You're doing the right thing. Just remember what we talked about. There's no need to mention your visit to Daddy's on the night he died. That will only raise the detectives' suspicions. We both know you didn't murder Daddy. You have nothing to fear. It will all be over soon."

She heard the words falling from her mouth and wondered which one of them she was trying to convince. She refused to contemplate the answer. They were there to present the police with the facts as far as Cody's movements were concerned. Once they'd heard what he had to say, the police would concede he wasn't their killer and would turn their focus elsewhere. At least, that's how she hoped it would go.

A door to her left came open and she looked up in time to see Detective Sullivan's large frame fill the space. Like it had the other times she was in his presence, her heart skipped a beat and her pulse picked up its pace in a combination of attraction and fear. It wasn't just that his sheer physicality was intimidating. It was also the aura of power that surrounded him. The certainty that wherever he was, he was in control. It filled her with a heady combination of fear and awe and confusion and together those things sent her heart racing. Meghan stood at his approach.

"Ms Chifley, it's good to see you again," he said, his voice smooth and unrevealing.

She nodded. "Detective Sullivan. This is my brother, Cody Chifley."

The detective turned to Cody and held out his hand. "Mr Chifley, it's nice to meet you. Thanks for coming in."

Cody shook the proffered hand and mumbled some kind of greeting. His gaze remained fixed on the floor. Meghan hurried to fill the silence.

"Detective, I managed to get in contact with Cody last night and told him about what happened to our father. He was just as shocked as I was and is here to assist you in any way he can. Both of us want to help you find the killer."

Zane nodded and turned his attention to Cody. "That's good. Are you ready to get started?"

Meghan glanced at her brother and gave him a reassuring smile. If anything, he looked even more nervous than he had earlier. Dread filled her stomach and she wondered if this was such a good idea after all.

Perhaps she should call Cody a lawyer? A lawyer experienced in criminal matters. But that would mean calling a halt to their meeting and waiting for someone else to arrive. It had been hard enough convincing Cody to come here in the first place. He'd only agreed because she'd assured him she'd be with him every step of the way.

If she suggested they find someone else to represent him, he might get up and walk right out the door and then where would that leave them?

The police would become even more suspicious of her brother and waste time looking into Cody when they should be looking for the person who actually committed the heinous crime.

She sighed, still unsure of what to do. The detective made the decision for her when he took a step backwards and suggested they move to an interview room. Without waiting for their answer, he turned his back to them and headed through the doorway from which he'd entered. In silence, she and Cody followed him.

Meghan stared at the detective's broad shoulders. He wore another perfectly fitting suit. This one was navy-blue and he'd paired it with a navy-blue-and-white striped shirt and a yellow-and-gray tie. His black boots were clean and shiny and he smelled pleasantly of pine needles and fresh air. Altogether, he was an attractive man and one she'd best avoid. She had a strong sense there could be something between them… But no. She had enough stress in her life already without taking on the challenge of a new relationship, even with someone as sexy as this detective.

Ahead of her, he opened a door that led into a small interview room. It had no windows and the only furniture was a table and four chairs. The dark-colored, industrial carpet muffled their footsteps as they entered the room. With a slight gesture, the detective indicated they take a seat and he immediately followed suit.

"Okay, so Mr Chifley, have you ever given an interview to the police before?"

Cody shook his head. "No."

"Well, this is how it goes. If you are agreeable, the interview will be electronically recorded. You'll see a camera up there on the wall."

He pointed and both Meghan and Cody looked up. An innocuous-looking camera was mounted on the wall and pointed toward them. Meghan swallowed another surge of nerves and noticed Cody did the same. Sympathy for her brother flooded through her. She prayed they'd get this over with quickly and then they could leave.

"As you're already in the company of your lawyer, we won't need to enquire about whether or not you want legal representation."

Meghan blinked and looked up at the detective. "I'm sorry, Detective. That's not quite right."

The detective cocked a single dark eyebrow. "Oh? You're not a lawyer?"

Meghan blushed. "No. I mean, yes, I'm a lawyer, but I deal with wills and estates. I certainly don't specialize in criminal matters. I'm here in the capacity of Cody's support person, his sister." She held the detective's gaze. "My brother has done nothing wrong. He doesn't need the presence of a lawyer."

The detective offered half a shrug, as if it were of no consequence. "Whatever." He turned and looked directly at Cody. "Just so you know, Mr Chifley, you're entitled to the services of a lawyer, if you want one. All you have to do is say the word."

Cody looked at Meghan, his eyes fearful, his expression torn. She could tell it was taking all his courage just to stay seated. Despite his recent fall into the darker side of life, being questioned by a detective who regarded him as a potential suspect in his father's murder was as foreign to Cody as it was to her. They needed to get this over with, and quickly, before Cody panicked and changed his mind. Lawyer or no lawyer. She just hoped they were both up to the task.

"Ask your questions and just get on with it," Cody muttered, keeping his gaze directed toward his feet.

Detective Sullivan pulled a notebook out of his jacket pocket and flipped through the pages. At one point, he paused and then asked his first question.

"Where were you on the night of October fifteenth?"

October fifteenth… So much had happened that night. Meghan closed her eyes on a wave of sadness and pain and then forced them open again when her brother responded.

"I can't remember."

Meghan blinked in surprise and a trickle of unease made its way through her veins. *What was he doing?* He was supposed to tell the truth. Well, everything except his visit to their father. Okay, so Cody's tale about his run-in with his dealer wasn't an endearing or glamorous story, but that's the way it was. Telling the truth was the only way they were going to remove suspicion. By offering vague answers as to his whereabouts, the police would only continue to prod and probe and ask their unending questions, motivated by suspicion.

Unless the story Cody had told her was all a lie...

Her mouth almost fell open at that shocking thought. The sharp-eyed detective's gaze zeroed in on her and she hastily rearranged her expression into something less revealing, all the while her mind continued spinning frantically.

Her brother had been shocked and devastated when she told him about their father. There was no way his reaction had been fake. He couldn't be that good an actor... *Could he?*

No!

She refused to think, even for a moment, that he was responsible for their father's death, though that very thought kept intruding time and time again. No matter their differences, Cody had *loved* their father. And their father had loved him.

Except, according to Cody, their last conversation had been full of anger and vitriol and awful things had been said. Love on either side had been sadly absent during what was to be their final conversation. The knowledge filled her with something beyond despair. She didn't think she could ever feel sadder.

"Think a bit harder. It was a Thursday night. Less than a week ago. Surely you must have some idea where you were."

The detective's harsh tone jarred her. Once again, she forced herself to concentrate on the two men who were squaring off against each other. Cody was relying on her to ensure the interview was conducted fairly and she could hardly keep her mind on the job. Some lawyer she was.

She turned to her brother and touched his arm. "Are you *sure* you don't remember?"

She kept her gaze trained on his, willing him to answer like he had in her apartment, but to her consternation, he shook his head and turned to address the detective.

"I'm sorry. I was probably high. I don't know if you know, but I've been that way for months. My wife kicked me out of my house. I've lost my job. My life's gone to shit. Getting high is the only way I get to forget."

"What about earlier that day?" the detective persisted. "Did you visit with your father at any time that day?"

Cody fidgeted and continued to stare at the floor. He picked at the scabs on his arms. One of them started to bleed. And then he glared at the detective.

"I've already told you! I don't remember anything! I don't even know what day it is most of the time, let alone where I was!"

"When was the last time you saw your father?" the detective continued.

Cody looked away and shrugged, his surge of anger gone as quickly as it came. Even to Meghan, he presented a pathetic figure.

"Let me guess; you don't remember." The detective's voice was thick with sarcasm. Meghan blushed in embarrassment for her brother, but Cody didn't appear to notice. And then the detective turned his attention on her.

"What about you, Ms Chifley? Where were you on the night of October fifteenth?"

Flustered, she took a moment to respond. "I-I worked late at the office. It was after midnight when I left."

"Can anyone verify that?"

"I didn't see anyone on my way out, if that's what you mean. There might be security footage of the building, though."

"Ms Chifley, did *you* visit your father on the evening of October fifteenth?"

His blue eyes bore into hers until it felt like he could look right into her soul. She froze instinctively under his probing gaze. She had nothing to hide and yet she still felt guilty. There was no doubt he was good at his job. She felt like confessing and yet she'd done nothing wrong. With an effort, she braced herself against the impact of his gaze and answered as calmly as she could.

"No. I didn't."

CHAPTER 10

Zane stared hard at the beautiful woman who sat across from him. There was something up with her and he was determined to dig deeper until he discovered what it was. She was almost as nervous as her brother and Cody was a singularly unimpressive candidate. He was fidgety, uncomfortable, clearly unwilling to look Zane in the eye. Zane couldn't yet work out if the nervousness was a sign of guilt or merely an aftereffect of the drugs. To top it all off, Cody Chifley had relied upon the old "I can't remember" response to everything Zane had put to him. And they'd barely started.

Why had the man bothered to come to the station? So far, he'd done nothing to assist Zane with his enquires. And Meghan was almost as bad.

Unwittingly, Zane's gaze swept over her. He catalogued each one of her perfect features and then did his best to thrust his interest in her aside. What she looked like didn't matter. What mattered was finding out what she and her brother had to hide.

He'd seen the way she'd reacted when her brother declared total memory loss of the night his father was murdered. Cody Chifley had lied about not knowing where he was. Zane was sure of it. And Meghan's reaction confirmed that. She'd been surprised by her brother's response, which meant he'd given her a different story. She knew way more than she was saying and that was beginning to piss Zane off.

They were in the middle of a murder investigation. The police were doing their best to find the person responsible for ending their father's life and yet neither twin appeared interested in doing their bit to assist them. It was infuriating.

Cody scratched once again at his arms. Right away Zane had noticed the sores and half-healed scabs so typical of an ice addict. While under the influence of the deadly drug, they often thought there were insects crawling under their skin and scratched themselves to the point where they drew blood. Over and over they attacked themselves until the wounds got infected. It wasn't a pleasant sight. Cody Chifley hadn't quite gotten to the point where his sores were oozing pus, but if he kept it up, it was only a matter of time. Zane had seen it too often to count.

And then Zane's gaze moved lower and it caught on the cut across the back of Cody's left hand. The wound was red, but it wasn't fresh. Maybe five or six days old.

"What did you do to your hand?" he asked,

taking care to keep his voice only mildly curious.

"I... I got cut."

Zane went still. It was the first question the man had deigned to answer and it was an important one.

"How?" Zane asked casually, keeping his gaze averted so as not to put the man off.

"I... I got into a fight. He had a knife. I got cut."

Zane nodded in sympathy. "Did you go to the hospital?"

"No. It was nothing. Just a scratch."

"It looks like it could have warranted a few stitches," Zane murmured.

Cody hid the offending hand under the table and remained silent. Zane knew he'd pushed the guy far enough. He'd get nothing more out of him about the wound.

"Tell me, Cody. Do you mind if I call you Cody?"

"That's fine," Cody mumbled.

"Tell me, are you left or right-handed?" Zane asked.

"Right."

On impulse, Zane turned to Meghan. "What about you, Ms Chifley?"

"I'm not sure how it's relevant, Detective, but I'm left-handed."

Zane concealed his surprise. Though Cody looked enough like his twin that he could see how someone might mistake them from a distance, there were also differences. Like their height. Cody Chifley was at least a few inches taller. He was also a little heavier. And unlike his sister, he was right-handed. Like their killer.

Was Cody Chifley capable of lifting the dead weight of his father? That was a definite possibility.

Meghan sat forward and leaned her elbows on the table. Against his will, Zane's gaze was drawn to the soft outline of her breasts. The T-shirt she wore stretched across her chest, clearly delineating the generous curves. Despite the gravity of the situation, his body reacted.

He gritted his teeth as blood rushed to his cock. She could be a fashion model or a movie star. No, she was too short for a model, but she was certainly beautiful enough.

Instead, she was a lawyer. Beauty and brains. It was a heady combination and one that could prove difficult to resist. Luckily she was way out of his league. Any startup with her would not end well, of that he was sure. At that realization, he was filled with a sense of disappointment that he irritably forced aside.

Zane eyeballed Cody. "Did you argue with your father about him writing you out of his will?"

From the corner of his eye, he saw Meghan become alert. She sat up in her chair and crossed her arms over her chest.

"Who told you that?" she demanded.

He waited a moment before turning his attention on her. "That's not relevant, Ms Chifley." Once again, he fixed his gaze on her brother.

"So, *did* you?"

"Don't answer that, Cody!" Meghan cried, her face flushed with anger.

Cody turned to face her. "It's all right, Meggie. I have nothing to hide, remember?"

The twins shared a long look. Meghan was the first to lower her gaze. Her face filled with resignation and something else. *Was it...relief?*

Zane pressed his advantage. "Talk to me, Cody. Did you argue with your father?"

Cody stared at Zane a moment and then his shoulders slumped on a heavy sigh. "Yes."

Zane felt a frisson of excitement. It was the second question the man had answered. They were on a roll. *Perhaps all was not lost after all?*

"When did you argue?"

"About a month ago. It was our birthday."

"What happened?"

"I needed money to support my drug habit. Dad wouldn't give me any. Things got heated. I... I punched him. On my way out of the room, he shouted that he was cutting me out of his will."

"And did he?"

Cody looked at him. "Well he said he would..."

Zane glanced at Meghan where she sat quietly in her chair. "Do you know anything about your father changing his will?"

Her eyes flashed. "Why should I?"

His gaze turned mocking. "You're an estate lawyer. It's a natural assumption."

She bristled, but forced herself to answer. "I was there at the party when Daddy made the threat, but no, I don't know anything about whether my father made good on his threat and actually instructed someone to prepare another will. He couldn't come to me. That would be a conflict of interests."

Zane lifted a single brow, but absorbed the

information in silence and then asked Cody another question. "Was your father the type of man to make idle threats?"

Cody's expression turned grim. "No. My father was a man who said what he meant and meant what he said. He was a hard man to like."

"Cody! Don't say anything else!" Meghan urged him.

Zane wouldn't be deterred. "Cody, do you think your father changed his will and removed you?"

Meghan shot her brother a look of warning. To Zane's relief, Cody ignored her and responded.

"Yes, he would have. I treated him abominably. He was beyond furious. He would have made good on his threat."

"You sound certain of that."

"As certain as I've been of anything in my life."

———————

After seeing the Chifley twins out of the building, Zane took the stairs to the squad room, two at a time, and threw himself down at his desk. He waited for Willie to end his phone call and then motioned him over.

"That was the technician handling the Chifley telephone intercept," Willie said as he took the vacant seat opposite Zane's desk. "Everything's in place. We'll be listening in on every call Cody Chifley makes from now on."

"Good. I just had him and his sister downstairs in an interview room."

"How did that go?"

Zane explained how Cody Chifley had initially clammed up, claiming to have no memory of the night his father died. "But somewhere along the way, he decided to cooperate. He still claimed not to remember anything about the night of the murder, but he did concede they'd argued last month about money and that his father threatened to write him out of his will."

Willie nodded thoughtfully. "That follows what Sarah Chifley told you."

"Yeah."

"So what's your take on the brother?" Willie asked.

"It's an interesting case. Cody probably has enough size and muscle about him to be able to pull off the murder. He has a serious drug habit and has no income to support it or plausible alibi. He's also sporting a cut on the back of his left hand. It looked like a knife wound to me and Cody verified that."

"What did he say about it?"

"Just that he got into a fight and got cut with a knife."

"Interesting. Is he right-handed?"

"Yes."

"Even more interesting. What about motive?" Willie asked.

"The thought is Daddy cut him out of the will," Zane replied dryly. "A drug addict with a serious problem is in need of extra cash."

"But how's that a motive? If Daddy acted on his threat and changed the terms of his will, Cody wasn't going to benefit from his father's death."

Zane nodded in agreement. "You're right, but whoever did this to Grant Chifley was angry. Extremely angry. They weren't thinking clearly. A drug-addicted son who's been tossed out of his house by his wife and whose father has just cut him out of a sizeable inheritance would likely be that angry. In fact, it doesn't matter if Chifley made good on his threat to change the will. What matters is that Cody Chifley believed he did. I think he should be on the top of our list."

"What about the sister?" Willie asked.

"Which one?"

"The hot-looking babe we met at the crime scene."

Zane tried not to take offense at the fact his partner had noticed how attractive Meghan was. Instead, he acknowledged Willie's comment with a nod. "You're right. She looks enough like her twin brother that I can understand why the neighbor wasn't sure which one of them she saw. It's funny, both twins deny being in the vicinity of their father's house the night of the murder, so either the inquisitive Mary-Beth Moore was mistaken, or one, or both of them, isn't telling the truth."

Willie rolled his eyes. "Surprise, surprise."

"Yes. One thing though, Meghan Chifley told me she's left-handed so that rules her out as the one who wielded the knife. Of course, she could have been the one who struck the initial blow to the head, but she also offered some sort of alibi for that night. She said she was working at her office until after midnight. Then she went home.

We can pull the CCTV footage of the Sydney Legal building and at least check part of what she said." He paused and then added, "Do we have the footage from Grant Chifley's place, yet?"

"No, but I put in a call to the security company. I'll chase it up."

Zane nodded. "Good. Let me know what you find. Let's hope it helps us nail this killer. Nobody deserves to die like that."

———————

Meghan glanced across at her brother from where he sat hunched in the passenger seat. They were on their way home from the police station and she wished she felt relief that they'd finally come clean to the police. The fact was, Cody hadn't come clean about everything and what he *had* said was probably the wrong thing. Admitting to the police he'd had an argument with their father, even a month earlier, was probably not the best information to offer them, even if it was the truth. Then again, what would she have him do? She'd told him to tell them everything, to tell them the truth. He'd only been following her instructions.

She shot him another concerned glance and then returned her attention to the road. Traffic was heavy and the going was slow and she cursed when a vehicle pulled out in front of her without warning. She hit the brakes and beeped the horn then quietly cursed under her breath.

"I don't think he heard you," Cody murmured.

Meghan blinked in surprise. They were the first words her brother had uttered since leaving the police station. "Excuse me?"

He turned to her with a grin. "I don't think he heard you. If you want to properly cuss him out, you need to put down the window, poke your head out and give him a mouthful and then follow up with a decent horn blast. It's the only thing that works."

A smile tugged at her lips. "That sounds like you're speaking from experience."

Cody's grin morphed into a chuckle and a rush of tears burned behind Meghan's eyes. She couldn't remember the last time she'd heard her brother laugh.

"Once upon a time, people actually had the courtesy to let someone in ahead of them and think nothing of it. Now it's every man for himself," she said.

"You have that right, Meggie. It sure as hell is a dog-eat-dog world."

"How did we get like this?" she mused quietly. "How did we get so impatient, so selfish, so *rude*? It didn't always used to be like this."

"You're right," Cody murmured his agreement. "But I sure as hell don't know what to do about it." With that, he turned to stare out his window at the traffic.

The lights up ahead changed and the traffic began to inch forward. Meghan reached over and squeezed her brother's hand. "Are you okay?"

"Of course. Why wouldn't I be?"

She shrugged. "It's just that, the interview didn't go exactly as I thought it would," she admitted.

"In what way?"

She sighed on a heavy breath. "Well, for starters, I thought you were going to tell the truth about the night Daddy died."

Cody remained silent for a moment before answering. "Yeah, well, the more I thought about it, the more that course of action didn't make sense. I mean, you wanted me to tell them that the very night my father was murdered, I had to front up to my dealer and confess I didn't have the money I owed him. The police aren't stupid. They know what kind of pressure I would have been under if I couldn't pay my debt. It only gave me extra motivation to ask dear old Dad for more money. It wouldn't take long for the detectives to join the dots."

She nodded sympathetically. "I understand, Cody. I really do. But I have a bad feeling about this. I know it was my idea for you to keep quiet about your visit to Daddy's that night, but what if the police discover you were there that night? I'm beginning to think it might have been better to come clean about that. At least they might have then been more inclined to think you had nothing to hide. After all, why else would you volunteer that kind of potentially damaging information?"

Cody made a sound of disgust in the back of his throat. "That's your problem, Meghan. You're too trusting. You expect everyone else to deal with others in the same way you deal with them fair and just and giving people the benefit of the doubt. The police don't work like that. Trust me. It's guilty before innocent and they'll make you fight hard to prove you had nothing to do with it. Especially when you hand them that kind of gold nugget: Admitting you're in the dead man's house, fighting with him, in the hours before he was killed."

Meghan sighed quietly. She understood the reasons why her brother had chosen not to be honest about what had happened the night their father died, but still… She didn't like it and it was all her fault. She'd screwed up and now there was nothing she could do about it. And then another thought occurred to her and her belly filled with dread.

"Oh, my God, Cody. We forgot about the security footage! Daddy has that place wired up like it's Fort Knox. No doubt the police will get access to the footage and then where will we be? They'll see you arriving at Daddy's house the night he died and they'll see you leaving again. It will be obvious you were there. Oh, Cody! I'm so sorry! I should have made sure you had a real lawyer, someone experienced in this kind of thing. This is all my fault!"

Cody sighed heavily. Reaching out, he squeezed her arm. "It's okay, sis. Don't beat yourself up. It's my fault as much as yours. I was more than happy to go along with your suggestion and I'm still fine with our decision not to tell them everything. I sure as hell didn't murder our father. I'm not going to put myself in the line of fire and make it easy for the cops to put the blame on me."

Meghan glanced over her shoulder and expertly changed lanes. She flicked another concerned glance at her brother. It wouldn't take the police long to work out her father had extensive security cameras along the perimeter of the fence that bordered his property. Cody's arrival and departure on the cameras would be clear for all to see. She just hoped he'd told her the truth when he'd said their father was well and truly alive when he left him.

She immediately hated herself for that thought. Her mind turned to the sharp-eyed, way-too-sexy detective. Meghan sensed there was no way he'd leave any stone unturned. If he saw the CCTV footage, he'd know immediately her brother had lied. Then the only question to be answered was why.

A shiver of fear arced down her spine. She was scared about what the detective might find. His intelligent blue eyes missed nothing. She was also scared by her physical reaction to him. Her heart raced when he was near. She was so aware of his masculinity. She'd never responded so viscerally to any man before.

And what was even scarier was the way he looked at *her*. There was definite interest in his shadowed eyes, even if he worked hard to hide it. She was desperate to find her father's killer, but at what price? What if she could protect her brother, but couldn't protect her heart?

That was yet to be determined.

CHAPTER 11

As Zane proceeded slowly up the tree-lined drive that led to the Chifley mansion, he was reminded of the yawning chasm between the life he'd known as a child and the one enjoyed by Meghan Chifley. He'd come from the poor end of town, had been passed from one foster parent to another and felt unwanted and unloved. Her childhood couldn't have been more different. He wondered if their different upbringings had forged their personalities.

She seemed so perfect, with her stunning good looks, intelligence and stylish designer clothes. Other than when being questioned, she appeared comfortable in her skin and confident about her place in the world. She had an imperceptible nonchalant attitude toward her father's wealth and no doubt was only remotely aware of how it had paved her future and had opened doors—and no doubt would continue to open doors.

The fact she'd chosen to go into law was surprising. It wasn't an easy job and it demanded time and impeccable attention.

His discrete enquires about Meghan among his friends in the legal fraternity had elicited even more surprises. It appeared she was not only good at her job, she excelled at it and many of the people Zane spoke to had nothing but praise and respect for the daughter of one of the richest men in the country.

Zane hadn't expected to like her. It was one thing to experience a purely male reaction to a beautiful woman, but now that he'd spent more time with her, he was dangerously close to admitting there was much more appeal to the exotic Meghan Chifley than first appeared. She wasn't just the spoiled daughter of a man with more money than he'd ever spend in a lifetime. She was a genuine woman who worked hard at her job and truly cared about her clients, and if the feedback he'd received was anything to go by, she had a compassionate heart and an intelligent mind and was an altogether nice person.

He wished his first instincts had been on the mark. That she was just another rich and spoiled brat whose every desire had been granted and who'd never been forced to grow up. He wasn't entirely comfortable with the knowledge that he'd misjudged her and that she wasn't at all like that. It made her so much more dangerous. So much more tempting.

The knowledge that his sexual awareness of her

might be reciprocated made things even more enticing. He'd heard the little catches in her breath and seen the telltale signs of a frantic heartbeat as a pulse in her neck whenever he got close. He'd caught her looking at him when she thought he wasn't aware and her frank interest had heated his blood.

Gritting his teeth, he swiped at the sweat that had popped out on his brow and continued up the drive. It was unwise to even contemplate a possible future with the beautiful Meghan Chifley. She was a potential suspect in his murder investigation. Okay, so he'd already ruled her out as the main suspect, but there was always the possibility she'd been an accomplice...to her brother.

Zane didn't want to contemplate the possibility that the twins had murdered their father, but it wouldn't be the first time a couple of disgruntled children had done away with a troublesome parent. His gut was telling him she wasn't capable of such cold-blooded killing, but he wasn't prepared to discount her, yet. He needed to see the CCTV footage from her building. See if that part of her story was true. Then they'd know if she was the twin Mary-Beth had seen calling on her father that evening.

He brought the squad car to a halt outside the wide stone steps and turned to Willie.

"We need to go over every inch of this mansion until we determine where Chifley was murdered. The killer might have done their best to clean up the scene, but our vic was stabbed more than forty times. No one can clean up that amount of blood and not leave some trace behind. We need to find it."

Willie nodded. "Did you bring the luminol?"

"Yes." Zane reached behind his seat and retrieved the satchel he'd obtained from forensics.

The two of them climbed out of the car and headed up the steps. Blue-and-white checked crime scene tape remained stretched across the entryway. Both men ducked under it and, after showing their credentials to the uniformed officer guarding the doorway, they made their way inside.

The grandeur inside was just as breathtaking as he remembered. With a conscious effort, he forced his mind away from all it represented and entered the study. Floor-to-ceiling bookshelves lined two walls. Another wall was graced with large pieces of art, no doubt originals by the masters. The fourth wall was taken up by wide picture windows that looked out onto a lush garden filled with exotic flowering plants that Zane could barely recognize, let alone name. A small waterfall trickled into a generous-sized pond filled with lily pads and other water plants and colorful black and red and white koi swimming slowly. It was a calming scene and one Zane could imagine Grant Chifley had enjoyed on many occasions. It was a shame he'd enjoy it no more. His mind drifted to the gardener...

Willie walked in behind him, his footsteps muffled on the thick carpet. He looked around. "It doesn't look like the scene of a violent crime."

"No. And it would be almost impossible to remove blood stains from the carpet. Still, we need to be thorough. We're going to examine each and every room until we're satisfied we know where Chifley was killed—or at least are able to rule out the house as the scene of the murder."

Willie nodded. "Oh, by the way. I followed up with the plumbers. I interviewed Riley Dorrington. His story matched that of his brother. I also looked into the fishing story. It turns out he told the truth. I spoke to both of the wives and two friends who all verify the Dorrington brothers' version of events, including their alibis. One of Harry's friends also had cuts on his hands from gutting fish. Plus, as far as I can tell, they have no motive. The bill was paid in full, right?"

"Right. I guess we can cross the tradesmen off the list of suspects," Zane replied and headed back out into the hallway.

Willie frowned in confusion. "I thought we were going to examine every room?"

"We are," Zane responded, climbing the stairs. "But we're going to start in the bedroom. Grant Chifley weighed two-hundred-and-sixty-five pounds. That's a hell of a lot of weight to lift. I can't imagine anyone carrying him up the stairs."

Zane reached the top of the flight of stairs and turned toward the master bedroom. The door was ajar and he pushed it open with his shoulder.

The room looked the same as the last time he'd seen it, except now black fingerprint dust coated every surface. A sliding door that led out onto a balcony that Zane had missed the first time round caught his eye. He strode over to it and opened the door and stepped out onto the terrazzo tile. The view of the ocean was breathtaking from there.

He stared out across the wide expanse of blue and slowly shook his head in awe. The smell of salt was so strong, it was like he was already riding the waves. The sound of them rolling in and crashing against the shore reached him clearly. He couldn't imagine what it would be like to wake up to such a sight and sound every day of his life.

"Find anything?"

Willie came up behind him and then let out a low whistle of appreciation. "Would you get a look at that? I can't believe there are people who actually live like this." He grinned ruefully.

Zane's lips tugged upwards in a smile. "Yeah. Pretty good, huh?" He chuckled. "Come on. We have a job to do. Let's go back inside."

The expensive cream carpet looked just as pristine as it had the first time he'd been there. It was difficult to believe Chifley had met with such a violent death and not a speck of blood had been left behind, but to the naked eye, that certainly seemed to be the case.

With a sigh, Zane pulled out the luminol mixture and began to carefully and methodically spray the room. Walls, bed, carpet, dressing room. Nothing was missed. Then he crossed the room and systematically closed all the drapes. Bit by bit, the light in the room was dramatically decreased to the point where he couldn't see an inch in front of him. Even Willie disappeared. Grant Chifley had obviously liked to sleep in the dark.

"Holy crap!"

Willie's soft exclamation filled the silence. Zane's gut tightened with dread. Though most of the room remained in darkness, a spattering of bright blue light appeared on the wall closest to the end of the bed. There were also patches of bright blue light on the carpet, visible beneath the tassels on a large red-and-cream colored rug.

Bending low, Zane lifted one corner. In the semi-darkness, he saw nothing, but he pulled out the luminol mixture once again and sprayed it on the spot.

In the pitch darkness, the carpet that had been hidden by the overlaid rug instantly lit up bright blue. Zane pulled the rug all the way out and Willie switched on the lights. A large dark red stain, showing signs of someone's attempts at cleaning it, met their shocked gazes.

"It looks like we found our murder site," Willie murmured, his eyes still wide with surprise.

Zane nodded grimly. He strode to the windows and pulled open all the drapes, flooding the room with light. The blood stain was clearly visible, now that they'd exposed it. Someone had tried to clean the carpet, but had given up on removing the stain and had then cleverly concealed it by placing the rug on top of the stain. He wondered where the rug had come from. Surely one of Chifley's children would know. Zane made a mental note to ask Meghan.

"I'd say our vic was struck across the back of

the head while he readied himself for bed. He fell to the floor and landed there. That's when his attacker went in with the knife," Zane murmured.

Filled with a surge of determination to bring the killer to justice, he prowled around the room looking for something that could have been used as a weapon. Samantha had said Chifley had been struck with a heavy, blunt object. His eye snagged on a solid glass paperweight that sat beside a lamp on the nightstand. He strode over to it, cursing under his breath that they'd missed it the first time. He guessed it was because the pyramid-shaped crystal didn't look out of place. It could have been a priceless sculpture, a work of art. Also, he'd been sporting one hell of a hangover that morning. He hadn't exactly been on top of his game. He clenched his jaw and shook his head.

No excuses. He'd slipped up. Again.

Pulling out a pair of gloves, he slipped them on and carefully brought the paperweight up to eye level.

"Well, I'll be damned. Willie, this is our lucky day."

Willie moved closer. "What did you find?"

"A paperweight. But more importantly, it's a solid heavy object and if I'm not mistaken, there are two hairs stuck to a corner with what looks suspiciously like blood."

Willie's face immediately lit up with comprehension. "You might have just found one of our murder weapons."

Despite his disappointment he hadn't found it

the first time round, Zane was filled with a surge of satisfaction. He grinned. "That's exactly what I was thinking."

———

With a word to the officer guarding the entrance, to ensure he wouldn't let anyone inside without authorization, Zane headed down the wide stone steps with Willie not far behind him. He'd bagged the paperweight and had it in his hand. He carefully placed it on the backseat of the squad car and climbed behind the wheel. Willie opened the passenger side door and slipped in beside him.

"So, where are we at?" Willie asked, pulling on his seatbelt.

"Well, we now know Chifley was killed in his bedroom. That means there was less distance for our perp to cart him into the bathroom, but still, it's a daunting distance to move such a weight. We've got to look at who might have had the strength to do that. Either that, or our perp had an accomplice."

Zane paused and then slowly shook his head. "But you know, I'm just not seeing that. According to Samantha, the multiple stab wounds were made with the same weapon and by the same person. It would be highly unusual for there to be more than one perpetrator involved in such a violent crime."

Willie regarded him solemnly. "Yes, but not

impossible," he murmured. "Don't forget someone clocked him over the back of the head first. That could have been done by the accomplice. What about the twins? It wouldn't be the first time twins took to their parents in a murderous rage."

Zane compressed his lips into a grim line. He didn't want to believe Meghan Chifley had anything to do with her father's gruesome murder...

"Let's go over what we know. Meghan Chifley found the body. By the time we arrived on the scene, she appeared genuinely distraught. Of course, all of that could have been an act. Still, we know she couldn't have been the one who stabbed her father and she has an alibi of sorts—she was working late. Have you got that footage from Sydney Legal, yet?"

"No," Willie replied. "They want a subpoena."

Zane grimaced. "Of course they do. Get onto it ASAP. What about the CCTV footage from Chifley's place?"

"I finally managed to speak to somebody at Warner Security," Willie replied. "They're happy to help out, but the thing is, they say they have no footage."

Zane frowned. "What do you mean, they have no footage?"

"Just that. The files from the night in question have been wiped."

"How the hell did that happen?"

Willie shrugged. "I'm not sure. It sounds like someone with inside knowledge of the Chifley security system got access to it before we did. No doubt, the killer."

Zane cursed quietly and stared out through the window across the wide expanse of perfectly manicured lawns. "Then that makes it even more certain Chifley's killer was part of his inner circle. No one else would have been privy to where the security files were kept. Whoever it was, knew where to access them and what they were looking for. They also knew what to do."

He looked at Willie. "Were any other files wiped from other time periods?"

"No. Apparently this is the only one."

Zane's lips twisted into a grimace. "Surprise, surprise. Whoever did that wasn't as smart as they think they are. They should have at least wiped a day or two either side. It would have looked a whole lot less suspicious."

"It's my guess the perp wasn't thinking straight," Willie replied. "If our theory's right, he'd just brutally murdered Grant Chifley. Someone he knew well. It must've shaken him up. It would have shaken anyone up. It's a miracle he managed to keep enough wits about him to clean up so well and that he remembered to dispose of the security footage at all."

"Yes, you're right," Zane agreed morosely. "Where are the recordings kept?"

"In the basement of Chifley's home."

"What about a backup? Surely Warner Security have one?"

Willie shrugged. "Apparently not."

Zane cursed. "What the hell do these companies get paid for? Why wouldn't they have a backup?"

"I was told old man Chifley didn't want them to have one. He preferred to keep his private life private."

Zane shook his head. "My gut is telling me it's more and more likely that a family member did this. Right now, not one of the three Chifley children has a decent alibi, except Meghan and her alibi relies on the CCTV footage from her building showing her leaving her office after midnight and no other time in between. We know from the undigested food in Grant Chifley's stomach that he was murdered somewhere between eight and nine o'clock."

Willie cleared his throat and spoke. "You're right. We need to see that footage, but if it supports her alibi, she's completely off the hook."

Hiding his relief, Zane nodded. "Yeah, you're likely right. What about the other two suspects? Let's talk about them. Cody Chifley. First of all, he's right-handed, like the profile suggests. He also has a cut on the back of his hand, albeit to the left hand. We know he had an argument with his father a month earlier. He admitted during the interview that he believed his father would have carried through on his threat to write him out of the will. Though he attended the police station of his own volition, he performed poorly during the questioning. He was clearly uncomfortable and nervous. He stared at the floor a hell of a lot and sure as hell looked guilty. The question is, guilty of what?

"Was he nervous because he was coming off a high? Was it just the fact he regularly engages in illegal behavior and he was closeted in a small interview room in a police station? That can be daunting for a lot of people. He's also of slight build. A couple of inches taller and a bit heavier than his sister, but I believe he's strong enough to lift a two-hundred-and-sixty-five pound weight.

"We know from the blood found on the carpet that Grant Chifley bled out in one spot and was then moved to the bathtub. There were no drag marks, so whoever did this had the strength to lift him off the floor and place him in the tub. That would have been no mean feat."

"Right," Willie agreed. "But it's possible Cody could have done it. He's no bodybuilder, but he's fit and lean and rangy and if he were angry enough, maybe it's possible."

"I agree," Zane added. "And he has a motive. He knew the access code to the security gate, the layout of the house and no doubt he was well aware of the security cameras. On top of that, he's smart enough to know how to wipe recordings off a hard drive."

"Yeah, and he didn't have any plausible explanation for his whereabouts on the night of the murder, did he?" Willie asked.

"No, he didn't. He relied on a convenient loss of memory. Of course, he might've been high as a kite when he committed the murder. That's not beyond the realm of belief. There's no question he's a drug addict. Maybe he truly can't remember anything about it. That doesn't mean he didn't do it."

Willie leaned back against the seat and sighed.

"Okay, that's Cody. What about the other daughter? Sarah. She definitely had issues with her father."

"Yeah," Zane replied, remembering back to the anger that had flared briefly in the eyes of the oldest Chifley child. "Then there was the cut to her hand. She said she'd injured it with a knife while she was cutting vegetables, but it could just as easily have happened during a fight with her father."

"She certainly looked strong enough to lift him," Willie said.

"What about a motive?"

Willie shrugged. "Daddy cut her off, remember?"

Zane scratched his head. "Yeah, but that was three years ago. I'm not buying it. Why would she wait so long? That murder scene was full of rage. Someone was well and truly pissed off. They'd been tipped over the edge. It didn't feel like the result of planning or a slow boil to me."

Willie slowly nodded. "Yeah, you're right. So where to from here?"

Zane sighed. He leaned over and switched on the ignition. "Let's go and talk to Meghan again. It appears she's the least likely to have done it. Maybe she can give us some insight on who might have."

With that, he pulled away from the house that held all the answers—but so far, was reluctant to reveal them—and slowly made his way down the drive.

CHAPTER 12

Meghan took a sip from her coffee cup and screwed up her nose in distaste. She set the cup on the low table that stood by the side of the couch. She'd made the restorative brew more than an hour earlier and had forgotten about it when she got caught up in dismal thoughts about her father and brother and sister. Now the coffee was cold.

It was seven days since she'd discovered her father's body. Seven days to sit and wonder who could have done such an awful thing. The truth was, she couldn't think of anybody and that was killing her. She wished she could point the police in the right direction, but all she could do was assure them the perpetrator wasn't close to home. There was no way either of her siblings could have done something like that. She'd had a moment's doubt about Cody, especially if he'd been high, but after his recount of the evening their father died, those thoughts had been pretty much put to rest.

Cody had insisted their father was still alive and well when he'd left the house. Someone had come in later and had carried out the deadly deed. But who? And why? If only she knew. She wanted to lay her father's body to rest, peaceful in the knowledge his killer had been found, was locked up, would spend a good part of the rest of their life behind bars. As it should be. But she had nothing. At this stage, she didn't even have her father's body.

As far as she knew, he was still at the morgue. Surely an autopsy would have been conducted by now? What was the hold up? Why hadn't she received a call that they were done with him so that she could make funeral arrangements?

The thought of her father's funeral sent a fresh wave of pain and grief coursing through her but, at least with the funeral, she'd have some closure. Right now, she had nothing but endless questions and no answers.

She'd fielded a call from one of her colleagues, the lawyer who had prepared her father's last will and testament. Though she was curious about the terms of the will, attending a reading and dealing with its contents was beyond what she wanted to do right then. The will would have to wait.

She wanted to call Detective Sullivan, but she was also afraid. She didn't want him to tell her they'd seen security footage of her brother leaving her father's property the night he died. She was also wary of the way her body reacted when he was near, a reaction she couldn't seem to control. Until now, she'd only ever dated safe men. Men who were pleasant and polite and intelligent. Not the dark, sexy type that made her heart beat faster and sent shivers of desire down her spine.

Zane Sullivan was dangerous. She'd best keep her hormones in check and steer well away from him. Yes, he was investigating the murder of her father. No matter the looks he'd thrown her way, she shouldn't be thinking about him that way. Her father wasn't even in the ground and she felt guilty for her steamy thoughts.

Sudden tears welled up in her eyes. She haphazardly dashed them away. *What she would give for a hug from her daddy!* A kiss on her forehead and a reassurance only he could give that everything would be all right. She didn't even have Cody to talk things through with. He'd left her apartment more than an hour ago, mumbling something about needing some air. She hoped he hadn't gone to get high. She couldn't stand to have him in her home in that state and right now she needed him sober in every sense of the word.

The sound of her front door buzzer startled her. She blinked and sat up straighter on the couch. She reached for the box of tissues she'd placed nearby and dabbed at her eyes and nose. The last thing she needed was a visitor. Perhaps if she ignored them, they'd go away? She sat quietly, determined to do just that.

The buzzer sounded again and she clenched her jaw against the intrusion. With an impatient sigh, she pulled herself upright and went over to the intercom screen near the front door. A grainy image of Detective Sullivan filled the small space. Her pulse went into overdrive.

Her hands went to her face and hair and then she glanced down at her clothes. It was mid-afternoon, but she still wore her pajamas. She hadn't gotten around to pulling a brush through her hair and she hadn't bothered with any makeup. She'd had no intention of facing the world when she'd climbed out of bed a few hours earlier. But now there was a hot-looking detective outside, waiting for her to let him in. It wasn't that she wanted to primp for him especially... She grimaced at the lie. *What should she do?*

The buzzer sounded a third time and she could almost feel his impatience in the overlong ring. Coming to a sudden decision, she picked up the handset, spoke to him briefly and then depressed the button to let him in.

With no time to make herself more presentable, she had no choice but to wait for his arrival. She still hadn't managed to get her heart rate under control when he knocked hard upon her door. Taking a deep breath, she unlocked it and stared at him.

His broad shoulders filled the opening. Tall, dark and handsome, he seemed to suck up all the air. His blue eyes were shadowed and lined with fatigue, like he hadn't been getting enough sleep. She frowned with misplaced concern and then shook her head, immediately annoyed that she cared about why he too looked so wretched. Taking a step back, she averted her gaze and promptly collided with the wall. She cursed at the heat that rushed to her cheeks and quickly turned her back on him and made a beeline for the kitchen.

"Thank you for letting me in," the detective said in his deep, rumbling voice as he joined her on the opposite side of the counter.

"Where's your partner?" she quipped.

"I dropped him off at the lab on the way over."

Meghan immediately tensed. "Did you find something that might help identify Daddy's killer?"

His face became a blank mask. She guessed he was used to dodging questions he wasn't prepared to answer.

"Maybe," came his non-committal reply.

"When will you know?" she persisted.

He looked around the room in response. "Where's your brother?"

She glared at him in irritation and then busied herself at the sink. "He's out."

The detective regarded her steadily. "Out where?"

Meghan gritted her teeth and counted to five. She should have known he'd press for more. He was a cop, wasn't he? Doing her best to remain nonchalant, she offered him a one-shouldered shrug.

"I don't know. He's not a child. He said he was going out."

"For how long?"

Irritation shot through her. She glared at him. "Aren't you listening, Detective? I'm his sister, not his keeper. He's free to come and go as he wishes. I don't know when he'll be back."

The detective's expression remained unperturbed. "You're not just his sister, you're his twin. Don't you have some sort of sixth sense about where he is?"

Now he was goading her. Meghan's stare got more pointed. Her annoyance morphed into anger. She narrowed her eyes at him.

"Why are you here, Detective?"

He stared at her, his expression passive. "I have more questions."

She clenched her jaw. She didn't want to answer any more questions, especially if they involved Cody.

"There's a very nice rug on the floor of your father's bedroom, right at the foot of his bed," the detective continued. "Dark red and cream. It looks expensive. Do you know the one I'm talking about?"

Meghan blinked, put slightly off balance by the question. "I'm not sure about a rug like that in his bedroom. I haven't been to his private suite for months."

The detective pulled his phone from his pocket and flicked through something on the screen. "Here's a photo."

Meghan took the phone from him. Their fingers touched ever so slightly, but it was enough to send a tingle of awareness down her arm. She frowned and blocked out the feeling and concentrated on the picture that filled the screen.

"Are you sure you saw this in my father's bedroom?"

"Yes."

"Well, that's strange. He must have done some redecorating."

"Why do you say that?"

"Because that rug was a gift from me and Cody for Daddy's sixtieth birthday. It's a genuine Persian rug. It used to be on the floor of his study."

"I see."

Meghan tensed and waited impatiently for him to say something more, but he wasn't forthcoming. At a loss, she offered him coffee and then cursed under her breath.

Why did she do that? Now he'd be there even longer. She wanted him out of there, not lingering over coffee... *Didn't she?*

To her chagrin, he accepted and she set about collecting mugs and filling both from the pot she'd made earlier.

"Cream and sugar?"

"No, just black."

She offered him the cup and he murmured his thanks. She tamed hers with cream and sugar.

"It must be nice coming from such a large family. You all seem quite close," he mused as he sipped his coffee.

Meghan frowned, taken by surprise by his sudden change in demeanor and his switch in the subject. Forcing herself to relax, she blew out her breath on a soft sigh.

"Yes, I guess it is. And you're right. We *are* close. Most of the time." She laughed disparagingly. "Of course, we're not without our problems. All families have them, right? I must confess, it's been difficult dealing with the fallout from Cody's drug problem and when Daddy tossed Sarah out... I'm sure he didn't mean it to be forever. Not that I didn't understand his decision. She's almost forty and she's never been employed. It's well past time for her to get a job. Stand on her own feet. Daddy was convinced she'd never do it while he kept paying her way." She shrugged. "Perhaps he's right."

"It's taking her awhile to find her feet. What's it been? Three years since your father asked her to leave?"

Meghan frowned. "Three years? Who told you that? Daddy only made the decision last month."

The detective put his hands on the counter and leaned closer. She could see tiny flecks of darker color in his blue eyes that were now filled with surprise. She wanted to take a step away from him, put some distance between them, but she was also determined to stand her ground. This was her kitchen, after all.

His voice rumbled out of his chest. "Last month? Are you sure?"

She shook her head and offered him a half-smile. "Of course I'm sure. I was there. It happened at my birthday. Cody and I were celebrating together. Twenty-six candles." She sighed at the memory. "Daddy and Cody got into an argument over his drug problem. You already know about that. Then Daddy turned on Sarah."

"What happened?"

She sighed again and crossed her arms defensively over her chest. "Daddy said some terrible things to Sarah and then he told her to get out. She'd been living in a wing of his house for as long as I can remember. He told her he was tired of her sponging off him. He wanted her gone that night."

"How did she react?"

"She was shocked, just like the rest of us. We didn't know what had gotten into him. First Cody, then Sarah. I did my best to calm him down. Then Sarah began yelling. She was upset and shocked and angry. I tried to intervene, I told her to leave it be. Daddy would come to his senses. In the meantime, I suggested she leave."

"And did she?"

Meghan's shoulders slumped. She could still picture the scene of anger and hurt as clearly as if it happened yesterday. Three out of the four of them weren't speaking to each other. The party was ruined. They hadn't even cut the cake.

"Yes. Eventually, I was able to convince her to go. But she and Daddy continued arguing until I was on the verge of tears. I hated it when they fought like that." Once again, she fell silent, remembering the anguish of that night. Now her father and sister would never get a chance to apologize, to reconcile, to forgive.

"Family's important to you." The wistfulness in the detective's voice was unmistakable.

She drew her gaze up to his. "Of course. They mean the world to me. Isn't your family important to you?"

A closed expression came over his face. "I have no family."

Meghan blinked in surprise. "What do you mean? Everyone has a family."

The detective stared down at his coffee cup. "Not me. I was supposed to be adopted at birth. My father didn't even hang around long enough for that. For some reason, the adoption fell through and I was moved from one foster home to another instead."

He grimaced, as if the memory pained him. Meghan stared at him, wide-eyed, her heart flooding with sympathy. For all her family's faults and failings, they were her *family*. She wouldn't change them for the world and she couldn't in her wildest imagination, think of not having them around.

"Oh, you poor thing! How awful!" she murmured.

"I didn't exactly help matters," he continued in a tired, defeated voice. "By the time I was eight, I had a chip on my shoulder the size of Mount Rushmore. I was as prickly as a cactus. I refused to allow myself to get close to anyone. Sooner or later I'd be moved, so what was the point of becoming attached? It was easier that way."

Meghan's heart broke at the thought of the callous way the detective had been treated from such a young age. She stared at him, appalled. He glanced at her and his expression hardened.

"Don't go feeling sorry for me. I survived and it made me all the stronger. I learned from an early age to fend for myself and I relied on no one for anything. It's held me in good stead all these years. It's not a bad way to live."

"It sounds heartbreaking," she whispered in a choked voice. All she could see was the little boy he used to be, unwanted, unloved. Hiding behind a tough exterior, refusing to let anyone in.

Was that how he'd gotten so good at concealing his emotions? Is that why she sometimes saw shadows in the depths of his eyes?

She looked at him through the tears that suddenly clouded her vision. Up close, she saw vulnerability in his eyes and how his lip firmed with the effort to hold back his memories—memories that could likely overwhelm him if he let them.

Without thinking, she reached out and touched his cheek. Her fingers tingled from the feel of his warm skin and soft, closely cropped beard. He pulled away like he'd been burned.

Her face flamed. "I-I'm so sorry," she stammered.

He moved away, jammed his hands into his pockets and turned his back on her.

"Zane." His name fell from her lips even though he had yet to invite her to use it. "I'm so sorry," she said again.

"Forget about it," he snapped. "It's my fault. And I shouldn't have said anything. This isn't about me. It's about your father and finding out who the hell stabbed him forty-seven times when one well-placed attempt would have sufficed." He turned on his heel and stared at her, his breath coming fast. "Who do *you* think did it?"

Meghan's heart stuttered. Her breath caught in her throat. She thought of Cody and immediately dismissed him. Still, she worried the detective might see the doubts in her eyes.

"I don't know," she whispered, keeping her face averted.

He came closer, so close she felt the whisper of his breath on her cheek. Taking her chin between his fingers, he tilted her head up until she was forced to look at him.

"I think you do."

"*No!*" The single word was wrenched from her in an agony of fear and panic. The detective's expression hardened.

"Someone let themselves into your father's house. They knew the security code to the front gates and they also knew he was there alone. They caught him by surprise. They used a heavy object to smash him over the head with enough force to leave a three-inch laceration that went down to the bone. He fell to the ground, incapacitated, but that blow wasn't what killed him. Oh, no. While he was lying there stunned and bleeding on his bedroom carpet, his killer stood over him with a knife. Over the next few moments, your father endured agony like he'd never known. The killer stabbed him forty-seven times. Ten of those stab wounds made it all the way through to your daddy's heart."

The detective's expression was filled with dogged determination as he continued. "Your daddy's killer was full of rage—perhaps angrier than he'd been in all his life. At some point, the knife would have been covered in blood. The handle would have been slippery. There's a fair chance your daddy's assailant cut himself."

Meghan stared at Zane in horror. The images he'd thrown at her bombarded her from every angle. All she could see was the blood. Her father's blood. Her chest was so tight, she couldn't breathe. And then the detective spoke again.

"Show me your hands."

His voice was low and commanding. It scraped across her skin. His eyes seared into hers. She gasped in shock at his demand.

"S-surely you don't think it was me?" she managed.

His gaze didn't waver. "Show me your hands."

She held them out. They trembled violently, along with the rest of her body. She'd seen her father's awful wounds with her own eyes, but hearing Zane describe them in such horrible detail brought the whole scene back to her in vivid Technicolor.

His gaze dropped momentarily to her wound-free hands and then flicked back up to her face.

"Are you happy now?" she cried.

His expression remained unchanged.

"Why do you keep referring to my father's killer as a man?" she demanded. "Do you *know* who murdered him?"

Zane eyeballed her, his face mere inches away. "Yes. And so do you."

Filled with panic, Meghan backed away. "No! No! No! You're wrong!" she cried.

He shook his head and the calm way he regarded her filled her with icy dread. "I don't think so, Ms Chifley. It was your brother, wasn't it? Your beloved twin."

"No!" Her cry of anguish echoed off the walls.

Spinning on her heel, she ignored the twinge of pain in her ankle and whirled around. Turned her back on him, buried her face in her hands. The sobs she'd been fighting so hard to hold back gripped her again with a force she was helpless to withstand. Her shoulders convulsed.

"No! No! No!" she cried. "It can't be Cody! I won't believe it! Not Cody! Please, not Cody!"

Her legs gave out and she slid down to the floor. She was beyond humiliated to have lost her composure in front of the handsome detective, but she couldn't help it. She thought she'd managed to convince herself that Cody couldn't have had anything to do with their father's murder and yet the detective appeared to have her brother firmly in his sights.

Did he know something she didn't? Had Cody left some vital evidence behind? Something linking him to the awful crime? Zane's partner had taken something to the lab. Something relevant to the crime. *Could it be linked to Cody?*

The thought that her beloved brother could be responsible for the death of their father was too much for her to bear. On a howl of pain, she pressed her hot face to the cool tiles and cried until there was nothing left.

CHAPTER 13

Zane stared down at the woman who had crumpled to the floor near his feet and felt torn. The urge to bend down and comfort her was overwhelming. The pain and desolation on her face, as she tried to convince him he was wrong about Cody, tugged at something deep inside. He wanted to soothe away her fears, tell her everything would be all right. But he was the lead investigator in an extremely violent murder investigation. It was highly probable her brother was the killer. Everything was far from all right.

Her mournful cries continued and little by little, his resistance waned. He knew what it was like to feel such devastation, like the world had ended right before his eyes. Time and time again it had happened in his childhood when yet another foster family cut their ties and sent him on his way.

He just didn't fit in... He was too difficult to love... Too defiant... Too damaged for them to help...

There had always been some excuse. He'd

learned to harden his heart against the pain, to not let anyone close. It was the only way he knew how to survive.

And now Meghan, beautiful, smart, vulnerable Meghan was crying hard enough to break his heart. Despite his best intentions, he found himself crouching by her side.

"*Shh. Shh*. It's okay." Hesitantly, he reached out and stroked her hair. It was soft and silky and bouncy and smelled like peaches and cream. Sweet. Sexy.

She tensed beneath his touch, but the crying continued unabated. Slowly, gently, he pulled her to her feet and into his arms. He had no experience in offering comfort. He'd made a habit of shunning human touch. But this felt so right. *She* felt so right, in his arms.

Her head fell against his chest. Slowly her arms crept around his waist. She clung to him, crying. Her perfume wafted on the air and filled his nostrils: exotic, sweet and tantalizing. His body hardened in response.

This was madness! What was he doing? Everything about this was wrong!

But there was nothing he could do about it. For the love of God, he was being swept away in the moment. He'd tried so hard to keep his distance. He didn't want to feel this way, to feel *anything* for this woman, but for all his brain told him to stay away, his heart and body wanted her close. His resistance was futile.

His arms tightened around her and he drew her up against him. He murmured quiet words of comfort against her hair. She felt so good, so right. Like she was meant to be there.

"*Shh, shh,*" he whispered.

Stroking her back, the curve of her hip, his hand moved in a rhythm that seemed to soothe her. The silk pajamas were soft beneath his hand.

Slowly, her sobs subsided. She gazed up at him. The moment seemed to go on forever. Everything but the two of them faded to nothing. He bent his head and grazed her lips with his. The lightest of pressure, but heat immediately ignited between them, snatching their breath.

She opened her mouth beneath his and kissed him back. Her mouth was soft, sweet, luscious. He couldn't get enough. Her hands stole around his neck and held him to her. He tightened his hold around her hips. Blood pumped to his groin, full and hard and wanting. He pressed her against his erection and for one mad moment imagined what it would feel like to plunge deep into her wetness and lose himself inside her.

And then she stiffened in his arms and tore her mouth away. Her breath came fast. She pulled back.

He dropped his arms to his side. And stared down at her, panting, doing the best he could to get himself under control. Her pajama shorts cut off mid-thigh. Her bare legs were slim and toned and muscular. It was obvious she worked out. His gaze moved lower, ending at her feet with toenails painted pink. He looked back up and paused at her face. Her eyes were red and swollen and tears still lingered in their depths.

Under his perusal, embarrassment flamed across her cheeks. She lowered her gaze.

"I'm sorry," she murmured. "I—"

"Don't be sorry," he interrupted hurriedly. "I'm not. Besides, you're upset. You turned to me for comfort. There's nothing to be ashamed of. With all that's happened… It's a lot for anyone to deal with. The possibility that someone close to you, someone you love, could do that to another person you love—it has to be horrifying."

He paused and then continued. "It's easier for me. It's not the first time I've seen a family member turn violently on another, but I understand how traumatic the realization is for you."

She looked up at him, her face a picture of desolation. "You speak as if you've already made up your mind that my brother's guilty."

He stared down at her, his gaze riveted on her face. He was loathe to add to her pain, but he also owed her the truth.

"Haven't you?" he asked softly. "I've examined the evidence available and I've come up with the most likely suspect. Your brother. I can see in your face, you want to believe Cody didn't do it, but you're terrified that's not true. I'm right, aren't I?"

Meg stared up at Zane, her heart thumping. She couldn't believe she'd sobbed all over him and then kissed him for all she was worth. Zane was almost a stranger and beyond that, he was the detective looking at her brother as a suspect for the brutal murder of their father.

But for all that, there was no denying his kindness and compassion and the way he looked at her turned her insides into liquid need. He'd just comforted her while she was at her lowest point and she could see from the look on his face he also wasn't happy about discovering her brother was most likely her father's killer.

"Talk to me, Meghan," he pleaded, his voice low.

She stared up at him, torn. She wanted so desperately to share her problems, to unload on him the burden she'd carried since Cody's call. *But what would happen when she told him? Would it make things better or worse?* Of course it would make things worse. That was the reason she'd told Cody not to tell him in the first place. Cody had fought with their father the night their father had been murdered. There was only one conclusion a detective would draw.

"Please, Meghan. Tell me what you know."

It was the sincerity in Zane's voice and the kindness in his eyes that finally convinced her. With a sigh, she gave in to the temptation to ease her burden and do the right thing. She moved toward the couch. Her brother was innocent. She was sure of it. She just needed to convince Zane of that.

But perhaps it was better if she left out the part where he'd argued with their father on the night of his death. Though she yearned to tell Zane everything, it would be safer if she left that part out. Decision made, she perched on the edge. His leg brushed hers as he took a seat beside her.

She looked at him, still beset with uncertainty, even as her leg tingled from his touch. "I don't know where to start."

Zane regarded her steadily, his expression encouraging her to speak. "Start at the beginning."

She closed her eyes briefly and drew in a deep, fortifying breath. Easing it out between taut lips, she began.

"You're right. I've had my doubts about Cody. And this is why. The night my father was murdered, I received a late-night phone call from my brother. He was distressed and in a panic and kept telling me he was sorry."

"About what?" Zane asked quietly.

"At the time, I didn't know. I asked him, but all he would say was that he was sorry and that he'd been forced to do it."

"To do what?"

"I pressed him, but he wouldn't give me anything else. And then he ended the call. For days, I tried to get hold of him. I called and left messages. I spoke to everyone he knew. I even spoke to Tanya, his estranged wife. Nobody had heard from him and nobody knew where he was. I was worried for him, worried for his safety and also worried about what he might have done."

"Did you call your father?" Zane asked.

Meghan shook her head, filled with regret. "No, but I wish I had. I often spoke to Daddy on the phone. At least a couple of times a week. But he hadn't spoken to Cody since their argument at the party. Every time I tried to bring it up, he shut me down. He didn't want to talk about Cody. He hated that my brother had become addicted to drugs and that it was destroying his life. He made it clear he didn't want to hear Cody's name mentioned again."

She sighed. "So, I didn't call him. I honestly didn't think he'd know where Cody was and I didn't want to give Daddy any more ammunition to hold against his only son. It broke my heart to see them at odds like that. Underneath it all, they loved each other."

"So, what did you do when you couldn't get hold of Cody?"

She ran her hands through her hair and sighed again. "Before I was able to locate him, I received the call from Arjun. My father's gardener," she added.

Zane nodded. "Yes. Mr Patel. I interviewed him the morning after you discovered your father's body. He's not a suspect in the murder."

Meghan was filled with relief. "Oh, thank goodness. I mean, I never suspected Arjun in the first place. He's like family to me. But I understand why you wanted to interview him. He had access to the mansion and he knew my father's movements well. He was also aware Mrs Abbott, the housekeeper, was away."

"Right," Zane agreed. "So, you received the call from Patel and then you went over to your father's house. That's where I came in."

Meghan nodded. "Yes."

"I assume you've since spoken to your brother about the phone call he made that night?"

"Yes, of course. I needed to get to the bottom of it. At first he didn't remember making the call, but finally he did. He told me he owed money to his drug dealer. The night of my father's murder, the man had come to collect. Gordo's his name. I'm sure that's what Cody called him. Anyway, Cody didn't have the money, but he told the man where he could get it."

"From your father's house?" Zane guessed.

Meghan shook her head. "No. Not for my father's house. He gave the lowlife the security code to my condo."

Zane's eyes widened in disbelief. "You've got to be kidding! Who the hell does that? He led a dealer right to your door? What would have happened if the asshole had followed through? Come in while you were home? He could have assaulted you, raped you, anything could have happened. What the hell was your brother thinking?"

She heard the anger in Zane's voice and understood it. She'd been angry, too. But she was also able to see things from Cody's point of view.

"You have to understand," she replied quietly. "Cody was high on drugs and he was desperate. He wasn't thinking straight. He offered the only solution he could think of to get the man off his back."

Zane cursed. "Bullshit. I'm not buying it, Meghan. Your brother's a coward and that is that."

"You might be right," she quietly conceded, "but that doesn't make him a murderer."

Zane stared at her, the anger still clear on his face. "When did you talk to Cody about the phone call?"

She frowned. "I raised it with him the same day we visited you at the station. We talked about what happened the night Daddy died and Cody told me what he remembered. He agreed to come with me to talk to you."

"And yet, when I asked your brother where he was the night his father was murdered, he told me he couldn't remember. He lied to me."

Icy fingers of dread curled themselves around her heart. She'd forgotten Cody had claimed memory loss in front of Zane. Though his actions had made her uneasy, she'd accepted his reasoning. It was the same reason she'd decided not to tell Zane about Cody's visit to their father's home.

She glanced at the detective and saw the expectancy on his face. He was waiting for an answer. Thinking quickly and ignoring the stab of guilt that pricked her conscience, she finally replied.

"Cody turned up at my place looking like a mess. It was obvious he'd been living rough. Though he wasn't high, I couldn't be positive he hadn't been shortly before he arrived. When he told you he couldn't remember where he was the night my father died, he was probably telling the truth. Perhaps his memory comes and goes? Drug addicts are known to struggle with things like that."

Zane's lips twisted in disgust. "Convenient memory loss, if you ask me. You haven't told me anything to make me change my mind that your brother could be the man who murdered your father."

Shocked, she leaned back against the couch and stared at him. "What are you talking about? Of course I have! I told you he was meeting with his drug dealer that night. He was already high. He was trying to negotiate his way out of a debt. There was no way he went through all of that, including calling me in the middle of the night to apologize, and then hightailing it over to my father's house."

"What did Cody say when you asked him about the phone call?" Zane asked, his voice flat.

"He told me just that. That he called me to beg my forgiveness about giving my security code to his dealer. He didn't even know Daddy was dead. Not until I told him."

"So you say," Zane replied, his eyes hard. "Now I understand why you gave me the wrong information when I asked you for Cody's phone number and address. You were stalling for time. For all I know you were trying to spirit him out of the country. After all, when money's no object, anything's possible."

Anger ignited in Meghan's chest. She pushed away from the couch and stood. With her hands on her hips, she hit him with the full force of her rage.

"How *dare* you! I know my brother! I saw the reaction on his face when I told him our father was dead. He was *devastated!* Beside himself with *grief!* He was filled with guilt at the knowledge he would never have the chance to reconcile with the man. No one can act that well, and *especially* not my brother. I might have doubted him in the beginning, but I certainly don't doubt him now. He had *nothing* to do with my father's murder and I had *nothing* to do with trying to help him escape...and if you don't believe me, you can go to hell!"

She advanced aggressively, poking him in the chest with her finger. "I don't expect you to understand," she cried, anger still dripping from every word. "After all, you don't know what it's like to have a family, do you?

"I've got you all figured out, Detective Sullivan. You had a rough childhood. Rougher than most. And it's tainted the way you see everyone around you. You think everyone is out to get you, that they're in it for themselves. Well, I'm telling you, *my* family's not like that. We love each other. We look out for each other. We have each other's backs. My father might have argued with my brother and sister shortly before his death, but if they'd been given time, they would have worked through it. That's what families do. They talk, they apologize, they forgive each other and then they wipe the slate clean."

His expression darkened like thunderclouds and hurt flashed in his eyes. She steeled herself against it. She refused to be taken in by another sob story.

"You think I'm talking nonsense," she continued. "That I don't have a clue what I'm talking about.

But you listen to me. You don't know what it's like to have a family. I feel sorry for you. I really do. Nobody deserves to go through life like that, but don't you *dare* put your misguided beliefs onto *my* family. My brother didn't do this! You need to remove him from the list of suspects and get the hell out there and find out just who did."

Her breath came fast. Zane had held his ground and now stood within an inch of where she was. His chest rose and fell in time with hers. Anger flashed in his eyes.

"This isn't about me or my family," he said in a deadly voice. "I'm sorry for even mentioning that to you. Obviously my bad. I should have known better. I won't make the same mistake again. As soon as I find your brother, I'm placing him under arrest. After what you've just told me, we have enough to charge him. I'll get a search warrant for his house. I'll turn the place upside down if I have to. It's time he stopped hiding behind his sister's skirts and faced the consequences of his actions, like a man."

With that, Zane turned on his heel and stormed toward the door. Meghan watched him go, her heart filled with despair. The door closed behind him with a decisive click.

For the love of God, what had she done?

———————

Zane stood outside Meghan's apartment complex and thought about all that had gone on and all that had been said. He couldn't believe he'd spilled his guts like that—talked about things so private, he'd never spoken to anyone about them before. *What was it about Meghan Chifley that had him opening his heart?*

Okay, so she was smart and kind and beautiful. She loved her family and wanted to protect them at all costs. He admired her dedication and loyalty, even if he believed it was misguided. He was more and more certain Cody Chifley was responsible for his father's murder and Zane wasn't sure how Meghan would react when that fact was proved beyond reasonable doubt. Being as close to her family as she was, the knowledge would likely devastate her.

A flood of compassion surged through him. He wished it didn't have to be this way. Despite everything, and though he was reluctant to admit it, he cared for the beautiful woman whose heart was being torn to shreds. If Cody Chifley had murdered his father, there was nothing Zane could do to ease Meghan's pain—and that was even if she let him try. It was a lose-lose situation, like so many others he'd faced in his past.

His past. He'd been surprised by Meghan's reaction after being told he'd been raised a foster child with no fixed place of abode. He'd expected her to be shocked and repelled, but though she'd appeared horrified at the way he'd been treated, he'd seen nothing but compassion in her eyes. He wasn't used to that kind of reaction.

Then in anger she'd thrown it all back at him and they were back to square one.

He'd learned a long time ago to keep his past to himself. In his teenage years, if anyone discovered his unfortunate upbringing, they'd look down their nose at him, dismiss him as a nobody. It was like discovering he had no one to look out for him, no one on his side, like that gave them permission to treat him badly. Teachers, employers, fellow students. It was only when he stumbled upon the police service and graduated with honors that he finally felt he'd landed on his feet. He was home.

His fellow police officers were his family. They looked out for him and he looked out for them. There was nothing he wouldn't do for his brothers in blue and he knew they felt the same. Any one of them would take a bullet for him and he would do the same. They were thicker than blood. It was just the way it was. The way he felt about his partner was no different.

He and Willie had only been partnered for about six months, but the young detective had Zane's back. He was certain of it—just as certain as Willie was that Zane would protect him with his life. They both hoped it would never come to that, but neither Zane nor Willie would hesitate if that's what it took.

With a sigh, Zane pulled out his phone and dialed Willie's number. As much as he hoped they found Cody Chifley's prints on the bloodied paperweight and would then be able to close their case, he was conflicted. Knowing how such a thing would affect Meghan filled him with dread. He'd find her father's killer, but he'd destroy her life in the process.

Could life get any more complicated?

"Zane, how are you doing?"

Willie's cheerful voice on the end of the phone was just what Zane needed to draw him out of his doldrums.

"I'm fine, Willie. How did you do at the lab?"

"They're overworked and backlogged to hell, as usual. The good news is, I sweet-talked one of the technicians. She's going to put a rush on our paperweight."

"Good work."

"Does this mean I get to go home early?"

Zane laughed at the mock hope that filled Willie's voice. "I hate to break it to you, partner, but your day's just beginning. Meghan Chifley admitted her brother told her he met with his bagman the night his father died. Apparently he owed the germ money.

"The point is, he went from remembering this in Technicolor detail, to having complete amnesia by the time he spoke to me at the station a few hours later. It's not too much of a stretch to imagine he might have paid a visit to good old Daddy to ask him to help him out. He was desperate for money. He would have been well aware how nasty his candy man would get if he failed to pay up."

"Interesting development," Willie murmured.

"There's more. He gave his sister some bullshit story that he'd given the lowlife the entry code to her apartment, but that just doesn't make sense. Daddy was rolling in money, a fact our Cody knew well. He knew where he could get his hands on the cash he needed. And fast. There's no way he'd put his sister at risk like that."

"Does this mean you think Cody did it? I checked in on the telephone intercepts. The twins have barely spoken on the phone and what has been said is of little consequence."

"That doesn't mean he isn't our guy. My gut's telling me he was in this on his own. He wouldn't be talking about the details with his sister."

"What do you want me to do?" Willie asked.

"Get an APB out on Cody Chifley and start drafting a search warrant for the house in Maroubra. He hasn't lived there for a while, but let's see what we can find. It's time we rattled this guy's cage."

"Righto. I'll get on it right away."

Zane thanked his partner and then ended the call. He was halfway back to the squad car when he came to a sudden halt. Cody Chifley stood a few yards away. He looked more untidy than he had when he'd shown his face at the station, but there was no mistaking it was him.

"Cody Chifley!"

The man's head came up. The moment he spied Zane his eyes widened with fear. A split second later, he turned and ran, knocking a teenager off his bicycle. The boy yelped as Zane sped past, unable stop.

"Chifley! Police! Stop!"

Cody glanced over his shoulder, but didn't stop running. Zane picked up his speed. Jumping over a concrete barricade, he made ground when Cody took the long way round. As soon as Zane was close enough, he dived through the air and landed on the fugitive with a thud.

Both of them gasped from the impact. Zane recovered first. Drawing his gun, he pointed it toward Cody, who remained panting and breathless on the ground.

"Cody Chifley, you're under arrest for the murder of Grant Chifley." Zane tugged out his handcuffs and secured the man's hands behind his back. Pulling him to his feet, he marched him to the squad car and shoved him into the backseat. Slamming the door behind him, he took a moment to catch his breath. Then he phoned Willie and gave his partner the good news.

Chapter 14

Zane leveled Cody Chifley a hard stare. They were ten minutes into the interrogation, but so far Meghan's brother wasn't saying much. Zane had been careful to play things by the book. He'd asked Chifley if he wanted a lawyer and to his relief, the man had merely shaken his head. Zane had even asked if Cody wanted to call his sister. Cody had just looked up at him with eyes filled with sadness and resignation.

"No. She's got enough to deal with. She doesn't need to add me to her troubles. All her life she's turned herself inside out for our family, playing the peacemaker, intervening in arguments between hotheaded members of our clan, including me. I don't want to drag her into this any further. She's already done enough. Besides, I didn't have anything to do with my father's murder. Ask your questions. I have nothing to hide."

Zane glanced at Willie seated beside him. Zane had brought Willie up to speed on what Meghan had told him. Between the two of them, they were determined to get Cody to crack. In a threatening move, Zane leaned forward.

"That's bullshit, Chifley, and you know it. Last time we talked you told us you were high the night your father was murdered and you couldn't remember anything. Now you're telling us you know you didn't do it. You don't know shit, and that's the truth! We've spoken to your sister. We know about your late-night chat."

The color leeched from Cody's face. Shock and fear filled his eyes. Zane stilled.

What the hell was going on?

Cody's reaction to discovering his sister had told the police about his phone call seemed way over the top. After all, according to Meghan, her brother had called to apologize for handing out her security code to a criminal. Apparently that call had nothing to do with their father and his untimely, violent death.

So why did the man who sat hunched over the table in front of them look so terrified?

"I-I don't believe you," Cody stammered. "There's no way Meghan told you about that. She knew what you'd think. Just like I knew what you'd think." He looked directly at Zane. "What you *do* think." With a sigh of disappointment, Cody ran a hand tiredly through his disheveled hair and then buried his face in his hands. Zane and Willie waited him out in silence. A few seconds passed, then he lifted his head.

"I still can't believe my sister told you," he said wearily. He sighed again and it sounded like he had the weight of the world on his shoulders.

Zane sat there, on edge. He'd interviewed enough suspects to know they were on the brink of a breakthrough. He glanced at Willie and could tell by the look on his partner's face that he felt the same.

Chifley scrubbed his hands through his hair and groaned in defeat. "So, Meghan told you what happened that night?" He shrugged when there was no response. "Okay, I admit it. I had an argument with my father. I should have told you earlier. The reason I didn't was because of *this*."

He threw up his hands toward the detectives. "Straight away you jumped to the conclusion since I was at my father's home on the night in question and we argued, I must be the killer. That's why you arrested me, right? Well, I'm telling you right now, I'm not your man."

Zane's jaw almost fell open in surprise. It was only with a supreme effort and years of experience hiding his emotions that he managed to conceal his surprise. The last thing he'd expected Cody to confess to was a visit to his father's house the very night the man was murdered. It was obvious Cody had misunderstood his reference to the late-night chat. Instead of the phone call Meghan had spoken about, Cody had owned up to arguing with his father the very night the man was murdered.

It was a gift Zane couldn't have anticipated, even as he was filled with anger at the knowledge Meghan had said nothing to him of the meeting when it was clear she'd known about it all along.

What else had she kept from him? Was she more involved in the murder than he'd supposed? Had he been taken in by her beauty and the air of sad vulnerability and forgotten basic policing along the way? Forcing aside his growing anger, he scrambled to gather his thoughts. It was time to turn up the heat.

"That's right," Zane snarled. "You turned up at your father's place, stoned from whatever you'd taken that night. You were desperate for money and you knew just where to find it. You keyed in the security code and made your way up the drive in your white Mazda."

He paused and then added, "Did you know one of the neighbors spotted you on the way in?"

Cody looked shaken. "No, I didn't. But I was only there to talk to him. He was still alive when I left. It wasn't me who killed him! You're wrong!"

Unperturbed, Zane continued. "You let yourself into your father's house. You weren't sure where he was, but of course, you're more than familiar with the layout of the house and you were also familiar with your father's habits. Eventually you found him in his bedroom, preparing for bed. You got into an argument. You wanted money. He refused to give it to you. It was more of what had gone on at your birthday party, wasn't it?"

Cody stared at them, his eyes imploring the two men opposite him. "No! Please, Detectives! You have to believe me! It wasn't like that!"

"But you already admitted you were there that night, Cody, and you told us the two of you got into a fight," Willie said, his voice like toughened steel.

"I said we *argued!*" Cody cried. "We *didn't* fight! Not like you're implying."

Zane took up where Willie let off. "Yes, you *argued*. Just like you had before. That time, your father threatened to cut you out of his will and you believed he'd follow through. You told us that, remember? The last time you were here."

Cody shook his head back and forth, becoming increasingly agitated. Zane pressed home the advantage.

"At some point, your father turned his back on you, dismissing you in such an arrogant way. That's when you reached for the paperweight and you clocked him with it on the back of his head. You hit him hard. He went down, right at the foot of his bed. You'd conveniently come armed with a knife—because you *knew* it was likely he'd refuse your request—after all, he'd done the same when you'd asked, a month before.

"Full of rage, you bent over him and stabbed him over and over again. Forty-seven times, in fact. Finally, you stopped. Maybe you'd worn yourself out? Whatever. It doesn't matter. Your father was dead and you were responsible. That's when the guilt started.

"Whether your high was wearing off or your conscience finally kicked in, all of a sudden you found yourself aghast at what you'd done. You gathered your father's body off the floor and placed him in the bath. You lovingly cleaned his wounds and washed away the evidence of your rage. You even covered his face with the washcloth when you'd finished so he couldn't bear witness to your shame."

Zane glared at him. Sweat had popped out on Cody's brow. His complexion was now a pasty gray.

Willie took up the narrative. "You then went downstairs and found a rug to cover the large bloodstain on the carpet that had accumulated beneath your father's body. You cleaned the walls. You got rid of the knife. You thought you'd gotten rid of all signs of your awful deed. To the casual eye, your father looked, for all the money, like he was sleeping in the bath."

Zane's lip curled up in disgust. "Except for the myriad of stab wounds decorating his chest."

"Yes, and the paperweight. Remember that, Cody?" Willie asked, his voice almost conversational. "Somehow, you forgot about that. We found it on your father's nightstand. It's still stained with his blood. It's at the lab right now, being tested as we speak. Once we find your fingerprints on it, you're done for. You know that, don't you?"

"No! No! You have it all wrong! It wasn't me! I swear! It wasn't me!"

Zane leaned closer, his body tense, his expression menacing. "The truth is, Cody, you don't know what you did that night. You were high on drugs. You don't remember anything. Only, bit by bit, it's been coming back to you, isn't it? That's why you were able to tell your sister about being there that night. It's the reason we couldn't find you. No one could. You disappeared, ran away to hide from your desperate shame."

Tears coursed freely down Cody's cheeks. Sobs of despair shook his shoulders and chest.

"No," he cried in a defeated tone. "No, I couldn't have! Even stoned, I would have remembered! I loved my father. We didn't always see eye to eye, but I loved him! I couldn't have murdered him like that! I just couldn't!" With that, he collapsed against the table and with his head in his hands he wept like a broken child.

Zane stared down at him in disgust. He glanced at Willie, who nodded. Zane tightened his lips and then in an emotionless voice informed Cody Chifley he was going to be charged with the murder of his father.

A knock on the door caught the detectives' attention. It opened and a junior detective appeared.

"Could I see you for a moment, Detective Sullivan?"

Zane looked at Willie who acknowledged the question with a slight movement of his head. Zane got to his feet and left the room.

"What is it, Watson?"

A blush stole up the young detective's neck. Zane swallowed his impatience.

"It's about Cody Chifley. We've executed the search warrant."

Zane felt a surge of anticipation. An examination of Grant Chifley's kitchen the morning his body had been discovered had revealed nothing was missing. It was highly likely the murder weapon had been sourced from Cody's house. There was also the question of where he'd discarded his bloodied clothes and the clothes his father had worn. There was no way he'd inflicted that kind of damage without both of them being covered in blood.

"What did you find?" Zane demanded.

"Well… We found nothing."

Zane frowned. "What do you mean, you found nothing?"

Watson shifted uncomfortably. "Just that. We tossed the place from top to bottom. We found nothing."

Zane gritted his teeth, filled with frustration. "Shit." He ran a hand through his hair and then eased his breath out on a sigh. He regarded the detective.

"Okay. Thanks for letting me know, Watson. I shouldn't be surprised. The man's estranged from his wife. He hasn't lived there for months. It doesn't matter. We have enough to charge him. And that's even before we get the results back from the lab."

Watson smiled in relief and handed Zane a copy of the search warrant for the file. Taking the paperwork and murmuring a few more words of thanks, Zane returned to the interview room and informed Meghan's brother he was taking him to the charge room. As they went through the motions of fingerprinting, photographing and cataloguing his personal effects, Zane's thoughts returned to Meghan.

She'd lied to him. More than once. Taken him for a sucker...

A flood of feral anticipation rushed through him. He couldn't wait to demand to know why she hadn't bothered to share with him the fact her brother had been in their father's house on the very evening he was murdered and not only that, that they'd argued—again—over money. From what her brother said, she'd known all about it and hadn't breathed a word.

Instead she'd given him some bullshit story about Cody meeting up with his dealer and handing over her security code. She'd batted her big blue eyes at him and had scrounged up a few tears and he'd fallen for it. Hell, he'd even felt sorry for her! And then that kiss... Every time he remembered the feel of her pressed against him, the sweetness of her mouth, it drove him wild.

Only, it had all been a lie... All along, she'd been playing him, covering for her brother, protecting him from being punished for his deadly deed. She claimed to have loved her father, but it was obvious no one came close to the love and devotion she had for her twin.

Depending on the answers she gave this time round, if she wasn't careful, he'd put her in handcuffs and drag her down to the station, too. She could share a cell with her beloved brother. That would give her plenty of time to contemplate how she'd miscalculated Zane's gullibility and for her to consider just how much time she could spend behind bars if she were found guilty of obstructing justice—or even of being an accessory to murder.

———————

Zane pressed the buzzer on the gate outside Meghan's ritzy apartment complex and waited impatiently for her to answer. He hadn't bothered to phone ahead. He didn't want to give her advance notice that he had a head full of steam and was on his way over to demand answers. This time, he wasn't leaving without the truth.

The speaker just above the buzzer remained irritatingly silent. He cursed and punched the button again. It was even more annoying knowing he only had himself to blame for falling for Meghan's perfidy. If his brain had been focused firmly on the case and the evidence they'd uncovered instead of letting himself be swept away by fantasies of him and her together, he would have seen through her lies.

She'd bamboozled him with her intelligence, her stunning good looks, her wealth. She'd dazzled him, period. A boy from the wrong side of the tracks had dared to dream just for an instant that there could be something between them. And now he'd been made to look a fool. Even now, she was probably laughing herself silly. His jaw clenched at the thought. He'd see who looked silly now.

The third time he depressed the buzzer, he kept his finger on it for almost a full minute, cursing the whole time. Finally, the speaker came to life and Meghan's voice came over the intercom.

"Detective Sullivan. I wasn't expecting you."

"I bet you weren't."

If she was surprised by his anger, it didn't show in her voice.

"Is there something I can do for you?"

"Yes. You can let me in. I need to talk to you."

"About what?"

"This is best left for the privacy of your kitchen. Surely you don't want the neighbors to hear?"

The sarcasm in his voice was unmistakable. With a click, the entry gate opened inward and Zane passed through. The foyer was empty and so was the elevator. In no time at all, he was pounding on her door.

She opened it and calmly stood there looking at him.

His gaze roved over her, as if he couldn't help but take her in. He guessed she'd taken a shower in his absence. Her hair was wet and hung in a riot of curls around her face, making her look even younger. She'd ditched the pajamas in favor of a worn pale blue T-shirt and a snug pair of white cotton shorts. The sight of her looking so cool and innocent and beautiful reignited his anger in a flash.

"Why didn't you tell me your brother was at your father's house the same night he died?"

The look of shock that passed over her face was deeply satisfying. While she grappled with an answer, he pushed past her and headed further into the open concept kitchen and living room.

Spinning on his heel, with his hands on his hips, he waited for her to answer him.

"How did you find out?" she asked dully.

So, she wasn't going to try and deny it... Until that moment, there had been the tiniest possibility she hadn't been aware of her brother's late night visit to their father. Now all his doubts were put to rest. He felt a stab of disappointment and quickly forced it aside.

"Your brother told me."

Her eyes widened in fear. "You found him?"

"Yes. It was quite fortuitous, really. I came upon him outside your place right after I left here. I guess he was on his way back. Too bad for him I was here, too. Just so you know, he's been charged with your father's murder."

She looked appalled. "Oh, no! Poor Cody! Where is he? I must go to him!"

"Right now, he's cooling his heels in a cell. I've suggested he might want to engage the services of a lawyer."

"You mean he's going to spend the night in jail? What about bail?"

Zane shrugged. "There's a presumption against bail when a defendant has been charged with murder, but I'm sure you know that, Counselor. Oh, that's right. You're not a real lawyer. You're an estate lawyer. Maybe you don't know that. Whatever. It's of no consequence. I'll let your brother sort it out with his lawyer. Besides, it's too late to take him over to the courthouse now for a bail hearing. He'll have to wait until morning."

She stood pale and silent with her arms folded defensively across her chest, staring blindly into the distance. A spurt of compassion filled Zane's veins, but he clenched his fists and stood his ground, determined to ignore it. He'd fallen for her vulnerable act once before and had been taken for a ride. He wouldn't fall for it a second time.

"You haven't answered my question." His voice was harsh in the silence of the room.

She looked at him half-dazed. "What question?"

He took two threatening steps toward her. "Why didn't you tell me about Cody's visit to your father? Instead, you gave me some bullshit story about him meeting with his lowlife dealer."

He moved even closer. Her chest rose and fell in time with her rapid breathing. She quickly averted her gaze.

"It wasn't bullshit. Cody told me that's what happened."

Zane's lip curled up in disgust. "Except he also told you he'd dropped by Daddy's place that night, didn't he?"

The slightest nod was the only indication she'd heard. Her hand came up to her mouth, as if holding back the words that might damn her brother forever.

He glared at her. "Did you know one of your father's neighbors saw Cody there that night?"

Meghan's eyes widened in shock. "No," she whispered.

"Well, to be more precise, she told me she saw one of the twins sometime after eight. She wasn't sure if it was you or your brother. After all, you do look similar. I can see how she might get confused."

Meghan hugged herself tighter and remained silent, but Zane wasn't finished.

"You still haven't told me why you neglected to share that bit of information with me. While you were pretending to bare your soul, you kept the best part from me. You were hoping to put me off Cody's scent, give him an alibi. Too bad for you I didn't buy it, and I want to know why you did it."

Zane's gaze bored into her. He wanted to take her by the shoulders and shake the answer out of her. Every time he thought of her deception, he got angry all over again. He wasn't sure any excuse she offered would be satisfactory. And then her face crumpled and tears flooded her eyes.

Zane steeled himself against her display of emotion. Still, it wasn't easy standing by watching while a woman he cared about far more than he should, or had a right to, slowly fell apart.

"I'm sorry," she sobbed, her tears coming faster. "I should have told you! I wanted to! Believe me, I did! It was just that… I knew what you'd think if you were aware Cody had been with our father in the hours before he was brutally murdered. And not only that, but they'd argued! It was like the party all over again! I couldn't bear to think about it and I couldn't bear the thought that you'd jump to conclusions and put my brother away for a crime he didn't commit."

She was crying in earnest now, with her head buried in her hands. With a supreme effort, Zane once again resisted the urge to go to her and offer her comfort.

"I don't understand your blind loyalty to him," he responded. "Okay, he's your brother, your twin, but that shouldn't mean you disregard common sense. Everything points to your brother being the murderer. He knew the code to get through the gate; he knew the layout of the house. By his own admission, he went there seeking money, knowing that your father would, more than likely, toss him out. It's not inconceivable that their argument turned physical, like it had once before, and that in the heat of the moment your brother struck out at your father and in a fit of rage, furious with him, he stabbed him forty-seven times." He paused and then added more gently, "It happens, Meghan. I've seen it all before. The people who most often hurt us are the ones that love us most. It's just the way it is."

She lifted her head and stared at him through eyes filled with pain. "I don't care what you say. I won't believe it. Cody's not capable of doing that, of inflicting that much hurt. No way. Never."

Her voice broke on another wave of devastation.

Cursing under his breath and against his better judgment, Zane stepped forward and took her in his arms.

CHAPTER 15

They came together fast and furious, with nothing holding them back. Meghan's heart pounded and she fought to catch her breath. Zane's relentless words, building a case against her brother, echoed in her mind, but she forced them aside and kissed Zane almost furiously with everything she had.

Cody had admitted to going over there, to getting into a fight. She only had his word that he'd turned and walked away and had left his father standing there, still very much alive. Despite everything Zane had said, she chose to believe her brother. He was her flesh and blood. He deserved her loyalty until it had been proved beyond reasonable doubt that her loyalty was misplaced.

Only then would she concede she'd been wrong. After all, everything Zane said was circumstantial. He still had no real evidence tying her brother to the crime. No weapon, no fingerprints. Nothing. Cody was family. She'd stand by him, no matter what. In the meantime, she needed an outlet, a way to release the tension that held her in its grip. It probably wasn't the smartest thing to get involved with the lead detective, but right now she had no desire to resist.

With that, she clung to Zane's broad shoulders and kissed him with all she had. His soft beard tickled her skin, unfamiliar, but nice. In some deep recess of her mind, she understood it was wrong to use him this way, but this is what she needed, and from the way his mouth moved against hers and the hard feel of his body, it appeared he needed this, too.

The night had crept up on them and the light was dim. The glimmer of lights from distant apartment blocks outside her window provided the only source of illumination. Zane took a couple of steps backwards, drawing her with him. A moment later, they tumbled together onto the couch. His lips found hers again and his tongue stole into her mouth. She opened her lips for him, relishing the feel and taste of him. Needing this, needing him.

His hands slid from around her hips and moved up until they cupped her breasts. His thumbs found her nipples and they hardened beneath his touch. She'd just stepped out of the shower and she wasn't wearing a bra. The plan had been to order some takeout, have a quiet dinner and go to bed. At the time she wasn't sure where Cody was or whether he'd be back and at that time she hadn't much cared. She'd been so weary, so tired of all that had gone on. The thought of her loss and her father's brutal death had left her heartsick. There were still so many questions...

Zane tugged her T-shirt off and his lips replaced his fingers on her breast. The feel of his hot, moist mouth on her nipple sent her thoughts scattering to the winds. She arched her back beneath him, giving him greater access to what he sought. Then he switched his attention to her other breast.

His teeth nipped gently at her soft skin and then he opened his mouth and drew the hard nub inside. He suckled it like a baby.

Hot white heat burned deep inside her, centering in her core. She moved restlessly against him. It had been a while since she'd had sex. Her body hummed with anticipation. She burned for completion.

"I want to feel you inside me," she growled, her voice husky and low.

"God, yes," was all he said.

With that, he sat up and loosened the tie around his neck. He flung it away and started on the buttons of his shirt. That quickly went the same way as the tie and she was left to stare at his broad chest.

Well-defined muscles covered in a light scattering of dark hair filled her vision. Her gaze dropped lower, past the washboard stomach and lower still to where a thin line of hair disappeared inside the waistband of his pants. She reached out and undid his belt buckle and slid it out of the loops. Next came the button and his zipper.

As if suddenly impatient, he brushed her hands

away and half-stood and shimmied out of his pants. Clad only in his underwear, he came back to her.

Reaching for her T-shirt, he tugged it up all the way over her head. Her shorts were quick to follow. A pair of brief, white lace panties were the only thing that hid the most intimate part of her from his gaze.

"You're so beautiful," he murmured. His eyes were dark with desire and heat flared in his gaze.

Answering heat ignited inside her. She reached for him. They came together, skin to skin and it felt better than she could ever remember. The hardness of his erection pressed against the softness of her stomach and sent a fresh wave of desire shooting through her. She squirmed, restless and impatient for the feel of him.

"I want to see you naked."

His words, spoken so quietly, sent a thrill of desire arcing through her. He reached down and took hold of her panties. She lifted her hips as he slid them down her legs. He tossed them away and then stared at her, his eyes drinking her in.

She should have felt embarrassed, shy, but she reveled in the feel of his gaze.

"Do you have a condom?" she rasped.

He hesitated and then nodded. "Yes."

With that, he climbed off her and picked up his pants. He fished through one of the pockets and pulled out his wallet. He pulled off his briefs and sheathed himself. In a brief moment he was back by her side. She sighed with pleasure at the feel of him on top of her.

Swooping down, he captured her lips with his and kissed her with a passion that left her breathless. At the same time, his cock probed her entrance. She lifted her hips in encouragement and with one swift movement, he found his way in. She gasped again as he filled her.

For a second, they both lay motionless, as if trying to get their head around it all. And then he began to move and pleasure poured through her again.

Long and strong he thrust inside her and with each stroke, he drew her higher, closer to the peak. She clung to his shoulders and rode him, her legs tight around his hips. Over and over he plunged inside her until she could bear it no more. Biting down on his shoulder, she reached her climax and cried out. With a gasp of relief, she toppled over the edge.

He thrust harder and faster. Sweat shone on his brow. The muscles in his arms bunched beneath the strain. Silently, she urged him on, clinging to his shoulders. Her muscles were still convulsing around him when he finally cried out himself. He pumped hard once, twice, three times—and then he collapsed against her. Breathing hard, they slowly drifted back to earth.

As reality sank in, Meghan burned with embarrassment. She'd just slept with the lead detective investigating her father's murder. The same detective who had her brother in his sights.

Oh, God. What had she done?

———

Zane's head was filled with the sweet smell of Meghan's perfume. Her soft body was still beneath him on the couch. He came up on his elbows, lifting his weight off her and then stood. Quickly disposing of the condom, he tugged on his briefs and pants. She put her hands up to cover her breasts and regarded him in silence. He understood how she felt. He didn't know what to say, either.

He'd never been in this position before; had never slept with someone involved in one of his investigations. It was totally unethical and just plain wrong. Still, he couldn't regret it.

It had been one of the most magical moments of his life. Fast and furious, full of desire and passion, it had sent him soaring for the skies. No matter what reality might impose on them, there was one inescapable truth: He was falling hard and fast for Meghan Chifley and there wasn't a damn thing he could do about it.

The thought was sobering. He could already see the regret that shadowed her eyes. Still, there was one thing that was certain: The two of them had unfinished business between them. This wasn't the last she'd hear from him. And under the circumstances, he felt the need to apologize.

"I'm sorry. I shouldn't have done that. It was unprofessional and totally out of bounds. I wasn't thinking."

A blush stained her cheeks, but he was encouraged when she looked him in the eye.

"I'm sorry, too. It's my fault as much as yours. You didn't force me. The truth is, I wanted you and I enjoyed this way too much."

Her words filled him with hope. He felt exactly the same way. What they'd just done was wrong on so many counts, but he couldn't ignore the way she made him feel. For the first time in his life, it was like someone cared, someone saw beyond the abandoned boy he'd been. He still wasn't sure how that had happened.

"What happens now?" she whispered.

In an effort to buy time, Zane bent down and picked up his shirt and slipped it over his shoulders. He wasn't sure what she wanted him to say. If it were up to him, he'd take up where they'd left off and love her all night long. But as the seconds ticked by... He was still the detective in charge of her father's murder investigation and she was integrally connected to his case. Her brother had just been charged with murder and she was in turmoil. Nothing he could do would change that.

With a quiet sigh, he picked up her clothing and handed it to her. She murmured her thanks and slid the T-shirt on over her head. Her underwear and shorts quickly followed. When she was dressed, she looked up at him again.

"I know this shouldn't have happened, but I refuse to say I regret it. It was... It was exactly what I needed. You helped me forget, for just a little while, the nightmare my life has become. I'll always be grateful."

Anger stirred inside him. He frowned down at her. "I don't want your gratitude, Meghan." His voice was rougher than he intended. Her words had taken him aback. She flinched.

"I'm sorry," he quickly added. "That came out harsher than I meant. The thing is, what happened between us had nothing to do with gratitude. At least, not on my part. I was attracted to you from the moment I laid eyes on you and nothing that's happened since has changed that. As far as I'm concerned, this was just a coming together of two adults who were drawn to one another, attracted and with a need that had to be quenched."

She regarded him steadily, her expression unreadable. "You're right," she said in an over-bright voice. "The sex was great. It served a purpose. Let's just leave it at that."

He narrowed his eyes. He didn't want her dismissing what had happened between them so easily. Still, what did he expect? She was still clinging to the fact her brother was innocent and Zane was doing all he could to put the man away for life. Even the thought he and Meghan could have something together was ludicrous. He'd known that from the start.

"I need to call Sarah," she murmured. "She's going to be as angry as I am that Cody's been charged with murder. It won't be long before the news comes to the attention of the media. I'd don't want Sarah to find out that way."

Zane's lips tightened, but he remained silent. There was nothing for him to say. At the mention of Sarah, he was reminded how she'd also lied to him. Why had she told him she'd lived independently for three years when it had been more like a month? What did she have to hide? While he was sure the right person was even now sitting behind bars, Sarah's dishonesty intrigued him. No one lied to police officers without a reason. He was determined to find hers.

He took a moment to sit beside Meghan while he pulled on his socks and shoes, then he stood once again.

"I need to get going."

She looked at him with resignation and nodded. Yes."

He leaned down and kissed her hard on the mouth. "I'll see you later."

And with that, he turned and left.

CHAPTER 16

Meghan listened to the click of the door announcing Zane's departure and sighed. She was a fool for succumbing to her need for release, in the moment, but like she'd told Zane, she refused to regret it. Yes, it made things more complicated, but they were two consenting adults who could surely set aside what happened and focus on what was most important: Cody.

The fact she and the detective were on opposite sides didn't matter. He had a job to do. She understood that. But she knew Cody better than anyone and she knew he wasn't capable of the kind of violence Zane had accused him of.

With a sigh, she reached for her phone and dialed Sarah's number.

To her relief, Sarah answered the call on the second ring.

"Meghan? What's the matter? It's past nine. Aren't you meant to be asleep? I thought you went to bed with the birds?"

Meghan heard the smile in her half-sister's voice and closed her eyes against a stab of pain. There would be no laughter for a long time in the Chifley household. Only a cold hard determination to set their brother free.

As quickly and as unemotionally as she could, Meghan gave Sarah the news. Her announcement was met with shocked silence. Finally, she braved the question.

"Sarah, are you still there?"

"Yes." Sarah's voice was flat and emotionless. Meghan hastened to reassure her.

"Of course, we both know the police have the wrong man. There's no way Cody's responsible for murdering our father. No way in the world. We need to band together and convince them they've made a mistake."

Sarah remained silent. Meghan was flooded with confusion and concern. "Sarah? Say something. You know as well as I do Cody's innocent. We need to go to the police, try and force them to see the truth."

"How do you know he's innocent, Meghan?"

The quiet words hit her in the stomach like a sucker punch. Meghan gasped for breath, but the band around her chest refused to ease.

"Wh-what are you talking about?" she wheezed. "Of course he's innocent!"

Sarah gave a derisive laugh. "Of course you're going to believe that. He's your twin. Accepting your beloved brother's a cold-hearted killer would just about do you in. But what about the evidence?"

"There isn't any evidence!" Meghan cried, unable to believe what she was hearing.

"So you say, but the police have charged him with murder. They don't do that without strong evidence pointing to his guilt."

Meghan's head reeled. "What are you talking about, Sarah? Whose side are you on?"

"*Tsk, tsk*. This isn't about taking sides. This is about facing the truth. It hurts, Meghan. It hurts a lot. I don't want to think Cody capable of murdering our father, either, but we need to be realistic. The police have charged him with murder. They obviously know something we don't."

Meghan thought of whatever it was Zane's partner had taken to the lab. Some new evidence that obviously linked her brother to the crime. Zane hadn't given her any indication of what he'd found, but whatever it was had been enough for him to lay charges. That was an indisputable fact.

Icy dread formed in the pit of her stomach. All of a sudden, she felt sick. "I'm sorry, Sarah. I have to go."

"Hey, how about I come over and keep you company? This has come as an awful shock to both of us. I don't know about you, but I'd rather not be alone right now."

"Sure," Meghan agreed readily, still fighting against her nausea.

"Are you at home?"

"Yes."

"I'll be there soon."

____

Zane absently reached across his desk and picked up his coffee mug. With his gaze still on the screen in front of him, he took a sip and then cursed as the steaming liquid burned his tongue.

"Shit!"

He'd forgotten he'd made the coffee a short time ago and it was still boiling hot. Already, he could feel the blister forming on his tongue. *Just what he needed, especially so early in the morning...* His shift had barely begun.

The squad room door opened and Willie came bounding in. "What's got you so chirpy?" Zane asked.

"We've got the lab results back on that paperweight." Willie's eyes gleamed with excitement. "I've also received the CCTV footage from Sydney Legal. It shows Meghan Chifley arriving at work at eight-fifteen the morning of the murder. She exits briefly around lunchtime and then we see her leaving at twelve-nineteen the next morning. It seems we can cross her off the list of suspects."

"You're right. She's not our killer." Zane's tone was matter-of-fact. Though he was glad there was now actual proof Meghan couldn't be the murderer, in his mind he'd already dismissed her as a suspect some time ago. No one as good and kind and loving toward their family as she was could have been responsible for such a heinous act.

"What about the lab results?" he asked, straightening in his chair. The proof of Meghan's innocence had already lifted his mood.

"I haven't opened them, yet. I thought I'd leave that honor to you. Seeing as you're the boss, and all." Willie grinned and Zane laughed reluctantly. Willie handed him the envelope and Zane took it from him eagerly.

Sliding his finger underneath the closure, his heart picked up its pace. Hopefully the paperweight held the indisputable evidence about the killer's identity, namely Cody Chifley. As Zane pulled out the single sheet of paper, he was filled with anticipation. He scanned the lines of type and his heart sank. Noticing the change in his expression, Willie frowned.

"What is it?"

Zane blew out his breath on a loud sigh of disappointment. "They're not his. It's not Cody Chifley."

"What you mean, it's not Cody Chifley?"

"Exactly that. It's not him."

"So there were no fingerprints?"

Zane grimaced. "Oh, yes, there were fingerprints all right. Just not prints belonging to our main suspect."

Willie's frown deepened. "What the hell? How can that be? It fits so well. Motive, means, opportunity. He even put himself there. How could it not be Cody Chifley?"

Zane compressed his lips into a grim line. He was just as surprised as Willie. "You tell me. All I know is that the lab found a partial print on the paperweight. They ran it through the system and didn't get a hit. Chifley's prints were taken when we arrested him. That means it doesn't belong to him."

It was Willie's turn to blow his breath out on a heavy sigh. "Shit. Did they find *anything* of use?"

Zane looked back at the typewritten results in his hand. "According to this, Grant Chifley's hair and blood were found on the paperweight. At least that means we know for sure this was the weapon used to inflict the initial blow to his head. They also recovered the partial fingerprint. It didn't belong to our victim, so we can only assume it belongs to the killer—whose identity still remains unknown."

Willie's lips compressed into a thin line of disappointment. Zane knew exactly how he felt. He couldn't believe the print didn't belong to Cody Chifley. Everything had seemed to fit. Now they were back at the drawing board.

"There is one possibility," Willie ventured.

Zane looked at him. "What's that?"

"Well, we're almost certain Cody Chifley murdered his father. It's possible someone else struck the initial blow. We've ruled out Meghan, but maybe someone else was involved? Maybe he took his bagman with him to show he was good for the money? Maybe it was that lowlife who administered the initial blow?"

Zane shook his head. "I'm not buying it. I don't believe a drug dealer wouldn't have a prior arrest record, which means his prints would be in the system. And don't forget: We pretty much discounted Chifley's story about meeting with his dealer as a tall tale he made up for his sister, to explain his whereabouts that night as well as the late-night phone call where he pleaded for her forgiveness."

Willie appeared deflated. "Yeah, you're right."

"Hey, don't take it too hard. We know from the autopsy that the stab wounds were all made by the same person, but there's still a slight possibility Cody went there with someone else who immobilized his father so Cody could stab him and finish him off. Someone who's clean. Somebody without a criminal record. Somebody we haven't yet considered."

"Either that," Willie said slowly, "or it wasn't Cody Chifley at all."

Zane clenched his jaw tight and swallowed a groan. He didn't want to contemplate the possibility they'd arrested the wrong man. A man who was even now cooling his heels in jail. It had been hard enough telling Meghan her brother was the killer. It was going to be even harder to admit that somehow he might have gotten it wrong.

Had there been a second assailant involved in the attack, or was he just clutching at straws? Could it have been Sarah Chifley? Was that the reason she'd lied?

One thing was certain, if the killer had acted alone, he sure as hell wasn't Cody Chifley and if it wasn't Cody Chifley, they were back to square one.

Frustration surged through him. With a groan, he rested his elbows on his desk and buried his hands in his hair.

"Fuuuuck!"

At that moment, all other words were beyond him.

———————

Meghan glanced across at her sister, sprawled out on the deck chair on Meghan's balcony, enjoying the midmorning sun. Sarah had arrived the night before looking even more unkempt than usual. Meghan had to admit, she'd been taken aback at the sight of her sister when she'd opened the door. Her hair was dirty and straggly and plenty of gray was showing through. The stained blouse she wore was pulled tight across her ample bosom and did nothing to conceal the unsightly belly fat that protruded from underneath. She didn't want to judge her sister too harshly, but it looked like Sarah hadn't been taking care of herself properly for weeks.

The last time Meghan had seen Sarah was at the birthday party. Sarah had been living at home at the time. Meghan imagined things had been tough since Sarah'd been thrown out by their father, but still, surely she didn't have to look like a homeless person?

Meghan felt a little ashamed at the thought she didn't know exactly where Sarah was now living, but surely she had the means to shower and wash her hair and clothes? Maybe her older sister enjoyed looking like she was a street woman? Maybe it was her way of thumbing her nose at their dad? Too bad he hadn't lived to see the result of his decision. He might have invited her back home.

Then again, maybe not.

Now they'd never know.

Over the course of Meghan's childhood, Sarah had mostly been absent. While she'd always lived in one wing of the mansion, she'd kept her own hours and had come and gone as she pleased. Meghan had rarely seen her, except for the sporadic occasions Sarah would join them for a family meal. Now, as Meghan thought back to those times, she realized her father often appeared disappointed, irritated and tight-lipped toward his eldest daughter.

As a child, Meghan hadn't fathomed his sudden mood change whenever Sarah appeared, but as Meghan grew older, she realized Sarah spent all of her time in idle pursuits, all financed by their father—and he resented footing the bill.

Endless shopping, hitting the nightclubs, drinking way too much. It appeared she had no intention of embarking on a career, or any kind of job, for that matter. As the years went on, Meghan understood more and more their father's attitude. Still, Sarah was her sister and there was nothing more important in the world than family.

Lifting the silver coffeepot off the tray that sat on the table between them, Meghan poured her sister a cup. "Are you still taking cream and sugar?" she asked.

Sarah responded with a grunt that Meghan took as a yes. "Two sugars. Plenty of cream."

Meghan did as she was asked and in silence handed the cup to her sister.

"Thanks," came the grudging reply.

Meghan swallowed her irritation with her sister's rudeness. After all, Sarah had been through a lot recently. She'd been tossed out of her family home and forced to fend for herself for the first time in her life. She'd also had less time than Meghan to process the enormity of what had happened to Cody and what it might mean for their family.

"What happened to your hand?" she asked, noticing for the first time the bandage that covered Sarah's hand.

"I cut it with a knife. Fixing dinner."

Meghan frowned. "Ouch. Was it bad?"

"Not really."

"Did you go to the hospital?"

"Yeah. It hurt like hell, so I ended up going to the emergency department. They put in a couple of stitches and gave me a shot in the backside. That hurt almost as much as my hand."

Meghan was filled with concern. She eyed the grimy, dirt-stained bandage. "A couple of stitches? That sounds bad. Are you sure it's okay?"

Sarah shrugged, as if bored with the conversation. "It's fine."

"Do you want me to take a look at it?"

"No. It's fine.

"Are you sure?" Meghan persisted. The last thing the wound needed was to get infected.

"Yes. I told you already. It's fine," Sarah snapped.

Meghan pulled back. This had been a tough day for both of them. She didn't want to antagonize her sister any more than necessary.

"Okay," she murmured and took a sip from her cup.

Silence fell between them as they took refuge in their coffees. In an effort to lift the mood between them, Meghan offered Sarah a tight smile. "Thanks for coming over, Sarah. It really means a lot."

Sarah's answering smile was as strained as Meghan's. "No problem." A moment later, she added, "I'm here for you, little sis. I want you to know that."

Meghan blinked in surprise. Sarah had never called her that before. Though Meghan had tried hard over the years to maintain a friendly relationship with her, Sarah had rebuffed her at every turn. Their relationship had always been prickly, to say the least.

As she'd grown older and could see things more clearly, Meghan had put her sister's attitude down to the resentment she must've felt upon the arrival of the twins. A new wife and two cute new babies must've been hard to compete with. Naturally, their father's attention would have been divided and perhaps he'd lavished that attention more generously on the twins. Though Meghan had no memory of this, it wasn't hard to imagine.

Sarah had been thirteen when Meghan and Cody were born. Three years before that, her parents had gone through a messy divorce. It was a tricky age to deal with so many significant life changes, not to mention the difficulties of a stepmother.

As Sarah watched her expectantly, she realized her sister was waiting for a response, gauging her reaction to the words. Meghan summoned a grateful smile, even as her mind continued to whirl.

"Thanks, Sarah. I really appreciate you saying that. Until Cody gets bail, you're all I've got." As the enormity of what had happened struck her anew, she slowly shook her head. "I still refuse to believe he did it."

Sarah shrugged. "I don't want to believe it, either, but we have to face facts. We both know how volatile Cody's been lately and the way he's been abusing those drugs... Who knows what he might have been capable of? He was so angry at Dad the last time he saw him. Maybe he went back there and exacted his revenge? Poor Dad."

Meghan closed her eyes in distress. Sarah's words brought to mind images of her father's last moments. Fending off blows from his only son, knowing his own flesh and blood was determined to kill him. *Was that the way it had happened? Was she naïve to think otherwise?*

Her mind rebelled at the thought, but a shiver ran down her spine. She glanced at her sister to see if she was equally affected.

Sarah's expression remained unreadable. She took another sip from her coffee and then set the cup aside. She stretched her arms above her head and then looked at Meghan. "Well, I guess I'd better be going. It's not like I can hang around here for the rest of the day."

Meghan sat forward in surprise. "Don't tell me you're leaving already? I thought you were going to stay for a bit?"

Sarah shrugged. "I don't want to outstay my welcome. After all, this is your place, not mine. We've already talked about what happened. What else is there to say?"

"You're right. But that doesn't mean I want you to leave. In fact, I'd really like you to stay."

Sarah frowned. "For how long?"

Meghan shrugged. "I don't know. Does it matter? Stay as long as you want. You're my sister. We need to look out for each other."

Sarah smiled and it was all Meghan could do not to grimace at the sight of her sister's stained and yellowed teeth. "Are you sure?" Sarah asked.

Shrugging off her misgivings, Meghan nodded. "Of course. It'll be great."

With a loud *whoop* of good cheer, Sarah enveloped her in a bear hug. Meghan nearly choked. Her sister's body odor was putrid. Despite Meghan's invitation to avail herself of the shower, Sarah had declined. What was even more surprising was Sarah's demonstrativeness. She'd never been one for hugs and kisses. It felt odd that she was doing it now.

Still, they were living in uncertain times and incredibly strange circumstances. *Who was Meghan to judge?*

Doing her best not to breathe in too deeply, she bravely returned Sarah's hug. There was one thing for certain: If Sarah was going to live with her, she was going to have to take regular showers and wear clean clothes every day. That was not negotiable.

Zane stared at the evidence board he and Willie had set up during the course of Grant Chifley's murder investigation. Each of their known suspects were listed, including a list of the factors that pointed to them. Cody Chifley acting alone had been their most convincing candidate, but that was now shot to hell. It was midmorning and he still hadn't told Meghan.

Knowing he'd put it off as long as he could, he strode back to his desk and picked up the phone. Gathering his courage, he dialed her number and waited as it rang out. He braced himself for it to go to voicemail and felt a jolt of surprise when he heard her voice.

"Meghan Chifley."

"Meghan, it's...Zane."

"Oh, Zane."

Though she sounded surprised, she also sounded pleased. A rush of nerves went through him.

"I hope I haven't caught you at a bad time?"

"No, of course not. I'm still on leave. I'm at home. What can I do for you?"

"I... I was wondering if I could come over. Something's come up in the case. Something we need to talk about."

"Can't we do that over the phone?"

He compressed his lips and briefly closed his eyes. This was going to be hard enough to admit to her, let alone doing it over the phone. He owed her a face-to-face explanation. Besides, despite everything, he wanted an excuse to see her again.

"If you don't mind, I'd rather not," he replied and hoped she didn't question him again.

"Oh, okay. Well, sure. Come over. You know where to find me."

CHAPTER 17

Meghan checked her reflection in the mirror and patted down a wayward curl. She was glad she'd taken the time to wash her hair earlier that morning. She still wore the short pink summer dress she'd put on straight out of the shower. She slipped on her favorite pink open-toed, low-heeled sandals.

The knowledge that Zane was on his way over filled her with a rush of anticipation and nerves. She hadn't seen him since their night of lovemaking. She wondered what he wanted to see her about and then decided she didn't care. Despite her casual dismissal of what had happened between them, inside she'd known it was a lie. She couldn't wait for him to arrive.

As if on cue, her front door buzzer sounded. Her heart skipped a beat and her belly did a flip flop. She hurriedly swiped some hot pink gloss across her lips, gave herself a final once-over and then turned to answer the summons.

Zane looked dark and mysterious and utterly

gorgeous on the intercom screen. He wore his usual suit and tie... but it was the unguarded flicker of desire in his eyes that did crazy things to her insides. She barely knew him and yet she wanted him with an intensity she'd never felt for any other. And it wasn't just the physical attraction that drew her to him. There was something about him, something aloof and unattainable that made her want him even more.

He was still such a mystery to her. She knew next to nothing of his past. Other than the fact he hadn't known his biological parents and that he'd spent years in and out of foster homes. It painted a lonely picture and she couldn't help but wonder if that vulnerability she glimpsed in him every so often was what drew her.

Family had always been important to her. She couldn't imagine what it had been like growing up without one. Some part of her, deep inside, wanted to give him what he'd been robbed of. She frowned and shook her head at the thought.

Where had that come from? He was doing his best to put her brother away for murder. They were on opposite sides of the fence. Besides, they'd known each other less than a week and here she was fantasizing about being a family. It was totally idiotic. If the sex hadn't been quite so spectacular, she probably wouldn't be giving him another thought.

Liar.

The sex *had* been spectacular, but that wasn't the reason why she couldn't get him out of her mind. She found him exciting, interesting, intelligent, wounded. It was a heady combination. She'd always been a sucker for the lost and the needy.

During her teens, she'd wanted to be a social worker. Her father had talked her out of it. He'd always been enamored of the law and bemoaned the fact he hadn't had the smarts to pursue such a career. He'd made it clear to her from an early age that he'd be thrilled with the idea that she pursue the career he had not.

And so she'd let go her aspirations for helping the poor and the needy and had gone to college and studied law. The day she graduated with honors her father boasted proudly to all who would listen.

She was thrilled to be offered a position at Sydney Legal. It was the most prestigious firm in the state, but she hadn't forgotten her socialist leanings and within two years of starting, she'd succeeded in convincing the managing partners to set up a pro bono program, where every lawyer in their employ donated a minimum number of hours every week to needy clients *gratis*. Meghan included.

The buzzer sounded again and she flushed with embarrassment. She'd been so caught up in her musings, she'd almost forgotten Zane waited for her downstairs.

"*Zane.*"

The sound of his name on her lips sent a shiver of anticipation down her spine, though she cautioned herself to stay calm. With her heart thumping, she pressed the button to let him in.

Meghan opened the door wearing a figure-hugging pink stretchy dress that ended mid-thigh. The color contrasted nicely with her tan. His gaze lingered on her smooth, slim legs and the fullness of her breasts clearly outlined beneath the tight fabric. Blood rushed immediately to his cock. Just like that, he wanted her—and then he remembered what he was there for. His excitement dissipated.

"Are you coming in?"

The expectant look on her face finally registered. He forced a smile and followed her inside.

"Would you like a cup of coffee, or maybe something stronger?" she asked, heading into the kitchen.

"No, I'm fine, thanks."

He spied a tattered coat lying across the arm of the couch. It looked so out of place, it immediately drew his attention. Meghan noticed him looking at it.

"That belongs to Sarah," she explained.

He frowned. "Your sister?"

"Half-sister," she corrected. "Yes. She came over. We're helping each other through this awful thing with Cody."

Zane grimaced and averted his gaze. He was still trying to find the words to tell her Cody was pretty much off the hook. "Where is she?" he asked instead, buying time.

"I asked her to stay here for a while. I... I could do with some company and I think she could, too.

She's gone back to her apartment to get a few things."

Zane acknowledged her comment with a nod. He recalled the dinginess of Sarah's digs. Living here in Meghan's luxurious condo with the sound of the waves lulling her to sleep every night was a fair step up in the world.

A part of him wished Meghan had turned to *him* for comfort. He quickly quashed the thought as ridiculous. They barely knew each other. Besides, he was the lead detective who'd been doing his utmost to put her brother away for murder. They might have slept together, but that didn't mean she intended or wanted anything long term, or anything more than a casual fling.

He was the one feeling needy; the one who in the darkest, loneliest hours of the night, longed for a family of his own.

For his own sanity, the best thing to do would be to say his piece, tell her about her brother and leave. What could have been would remain a question that forever went unanswered. Better that than laying his heart on the line—only to be rejected. He'd been rejected all his life.

He couldn't go through that again. Not with Meghan. She was special. More important to him than any other woman who'd come into his life. No, he'd best keep things on a professional level.

If only she wasn't looking so desirable in that sexy pink dress and matching shoes. If only he hadn't noticed the pulse that beat frantically in her neck and her pebbled nipples that strained against the stretchy fabric. If only she wasn't looking at him so expectantly, like she wanted him to kiss her again. If only he could ignore the fact he was as hard as a rock...

Something in his expression must have triggered an answering call deep inside her. Her lips parted and the tip of her pink tongue came out. She took a step forward. His heart thumped as she closed the distance between them.

She stood so close he could see the rapid rise and fall of her chest. Her long lashes were dark and spiky. Her skin was as clear as the summer sky. The pulse he'd noticed earlier continued to beat frantically under her skin. In response, his heart rate lifted its pace.

He stared at her, unable to drag his gaze away. "How long ago did your sister leave?" His voice was deep and gravelly, rough with desire.

Her eyes flared wide with answering need. "About ten minutes ago."

His belly somersaulted. Need, hot and visceral, kicked in with a jolt. Sarah Chifley lived in Macquarie Fields. It would take her at least a couple of hours, probably more, to get there and back. No doubt Meghan knew that as well as he did.

His gaze meshed with hers as awareness continued to build between them. All he could hear was the pounding of his heart and the rush of blood through his veins.

She moved and all of a sudden, there was no distance between them. Her hips brushed his. Her breasts, soft and luscious, pressed against his chest. He wanted her so badly, it was all he could do not to tear her clothes off.

But that wasn't what he'd come there for. Well, not the primary reason, anyway. He had to tell her about Cody. It was only right. Zane had played a major part in her brother's arrest. It was only fair he tell her right now he'd been wrong.

It meant her father's killer was still out there, but it also meant her brother would now go free. He owed it to her to share that information now, before anything else happened between them. Whether it changed her opinion of him or how she felt about them being together, he'd have to cross his fingers and hope for the best.

With a strength born of years of honing his self-control, he drew in a deep breath and eased it out. Though it almost killed him, he forced aside the desire burning through him and rested his hands lightly on her shoulders.

"There's something I have to tell you," he said. "It's the reason for my visit."

She frowned impatiently. Two little grooves marred the otherwise perfect skin of her forehead.

"I don't care why you came over. All I care about is that you're here. I want you, Zane. I want you now. I've been living through the worst week of my life and it still isn't over. Please help me to forget."

Before he could respond, she came up on her tiptoes and dragged his head down to hers. Her lips pressed against his with hot urgency, a silent plea he couldn't ignore. In her kiss he felt all the pain and the passion she held way deep inside. She needed him to help her block out the world, forget her anguish, even for a little while.

Her hand stole down his chest and slipped in between the buttons of his shirt. Unerringly, she found his nipple. Her fingernails scraped across the sensitized flesh and it was all he could do not to cry out.

"Tell me how much you want me," she whispered.

With a groan, he crushed her to him and met her kiss for kiss. She'd blown his self-control to pieces. Desire raged between them until at last, they pulled away, gasping for breath.

"Bedroom," Meghan managed, and in one swift movement, tugged her dress up over her head.

She wore a scrap of black lace to cover her femininity and a matching black lace bra. Zane's breath caught in his throat. A fresh wave of hot desire rushed through him, snatching what little breath he had. Without pause, she unclasped her bra, tossed it to the floor. A moment later, she stepped out of her panties and stood naked and glorious in front of him.

With no further thought other than the need to bury himself deep inside her, he tore off his tie and shirt and pants and underwear until he stood equally naked before her. Sweeping her up in his arms, he detoured to the couch and lowered her gently down on it.

"No bed?" she asked, laughter glimmering in her eyes.

"No time." With a husky growl, he buried his face between her breasts.

Licking and nipping and sucking her nipples he

loved her breasts with his hands and his mouth. She moaned and buried her fingers in his hair, holding his head in place. With his hard thigh pressed against the sweetness of her femininity, he worked his cock against the softness of her belly. The excitement on the tip of his cock lubricated the way.

She moaned again beneath him and tightened her hold on his head. He slid his cock through the slick moisture, loving the feel of her silky skin against his. Thrusting his hips forward in time with the movement of his mouth on her breast, she ground herself against his thigh with increasing abandon. Tension began to build.

The effect was electrifying and he didn't know how long he could last. Foggy with desire, he somehow remembered they needed protection.

In his wallet... Pants... Needed to find them... Where had he left them...?

Clenching his jaw, he drew away and was pleased when Meghan's made a sound of distress.

"Condom," he muttered by way of explanation.

She nodded her understanding. Quickly he searched his pants pocket for his wallet and found what he was looking for. Tearing the packet open, he sheathed himself and within seconds was back at her side.

This time, he settled himself between her thighs, which were wide open and waiting for him. He probed her entrance and then ran his cock along her wet slit, teasing, tantalizing, dragging out the moment when they'd both find ultimate fulfillment.

"Please, Zane. Please, I need you."

"Do you want my cock?" he growled, his voice husky with need.

Her eyes flared wide with answering need. She nodded, but he wasn't prepared to let her get away with it that easily.

"I want to hear you say it," he demanded. "Do you want my cock?"

This time, her expression grew tumultuous with desire. She nodded almost frantically, moving restlessly beneath him. "Yes, Zane. I want your cock. *Now!*"

With that, he thrust deep inside her.

Their breath was stolen away. Moving hard and fast and with ever-growing need, he plunged inside her. She clung to his shoulders, moaning with need. Her fingernails dug into the side of his neck. He welcomed the stinging pain, even as he continued to thrust inside her, building toward their common goal, the pinnacle of completion.

"Faster, harder," she muttered.

He did as she asked. As his hips moved rhythmically against her, he leaned forward and captured one of her nipples in his mouth. She cried out and bucked against him and the need inside him grew too strong for him to ignore. As her inner muscles contracted around him, he could hold back no more.

Over and over, he thrust inside her until, moments later, he reached his peak. With a cry of triumph, he climaxed and then collapsed against her with a groan of relief.

So much for keeping things professional...

Right then, and there, still surrounded by her

heat and the scent of their lovemaking, he didn't give a toss.

Meghan woke up with a start, her heart pounding. She looked at the clock on her nightstand and gasped. Sarah would be back any minute. Zane lay sprawled out, asleep, beside her.

Somewhere during their second bout of lovemaking, they'd made it back to her bed. He'd loved her with his mouth, his tongue, his hands and his cock until she couldn't take a moment more. At last he'd given in to urgings and had seated himself home. They'd orgasmed together, a magical feat she'd only ever read about in romance novels. Now she knew it was true.

He had one arm flung out over his head, like he didn't have a care in the world. Relaxed in sleep, his usual guarded countenance was gone. She wanted to take the time to catalog his features— the thick, dark hair that curled below his ears; the longest, thickest lashes she'd ever seen. The dark beard and moustache he kept neatly trimmed that felt so soft against her skin.

She blushed at the memory of him going down on her. She'd expected it to tickle. She hadn't expected the incredible sensations his whiskers would have on her womanhood. It was like nothing she'd ever experienced and she longed for him to do it again. But not now, not with her sister expected home.

Regretfully, she leaned over and gently nudged him with her hand. "Zane. You need to wake up. My sister's due back any minute."

Slowly, his eyes came open and he looked around. He frowned, as if disorientated by his surroundings. A few seconds later, his gaze sharpened and he sat up. "Did you say Sarah was back?"

Meghan shook her head. "No, not yet," she assured him, "but she can't be too far away. Look at the time."

He followed her gaze to the nightstand and his eyes widened. "Shit. How could I have been asleep for so long?"

The words were muttered under his breath and she knew he didn't expect an answer. Without a hint of embarrassment, he pushed away the bedclothes and stood, naked.

"Where are my clothes?" he muttered, looking around.

Not quite as comfortable with her nudity as he was, Meghan wrapped the sheet around her and climbed out of bed. "In the living room. Remember?"

He grinned and there was a wicked gleam in his eyes. She couldn't help it. She grinned back. It felt like they were two naughty schoolchildren, truanting from class. She'd taken two weeks' leave after the death of her father, but it felt like months since she'd been to the office. With a start, she realized she wasn't sure she ever wanted to go back.

What a ridiculous thought... Of course she wanted to go back. She loved her job. Apart from her family, her job was everything. Countless women juggled challenging careers and family life every day. There was no reason she couldn't do both.

She shook her head with a wry smile. Just because she and Zane had shared a few tender moments, didn't mean he was thinking what they had together might be in any way permanent. She'd best remember that before her heart got too involved.

What was she thinking? It was too late for that...

With a resolute sigh, she pushed the mop of messy curls out of her eyes and padded to the living room. Zane had already pulled on his pants and was buttoning his shirt.

He looked at her quizzically. A grin tugged at the corners of his mouth. "I thought your sister was due any minute? Shouldn't you get dressed?"

Meghan blushed. "You're right. I should." Instead, she remained standing there staring at the beautiful expanse of his broad, tanned chest. Even now, she could remember what it felt like to touch, to taste, to kiss. Her fingers tingled.

As if aware of the direction of her thoughts, his eyes darkened with desire. "Meghan, quit looking at me like that or you're going to have a hell of a lot of explaining to do when your sister arrives."

She laughed. It seemed as far as Zane was concerned, she couldn't get enough. Still, the thought of having to explain him to Sarah was a little bit too much to take on right then. She wouldn't even know where to begin to explain his half-naked presence in her living room.

"You're right. It's probably best you got going," she replied and was a little surprised at the disappointment that flickered briefly across his face.

Surely he understood her reluctance? After all, what would she say to Sarah? She had no idea what they meant to each other. Were they fuck buddies? Friends with benefits? Something more? How would she know? It wasn't like he'd given her any indication he was in this for the long haul, or even for a night or two. It was way too confusing and far more than she could deal with right now. And there was still Cody's situation to consider...

Filled with a sudden surge of confusion, she bent and collected her clothes where they lay scattered on the floor and turned on her heel and escaped to her bedroom. Dressing quickly, she took a few more moments to straighten the bed and return things to normal, just in case Sarah got curious and wandered into her room. By the time she made her way back out into the living room, Zane was fully dressed and stood with his back to her, staring out at the ocean through the tall windows.

Meghan suddenly remembered he'd come over to talk to her. "What is it you wanted to see me about?" she asked.

Slowly, Zane turned to face her. The teasing light in his eyes had disappeared and had been replaced by a neutral expression. His lips tightened. It's about Cody."

Her heart skipped a beat. "What about Cody?"

He stared at the floor a moment and then reluctantly lifted his gaze to hers. "We found a bloody fingerprint on one of the weapons that was used to hurt your father. It turns out the print doesn't belong to Cody. We haven't completely ruled him out as the killer, but he certainly wasn't the man who struck the initial blow. Either he had an accomplice..."

His voice drifted off. Meghan's heart pounded. "Or else he isn't the killer at all," she finished. Relief flooded through her, followed closely by anger. Her body went taut. "You arrested him and charged him with murder! You were so sure he was your man. You refused to accept anything different, even when I begged you. Now you're telling me there's a strong possibility he wasn't involved at all?"

Zane's expression remained inscrutable. "Yes, that's definitely a possibility," he conceded quietly.

She stared at him in amazement. "Why didn't you tell me this before?"

"I tried to, remember? You had other things on your mind."

"Don't put this back on me!" she shouted. "You should have—"

She closed her mouth on the rest of the words that threatened to spill out. Of course he was right. He'd tried to talk to her about the reason for his visit. It was she who'd shut him down. She was the one who had only one thing on her mind. Getting naked together. And fast. She had no one to blame but herself. Embarrassment flooded through her.

"I'm sorry," she muttered. "I should have let you say your piece. Instead, I jumped you like a woman starved for an orgasm." Her face flamed with embarrassment. "I'm sorry," she mumbled a second time.

"Don't be sorry. I was a willing participant. Besides, before you get your hopes up, we still haven't completely ruled out Cody's involvement," Zane replied. "It's possible he had an accomplice. Someone who caught your father by surprise and landed the first blow. Once your father was incapacitated, it allowed Cody to go in for the kill."

She winced. No matter how long she lived, the memory of the awful wounds her father had sustained fighting for his life would never leave her.

"I know you don't want to think about that," Zane continued quietly, "but we have to look at this from every angle. And right now, though I'm doubtful it happened that way, it's a possibility. I know I've asked you this before, but is there anyone you can think of who might have had a beef against your father? Someone who might have been willing to assist Cody like that? What about Sarah?"

Meghan shook her head in confusion, her mind still reeling with images of the crime scene and all that had gone on. She'd never believed Cody was involved in the murder in the first place... She certainly didn't believe he'd engaged the services of another to help him carry out the deadly deed. And Sarah... No, it couldn't be Sarah. Sarah loved their father as much as any of them. The thought that she might have teamed up with Cody to do away with their father was ridiculous.

Before she could formulate a reply, the front door buzzer sounded. She jumped and her gaze flew to Zane. "It must be Sarah."

He nodded. She remained rooted to the spot, her mind still full of Zane's fresh revelations. The buzzer sounded again.

"Are you going to answer that?"

Zane's quiet question finally broke through the fog of confusion in her brain. She nodded and walked in bare feet toward the intercom. Confirming the visitor was Sarah, she pressed the button to let her in.

Sarah's surprise at finding a detective in her sister's living room was plain for all to see. Her eyes went wide and deep frown lines creased her forehead. Her gaze went from Zane to Meghan and back again, a calculating look in her eyes. In silence, Meghan bit her lip, praying her sister would sense nothing was awry. She wasn't in the right frame of mind to face unwanted questions.

"Detective Sullivan, what are you doing here?"

Before Zane could reply to Sarah's question, Meghan averted her gaze and hurried to answer.

"Detective Sullivan dropped by to ask a few more questions and to give us an update on the case. He now thinks Cody might not be guilty or he might've had an accomplice." She forced herself to look at her sister. "Can you think of anyone who might have been willing to fill that role?"

"I can't think of anyone off the top of my head," Sarah replied slowly and then paused and frowned again.

"I suppose it could have been Arnold. He'd do anything if there was money involved and I'm guessing Cody offered the person a substantial sum if they came on board."

Meghan frowned. "Who's Arnold?"

"Arnold Blackwell. He's one of Cody's buddies. They like smoking pot together."

Meghan grimaced in disgust. She still couldn't bring herself to accept her brother's illegal lifestyle. It was so far removed from the successful, respectable stockbroker he'd once been. She wondered if she'd ever get that real version of her brother back.

Zane pulled out a notebook from his shirt pocket and dutifully took down the details of Cody's friend. After thanking both of them for their assistance, he went to take his leave. Meghan showed him to the door. As he slipped on his jacket, he shot her a long look that spoke volumes. Once again, her heart skipped a beat and excitement raced along her veins.

Okay, so maybe he wanted to see her again... Was she reading that right? Oh, God. She might have it all wrong. She wished she could just come out and ask him, but Sarah was nearby, listening and watching. That would have to wait.

"I'll call you later, okay?" he murmured.

She nodded. "Of course. I'm here to help in whatever way I can. We need to find my father's killer." Unable to help herself, she reached out and touched his hand. "Please, call me. Anytime."

He nodded and with one last lingering look, he was gone. Meghan made her way back into the living room. Sarah stood by the kitchen counter. She shot Meghan a sly look.

"So, what's with you and the hot detective?"

Embarrassment immediately flamed across Meghan's cheeks. With her face averted, she moved past her sister and busied herself in the kitchen refilling the coffee pot. To her consternation, Sarah followed her.

"So, are you going to answer my question?"

Irritated a bit, Meghan tried to brush her off. "I don't know what you're talking about. There's nothing going on. He's the lead investigator in Daddy's murder case. He stopped by to ask some questions. That's all."

Sarah continued to regard her quizzically, a look of cunning clouding her eyes. "Yeah, right."

Meghan gritted her teeth as irritation flooded through her. It was none of Sarah's business who she did or didn't date. She wasn't ready to share information about her relationship with Zane, with anyone... Especially not her half-sister. The two of them weren't exactly close. Just because they were the only family they had left didn't mean she was going to start sharing confidences like that.

Besides, even *she* didn't know what the hell was going on with her and Zane, so how could she explain it to anyone else? As firmly as she could, she changed the subject and prayed her sister would leave it at that.

CHAPTER 18

"How did you do with Meghan Chifley?" Willie asked as he leaned against Zane's desk and chomped on a doughnut.

Images of Meghan naked and writhing beneath him immediately flooded Zane's mind. With an effort, he forced the memories aside and formulated an answer.

"Fine. She's still convinced her brother isn't the murderer, and the news about the fingerprint was a confirmation of his innocence, in her mind. She didn't like my suggestion that Cody might just have had an accomplice."

"Did she come up with any names?"

"No, but her sister did. Sorry, her half-sister did."

"You mean, Sarah?"

"Yes."

"I didn't realize you were making a trek out to Macquarie Fields," Willie replied around another mouthful of doughnut. "No wonder you were gone so long."

Heat crept up Zane's neck before he could stop it. He concentrated hard on willing it away before it reached his face. He cleared his throat and responded.

"I didn't. She's staying with Meghan. I spoke to her there."

"Wow, I bet she's loving that! Who wouldn't? City living. Ocean views. It's a far cry from her last lodgings."

"Yeah."

Zane frowned. With Sarah in residence, he and Meghan would have to find somewhere else to spend time together. He wondered what she'd make of his modest inner west apartment. *Would she even be interested in going to see where he lived? Would she be interested, period?*

She'd been quick to get him out of her condo. It was almost like she was ashamed of them, or of the possibility her sister might put two and two together. Either that or she just wasn't ready to answer questions about them. Either way, it didn't fill him with confidence that this was anything more than a short-lived good time. The thought depressed him more than it should have.

Hell, they'd known each other six days. He shouldn't have fallen so hard. It was his own fault if she didn't feel the same way. No one fell in love with someone they'd just met. It only happened that way in the movies and everyone knew how real those were.

Besides, how did he know this was the real deal? He'd never been in love before. There had been women in his life, but no one he felt close to or who he wanted permanently in his life. With his past, he was more than happy with that.

But with Meghan it was different and he didn't quite know why. What he did know was that he'd be devastated if this thing they had between them didn't go anywhere.

He cursed quietly under his breath. He was being stupid. Beautiful, rich girls like her didn't spend their lives with men like him. They might dally with him for a while, but when they got bored, they moved on. And that was a fact.

"So, who did Sarah suggest might have been her brother's accomplice?"

Willie's muffled question jolted Zane from his thoughts. He glanced at his partner who had swallowed the last bite of his doughnut and was now licking sugar off his fingers.

"She gave me the name of a guy called Arnold Blackwell. Apparently he and Cody Chifley are dope heads together."

"Is he in the system?"

Zane shook his head. "Nope. Not under that name, anyway. Besides, if he's the perp we're looking for, that fingerprint should belong to him. If he was already in our system, we'd have identified him by now, no matter what name he's under."

Willie nodded. "You're right. If what Sarah says is true, he must be either new to the game or he's a lucky sonofabitch who hasn't gotten himself caught. How reliable is your information?"

Zane shrugged. "Meghan Chifley didn't know about him, but Sarah seemed to know a lot.

Maybe she's spent more time with her brother since his fall from grace?"

"Yeah, maybe they had that in common. They could sit around and bag out the old man—or plot his murder."

"Then again, we already know she's lied to us in the past. There's no guarantee she's telling the truth now. I guess we ought to go and bring Blackwell in for questioning," Zane added. "Sarah gave me an address in Coogee. It's close enough to Maroubra that you can imagine he and Cody might have crossed paths, particularly if they have a common hobby."

Willie whistled, impressed. "This guy must have something behind him. Real estate in Coogee doesn't come cheap, even if it's only a rental."

"I'm guessing he doesn't have ocean views," Zane said dryly.

Willie grinned. "Right."

Zane pushed away from his desk and stood. "Are you ready?"

Willie nodded. "Let's go."

In the late afternoon traffic, it took them almost an hour to reach the trendy beachside suburb of Coogee. He followed the GPS directions and pulled up beside the curb outside an old three-story walk up that had definitely seen better days. With overgrown yard, faded and crumbling brickwork and paint around the window cracked and peeling it wasn't hard to understand how an illegal drug user could afford to live in such a place. While much of the suburb had been gentrified over the years, there were still pockets of neglect, like this one, as you went further away from the beach.

Zane flipped the latch on the gate that had the same overall appearance of neglect as the rest of the place. The gate squeaked a protest as they pushed it open and made their way up the cracked and stained concrete path. According to Sarah, Blackwell lived on the third floor.

Taking the stairs two at a time, Zane and Willie were only lightly panting by the time they reached the third floor. The door to number six was as equally rundown and grimy as those they'd passed on their way up. The worn red carpet barely covered the old floorboards that creaked beneath their feet. The Coogee address was misleading. This could have been any dump.

Zane lifted his fist and pounded on the door. "Arnold Blackwell? It's the police. Open up."

They were met with silence. A door opened further down and an old woman with a cloud of white hair and a wizened face eyed them curiously.

"What do you want with Arnold?" she asked, her voice husky with age and a lifetime of cigarettes.

"We're detectives," Zane explained. "We just want to talk to him."

The old woman squinted at them through the dimness. "Is he in trouble?"

"No, ma'am. We're just here to ask him a few questions," Willie replied.

"Then you'll have to bang louder than that. Arnold's getting hard of hearing. He keeps forgetting to wear his hearing aid. Here, how about I help you?"

The woman opened her door wider and walked toward them with the aid of a cane. When she arrived at Blackwell's door, she reached into the pocket of her housedress and pulled out a key.

"Arnold gave me this a few months ago. He got sick of locking himself out. Along with his hearing, his memory's shot. If it weren't for me, he'd have slept rough on the streets more often than not."

"It's good of you to look out for him," Zane said. It was a sad fact of life that it was unusual for people to show so much kindness toward their fellowman these days, neighbor or no neighbor.

The old woman merely shrugged off his praise and inserted the key in the door. Stepping back, she let the detectives enter. Zane was the first through the doorway. He spied who he assumed to be Arnold Blackwell, lying sprawled out, asleep on the couch. Zane clapped his hands loudly in front of the man's face and the guy came to with a start. His eyes were bleary from sleep or something else. Zane couldn't tell. He spied old-fashioned hearing aids in the man's ears. At least he'd be able to hear them.

"Are you Arnold Blackwell?" Zane asked.

The man eyed him suspiciously, fiddled with his hearing aids, and brushed a hank of dirty gray hair from his face. "Who wants to know?"

"I'm Detective Sergeant Zane Sullivan and this is my partner, Detective Willie Whitehouse. We're investigating the murder of Grant Chifley. We'd like to ask you some questions."

The man's eyes went wide with fear and he scrambled to get off the couch. "M-murder? What are you talkin' about? I ain't got nothin' to do with no murder."

"Do you know a man by the name of Cody Chifley?" Willie asked.

Blackwell frowned. "No. Should I?"

"Someone told us you were a friend of Cody Chifley. Are you sure you don't know him?" Zane persisted.

"Who told you that? They're lyin'. I've never heard of 'im."

Zane glanced around the small, cramped apartment. Though there were dirty dishes in the sink and the trash can overflowed, the countertops were bare and the rest of the place was relatively clean and tidy. Not quite the filth and squalor he was used to when attending the premises of a known drug user. Also absent was the familiar sweet smell of marijuana or any other sign that the man habitually indulged in illegal drugs.

"Do you know a woman by the name of Sarah Chifley?" Zane asked.

Blackwell's expression bloomed with guilt, but he hastily turned his face away. He frowned once again and then shook his head. "No. I've never 'eard of 'er, either. You got the wrong bloke."

It was obvious he was lying that time. Zane glanced at Willie. His partner gave him a slight nod, correctly interpreting Zane's look. Zane turned back to Blackwell.

"Well, then, I guess that means you won't mind coming down to the station so we can fingerprint you. That's one way of clearing this up very easily."

Blackwell's short burst of courage faded. He looked scared and uncertain. "My fingerprints?"

Zane eyed him steadily. "Yes. Your fingerprints. And a DNA sample while you're at it," he added.

Blackwell looked from one to the other. His shoulders slumped in defeat and then he sighed heavily.

"Okay. I know Sarah, all right. We 'ang out together sometimes. But I've never 'eard of the other. I mightn't always live within the law, but I ain't no murderer. I'll come down to the station. You can take me fingerprints, DNA, whatever you want. I 'ave nothin' ta 'ide."

Meghan stared at the mess in her kitchen and swallowed a sigh of irritation. It had been two days since Sarah had moved in and already, tensions between them were riding high. Meghan wasn't exactly a neat freak, but she liked things clean and tidy, and especially when there was the possibility Zane might stop by again. She hadn't seen or heard from him since the last time he'd been in her condo. She didn't know if the silence was because he wasn't sure how involved he wanted to get with her or if he was just too busy to call. Either way, she missed him.

With another sigh, she put the lid back on the bottle of milk and returned it to the fridge. She collected dirty plates, two bowls and three coffee mugs and dumped them in the sink. A pizza Sarah had ordered for herself the night before lay half-eaten in its box, abandoned on the counter. Two flies buzzed over it. Meghan picked it up and dropped it into the trash can. Her annoyance grew by the minute.

She could see her sister out on the balcony, enjoying yet another cigarette. That was another thing they'd argued about. Sarah had expected to be able to smoke in Meghan's living room. In no uncertain terms, Meghan had set her straight. Sarah had huffed and puffed and stormed outside, eventually settling on the balcony. Meghan wasn't happy about her sister smoking out there, but at least it wasn't inside her home.

Two days and already she was sick of having Sarah living with her. *So much for family sticking together...*

She was immediately beset with guilt. She needed to try harder to get along with her half-sister because that's what family did.

They were there for each other through thick and thin, the ups and downs, the ins and outs. They didn't ditch each other at the first inconvenience or at the first load of dirty dishes that didn't make it to the sink. Drawing in a deep breath, she made a silent vow to try harder to get along with Sarah. With that thought in mind, she pasted a smile on her lips and stepped out onto the balcony.

"Good-morning, Sarah. I hope you slept well."

Sarah merely glanced up from the newspaper

spread out on her lap and grunted. Despite the less-than-civil greeting, the morning sun was warm and bright on Meghan's face and the sunshine immediately lifted her spirits. She was determined to get things back on track with her sister. Then she spied an overflowing ashtray on the table beside the deckchairs and once again, her mood soured.

"Sarah, do you think you could empty that once in a while?"

Though Meghan meant to keep her voice neutral, it came out sounding almost accusatory. Sarah's expression darkened.

"Oh, so you won't let me smoke in your condo and now I can't even smoke out here. There's just no pleasing you is there little Miss Princess Perfect. Why don't you just come out and say it? You don't want me here."

Meghan stared at her, horrified. At the same time, she was flooded with guilt. "No, Sarah!" she hurried to assure her. "That's not what I meant at all. I'm sorry. It's just that... I'm not used to sharing my space and it's taking some getting used to. You and I might have lived under the same roof at Daddy's house, but we never shared the same space. I hardly saw you while I was growing up and...it felt like you wanted it that way."

Sarah's expression turned ugly. "Of course I wanted it that way! Why would I want to hang around a snotty-nosed brat like you? You *and* your brother, the apple of my father's eye. We were fine until you two came along. The perfect, golden-haired, blue-eyed twins. Everyone who met them, adored them. My father included. I didn't stand a chance."

The bitterness in Sarah's voice surprised Meghan. She had no idea her half-sister felt that way. It was true Sarah had always kept herself apart from their family, but Meghan had thought that had been by choice—after all, Sarah was thirteen years older. She had very little in common with the twins.

Now it seemed Sarah felt she'd had no choice at all. Meghan had had no idea her half-sister's resentment ran so deep. She was once again flooded with guilt. It was her job to keep the family together, to maintain the peace. Right now she felt like she'd failed miserably at that. Sarah was all she had now. She needed to work harder to keep them happy and together.

"I'm sorry, Sarah. I didn't realize you were so unhappy while we were growing up; that you felt so left out. We didn't mean for you to feel that way. I promise. Daddy loved all of us equally."

Sarah's lip curled up in disgust. "Yeah, right." With that, she pushed herself up out of the deck chair and putting her cigarette butt out on the ledge of the balcony, she flicked it over the side. "I can tell when I'm not wanted. Don't worry, I'll have my things packed and be out of your hair before nightfall. Are you happy now?"

Sarah's angry words lashed Meghan like a whip. She gasped in shock and took a step back. Tears threatened. With her heart beating fast, she held her breath until Sarah was out of sight. With a cry of relief, she collapsed onto one of the deckchairs and put her head in her hands.

Now what was she going to do? Her sister hated her. That much was clear. Okay, maybe she was being a bit melodramatic, but she'd managed to alienate the only family she had left. Her father had been brutally murdered and was still sitting in the morgue. She hadn't even been able to give him the dignity of a funeral. Her brother was sitting in jail. To top things off, she hadn't heard from the man she was fast falling head over heels in love with and she didn't have a clue how he felt.

Could life get any worse?

Sarah Chifley fumed in silence from her position deep in the shadows across the street. The lights from Meghan's hoity-toity condo complex winked at her teasingly, egging her on. Sarah's anger flared brighter, burning out of control.

How dare the little bitch throw her out! Complaining about this and that and everything in between. Who the hell did she think she was?

That was the problem with spoiling the brats rotten. She hadn't been lying when she'd accused Meghan of stealing all their father's love. Between her and her equally bratty brother, there had been nothing left for Sarah. She'd gone from being an only child, her daddy's adored and treasured little girl, to fading into the background when a new wife and two new babies came along.

That had been the beginning of the end. As the years went by, the twins only got cuter. It was like they could do no wrong. Meanwhile, Sarah was left to work things out on her own, motherless, alone, unloved.

The hurt and pain grew and festered until it almost consumed her. She wanted to scream and shout and protest her treatment, and every now and then she did. But her father refused to accept she had a valid point of view. He dismissed her arguments as fanciful, told her to get a life and first and foremost, he demanded she get a job.

The last was the most hurtful of all. His current wife swanned around from one social engagement to the next, wearing the latest designer couture and Daddy didn't lift an eyebrow. He didn't expect *her* to work, so why did he expect his child to?

Of course, the second Mrs Chifley had an untimely death courtesy of an unfortunate car accident, but that didn't make things any better for Sarah. Daddy turned to the twins to help him through his grief. It was the twins he gave his attention to, even more than he had in the past. Sarah was left to deal with life and the wealth of issues she faced on her own.

Well, she was sick of it. Now that Daddy was dead, things were going to change and it was going to start with Miss Princess Perfect Meghan. The little bitch had tossed her out and there was no way in hell Sarah was going to take that sitting down. No, she'd find a way to make Meghan pay...or die trying.

CHAPTER 19

"Shit, shit, shit!"

Zane stared at the lab results in his hand and tried to curb his aggravation. Willie looked over at him from his position behind his desk.

"Bad news?"

Zane held up the single piece of paper in his hands. "Arnold Blackwell's lab results. The print left on the paperweight doesn't belong to him."

Willie nodded once, his expression grim. "Well, he already denied knowing Cody Chifley. I guess this proves he's not Chifley's accomplice. To tell you the truth, I think we're clutching at straws. We're going to have to spring him."

"I agree. And it's too late for that. Chifley's lawyer got him bail earlier this morning and once the counselor gets news of these lab results, he'll be filing a motion to dismiss and he'll have just cause to do so," Zane muttered sourly.

He let out a growl of frustration. It had been two weeks since the murder and they still didn't have a firm suspect in their sights. It was beyond infuriating. Everywhere they turned they hit a brick wall. With nothing concrete to go on, he hadn't dared contact Meghan and that was eating at him, too.

He wanted to see her, hear her voice, touch her, but what would he say? She was relying on him to find her father's killer and so far he'd come up empty. Not even the Blackwell lead had panned out. Either Sarah Chifley had been mistaken or she'd deliberately given them the wrong name.

But why would she do that? It was her father who'd been murdered, too. She seemed to want him to find the killer as much as Meghan did. It didn't make sense. Except this appeared to be the second time they'd caught her in a lie…

"We need to track down Cody Chifley and ask him about Blackwell. His sister named Blackwell as one of her brother's buddies, but Blackwell swears he's never heard of the man. The print certainly doesn't belong to Blackwell, so he sure as hell wasn't the perp who clocked our vic over the head. It's strange that Sarah suggested Blackwell as a possible accomplice. Let's see if Cody even knows him."

"Sounds like a plan," Willie agreed. "Do we have any idea where Cody is?"

"No, but I still have his number. Let's hope he picks up."

With that, Zane tapped in Cody's number and waited. The call rang out once, twice, three times, four. Zane braced himself for voicemail.

"Hello?"

Zane blinked in surprise. "Cody?"

"Yes. Who's this?"

"It's Detective Sergeant Zane Sullivan. I—"

"Have nothing to say to you, Detective. In case you didn't hear, I'm on bail. I don't have to talk to you. Good—"

"Cody, wait! Don't hang up! I'm sorry about the charges. We're only doing our job. And now I'm not entirely convinced you're the one responsible. Tell me, do you know someone by the name of Arnold Blackwell? Apparently he's a friend of yours."

"Arnold Blackwell? No, I don't think so. Who told you we were friends?"

"Your sister, Sarah."

"That's strange. I can't remember anyone by that name. What does he look like?"

"Mid-fifties, gray hair, paunch. Lives in Coogee."

"It still doesn't ring any bells. Are you sure Sarah said we were friends?"

"Yes. In fact, she said you and Blackwell smoked dope together."

"She must be mistaken. I don't smoke pot. Never have. It's not my style. Heroin was my drug of choice. Then I switched to meth. I leave the dope smoking to my sister."

Zane tensed. "Meghan?"

"No, of course not! Meghan's as straitlaced as they come. Why do you think she's so disapproving of my drug habit? No, I was referring to Sarah."

Zane stared at the phone in shock. "Sarah smokes marijuana?"

"Yes. Not around Dad or Meghan, but I guess I don't count. Even before my life spiraled out of control, she was dope smoking. She used to come around to my place. She said she got sick of smoking in her rooms. She was afraid Dad would smell it and would kick her out for good. Come to think about it, Sarah's more likely to know someone like Arnold Blackwell than me."

Zane's heart skipped a beat and then took off at a gallop. Thanking Cody for his information, Zane ended the call, dazed. His mind was awhirl with all he'd discovered.

"What is it? What did you find out?"

Willie's questions broke into his busy thoughts. He swiveled in his chair, still shocked. "Cody Chifley doesn't know Arnold Blackwell, but he thinks the man might have some connection to his sister."

"To Meghan?"

"No. To Sarah."

Zane went on to explain all he'd been told. When he finished, Willie looked equally shocked.

"Blackwell did admit he sometimes hung out with Sarah. Do you think Cody's telling the truth?"

Zane tightened his lips, feeling grim. "Who knows? What we do know is one of the Chifley siblings sure as hell is lying. The question is, which one?"

"Cody might be out on bail, but he's still facing a murder charge. He has nothing to gain by lying about his accomplice. If anything, he could use the guy to help shoulder the blame. What does Sarah Chifley have to gain by lying?"

Zane stared at Willie. His partner had hit the nail on the head. They needed to look at it from the point of view of who had the most to gain. People lied for many reasons, but mostly to cover their ass.

What was Sarah hiding? Was she protecting her brother, or someone else? They needed to find out.

"Let's go and have another chat with Sarah. We need to see her reaction when we tell her about Blackwell and the fact we've become aware of her ongoing drug problem. Plus there's the little tale she told about how long she's been fending for herself. Let's see what she has to say. She does have that cut on her hand, after all. We only have her word it was done while she was cutting vegetables."

A spark of excitement lit up Willie's eyes. "You're right. All this time we've been focused on the son, but it could have just as easily been Sarah. Let's go."

———

Zane and Willie made good time in the late afternoon traffic and arrived outside Meghan's apartment complex in just over an hour. Pressing the buzzer outside the front gate, Zane waited nervously for her to answer. Even though they were there on official police business, his gut somersaulted at the thought of seeing her again.

It had been five long days since he'd seen her. Way too long.

The intercom crackled to life and he braced himself for her voice.

"Zane."

From the corner of his eye, Zane caught the look of surprise on Willie's face at the casual use of Zane's first name. He blushed and tried to stem the heat that rushed to his cheeks.

"Ms Chifley, I'm here with Detective Whitehouse. We have a few more questions for your sister, Sarah. Can we come up?"

If she was surprised by his formal address, it didn't show in her voice. "I'm sorry, Detectives. Sarah isn't here."

"Oh," Zane replied. "Do you know when she'll be back?"

There was a pause and then Meghan said, "No. The thing is, she moved out last weekend. Things just didn't work out."

Zane couldn't say he was surprised. The two sisters were polar opposites. He couldn't imagine them cohabitating with any degree of success.

"Do you know where she is?" he asked.

"No. I guess she moved back to her place in Macquarie Fields. I haven't heard from her since she left."

Zane looked at Willie as he tried to hide his disappointment that he couldn't see Meghan at the moment, even under the pretext of talking to her sister.

"It looks like we're headed for Macquarie Fields," he muttered, not bothering to hide his irritation.

"Why don't I go?" Willie offered. "I live out that way. You don't. By the time I finish with her, it will be almost knock off. Let me go and ask Sarah the hard questions. I'm up for it, boss."

Willie shot him a smile. Zane stared at him in surprise.

Misunderstanding his reaction, Willie looked embarrassed. "Of course, if you don't think I can handle it, I'm happy for you to come along," Willie hurriedly added. "I just thought I'd save you the trip, that's all. The only thing is, if you decide not to come with me, you'd have to make your own way back home because we're traveling in the same car."

Zane grinned widely. He couldn't believe his luck. Here he was standing outside his woman's place and, until that second, he was convinced he wasn't going to be able to go inside. Now Willie had offered him a treasure on a plate made of gold.

Of course, it wouldn't do for Willie to realize Zane had something going on with Meghan. Though she was no longer on the suspect list, he'd still prefer to keep their burgeoning relationship a secret until after they'd closed the investigation— just as Meghan had held off telling her sister about them.

"Of course I'm confident you're up to it, and I can always catch a cab, but are you sure?" he asked, keeping his tone casual.

"Yes. Like I said, I don't live too far from there. It's hardly out of my way. Besides, there's no sense in both of us getting home late."

Zane fought to keep the elation off his face. "Well, if you're sure."

"Give me Sarah's address."

Zane provided Willie with the details. A few minutes later, he waved his partner off. With a jolt of anticipation in his belly, he turned back to Meghan's intercom and pressed the button again.

Meghan heard the front door buzzer sound again and her heart skipped beat. Her pulse still hadn't returned to normal since she heard Zane's voice. When she realized he was with his partner and they were there for Sarah, she'd been filled with disappointment. Now there was a chance he was outside her front gate again. She headed over to the intercom and saw Zane's profile on the screen. Her belly somersaulted with need.

"Zane. You're still there."

He stared into the camera. "Yes."

"Where's your partner?"

"He's gone to interview Sarah. We have a few more questions about the case."

"What kind of questions?"

Zane sighed. "Do you mind if we don't go into that right now? I'd really like to forget about everything but you for a few hours. Would that be okay?"

Meghan's pulse went into overdrive. Nerves fluttered in her stomach. Her mouth went dry and she licked her lips. She saw his eyes flare wide and heard his soft groan. Heat pooled between her thighs. There might be so much that was yet to be said between them, but right now she wanted him more than she could bear. Pressing the buzzer, she released the gate and waited impatiently for him to arrive.

It took longer than she expected and her nerves were strung taut when he finally knocked on her door. She flung it open and stood there, drinking him in.

He wore his usual work outfit—a nice suit and tie—but he could have worn a sackcloth for all she cared. His hair was mussed, as if he'd run his fingers through it more than once and there were fatigue lines around his eyes. Still, he looked gorgeous. She had to touch him.

"I'm sorry," he said by way of greeting. "There was a lineup for the elevator. Then it stopped at every floor. I didn't think I was ever going to get here."

His voice dropped to a low drawl, deep and husky with need. Unable to help herself, wordlessly she reached for him and drew him inside. He kicked the door closed with his foot. She brought his mouth down to hers and kissed him hard and passionately. Tongues entwined. Breaths came faster. In some distant part of her mind, she cautioned herself against such reckless behavior, but she blithely ignored the silent words and continued with her exploration.

His arms came around her and he lifted her off her feet until she was snug and tight against him.

The hardness of his erection pressed into the softness of her belly, filling her with heat. With her arms around his neck, she clung to him, giving him everything he demanded and taking the same from him. When they finally broke apart, they were both breathing hard and Meghan struggled to come back to reality.

"I guess that means you missed me." The teasing light in his beautiful eyes and the soft smile on his lips turned her insides to mush. She pressed a hand against his shirt, feeling the beat of his heart.

"More than you could know," she whispered.

She moved her hand and flicked his nipple through his shirt, with her fingers. She heard him gasp. His eyes went dark with desire. And just like that, the fire reignited and they tore at each other's clothes.

Kicking off shoes, socks, belts, dresses, shirts, pants and underwear, they didn't stop until both of them were naked, their chests heaving with the effort. Meghan's gaze ran over him from the top of his head to his feet. Every single part of him was perfect. The dark hair, almost as black as midnight. The blue eyes that carried secrets and yet seemed to look into her very soul. The broad shoulders and muscular chest. The washboard stomach that was testament to hours in the gym. The light scattering of dark hair that covered his pectorals and then moved lower into a thin line that ended at his groin.

She stared at his erection—thick and long and hard. Jutting from a nest of dark curls. The memory of how it felt when he was deep inside her sent liquid honey running through her veins.

His legs seemed to go on forever. Muscular and yet also graceful. He had the legs of an athlete. Even his feet were nice.

"Are you done?"

His eyes were heavy with desire. His voice was rough with need. She didn't need to be told how much he wanted her. She could see the evidence. Slowly, she nodded.

In one swift movement, they came together, pressed skin to skin, heated mouths, heated flesh. He bent his head and suckled one of her nipples and she couldn't suppress a groan.

"You taste so sweet," he muttered and moved to the other breast.

She dropped her head back to give him greater access, relishing the feel of his hot mouth on her skin. He took full advantage, cupping and kneading her breasts in his hands. His mouth continued to suckle.

Without warning, he bent and put his arms under her knees and gathered her up against him. She clung to his shoulders and nibbled at his neck as he made his way to her bedroom. She cringed when she spied a wet towel from her recent shower lying piled on the floor, along with the clothes she'd worn that day. Zane merely kicked them out of his way and continued to her bed.

Releasing her slowly, he set her down by sliding her along his body. Every hard, hot inch of him branded itself against her skin. Once again, she reached up and dragged his head down until their lips met in another searing kiss.

Walking her backwards, Zane pushed her gently onto the bed. He followed her down, covering her with his body, claiming her with his weight. She opened her legs and tightened them around his hips, welcoming his invasion. With his cock pressed against her moistness, he returned his attention to her breasts.

Licking and sucking and tugging, he loved them with his mouth. She squirmed against him, restless to assuage the need that burned within.

"Not so fast," he murmured and captured her mouth in his.

His hand stole down between their bodies and fondled her wet folds. Then he slipped one finger, then two inside her and imitated the stroking of his tongue. Heat exploded through her blood and she writhed in ecstasy against his hand. All the time his hot wet mouth suckled at her breast.

Desire welled up inside her, building to a crescendo. When his tongue replaced his fingers in the depths of her femininity, she could stand the sensual pleasure no more. As her orgasm gripped her in its power, she bucked against his mouth. Still he continued to love her until at last, she collapsed against the sheets, spent.

He lifted his head and looked at her, grinning. "Good?"

"Wonderful," she gasped. It was all she could manage.

With a satisfied smile, Zane moved to lie down beside her. He took her hand and brought it to his lips. He brushed a tender kiss across her knuckles. Her heart flipped over with love.

She was a goner.

When she finally felt able to move again, she turned on her side to face him. His eyes were closed, but as soon as she touched him, she heard the quickening of his breath. She ran her hand over his chest, flicking at his nipples with her nails. They pebbled beneath her touch, tiny hard nubs amidst a scattering of soft chest hair.

Leaning over him, she stroked her tongue in circles around his nipples. Each circle was smaller than the last until finally, she took one nipple in her mouth and suckled it, just like he'd done to her. He arched his back and groaned with pleasure. She smiled, still in awe of the power she had over his body, and moved to concentrate the same kind of attention on the other one.

"You're a witch, a temptress, a siren and I can't get enough of you," he muttered, his eyes dark and hooded with desire.

Her smile widened. She looked at him from beneath her lashes. "And I haven't even started yet."

With that, she once again bent her head and kissed her way across his broad chest. Kiss by kiss, she moved lower, over his rib cage, down his sternum, his flat belly, his hip bone. Her mouth tasted and savored and suckled and the moans of desire coming from his mouth continued. Burying her face in his soft pubic hair, she took his erection in her hand and then slowly lowered her mouth over the tip.

She took the long, hard length of him all the way to the back of her throat. Then squeezing the base of his cock, she sucked hard on the engorged head. He tasted salty and warm and delicious.

With her tongue, she laved the side of his cock, long strokes that were meant to drive him wild and from the way he was twisting his head from side to side with his hands clenched into fists, it was obvious she was succeeding.

"That feels so good," he moaned. "Your mouth is magic."

Encouraged by his reaction, she renewed her efforts and sucked until her cheeks were sore.

"I'm gonna come if you keep that up," he muttered.

She wanted to taste all of him, feel the hot jets of his excitement fill her mouth, but she also needed him inside her, thick and hard and urgent. Though she'd climaxed already, she could feel tension building once again deep in her core. Heat burned through her veins. She needed him inside her to fill her completely, to satisfy her like no other had.

Releasing his cock, she gave him a few moments to sheathe himself and then straddled his hips. She reached between their bodies and took hold of him once again and worked his erection toward her moist center. He opened his eyes and stared up at her, his expression raw with desire. With his gaze still on her, he groaned and thrust up inside her. She gasped from the sweet intrusion.

"Zane," she breathed. "You feel so good."

Slowly, she began to move. Rocking her pelvis forward, she savored every sensation of his hardness deep inside her. With his eyes closed, he reached up and took hold of her hips. Lifting her up and down on his cock, he increased the speed and pressure. She willingly went along for the ride.

With her breath coming fast, she rode his cock, faster and faster until she was gasping. As she neared her peak, her muscles clenched. Zane's eyes flew open. Sensing she was close, he thrust harder and cried out just as she toppled over the edge. Together, they floated slowly back to earth, satiated beyond belief.

Exhausted, Meghan collapsed against him. The words *I love you* were on the tip of her tongue, but she quickly closed her mouth on them. It was far too early for words like that. They barely knew each other and though he'd connected with her in a way no other man had, they needed to take things slow.

There was so much going on in their lives right now, complicating things. A relationship was the last thing either of them needed. Still, she quietly hoped he'd be up for the challenge and would at least agree that they could see each other again.

His arms tightened around her. "You've gone quiet," he murmured. "Is everything okay?"

She forced a smile. "Of course."

He probed her gaze, as if trying to read what was on her mind. "I really like you, Meghan. I hope you know that."

Immediately, her heart filled with happiness. Her doubts were swept away by his words. "I really like you too, Zane."

His gaze remained fixed on hers. "Where do we go from here?"

Relief flooded through her. He'd asked the question, opened the conversation, like he wanted them to have a future. That was a good start.

"I'm not sure," she answered honestly. "Where do you see us going?"

His expression remained solemn. "I know it's probably too soon, but I've never felt like this about anyone before. It scares the hell out of me, but there's nothing I can do about it. Years of experience in the police force haven't prepared me for how it feels to fall for a woman I'm not sure is meant for me."

She frowned. "What do you mean, not meant for you?"

He turned his face away. "We're from different worlds, Meghan. Neither of us can deny that. Ordinarily, our paths would never have crossed. The fact that they have is moot."

She frowned and came up on one elbow. "What's that supposed to mean?"

He turned back to face her and shrugged. "I don't know. You're way out of my league. We both know that. This…thing between us… It seems we can't help that. It doesn't mean we're suited to each other for a lifetime."

"Who said anything about a lifetime?" she quipped, feeling churlish.

Hurt and disappointment clouded his gaze. She immediately wished her words back. She'd had no intention of hurting him. *Hell, she was well on the way to falling in love with him! Couldn't he see that?*

His expression remained somber. He stared at her for long moment and then once again looked away.

"Being with the same person forever is an old-fashioned idea, but in a lot of ways, I'm an old-fashioned kind of guy," he said quietly. "I believe in marriage even though most people our age think it's outdated and I never saw a successful one during the time I was growing up."

He paused and she wondered if he was beset with old memories. When he spoke again, his voice was rough with emotion.

"Of all people, I should be the one to run a mile from commitment, but the truth is, I want a family of my own. I want safety and security. I want someone to love me and to always have my back. And I want to love them in the same way. I *need* that security, Meghan. I need to know the woman I give my heart to is in this for the long haul. I can't give myself to you in a relationship if I know you're only in this for the short term."

Her irritation dissipated as quickly as it had appeared. He'd had a tough childhood. He didn't know what it felt like to be loved. His life had been filled with disruptions and insecurities, being moved on from one foster family to the next. She couldn't imagine what scars it left behind on someone who had never felt wanted or loved in their life, or what it had taken for him to want to risk everything and share his life with her.

Reaching up, she lay her hand against the roughness of his cheek. "I swear to you, Zane, what I feel for you is real. You're right, we come from very different backgrounds and if my father hadn't been murdered, we probably would never have met. But we can't change what's happened and I, for one, don't want to. I'm *glad* we met. I don't know what this is we have between us, but I know it's real."

Slowly his face was transformed by a smile. His eyes were wide, as if he hardly dared believe what she was saying.

"You do?"

She grinned and nodded. "Yes, I do. And I agree, planning a lifetime together is old-fashioned, but I'm an old-fashioned girl, too. I believe in love and marriage and I believe it should be for a lifetime, the good and bad, the ups and downs, in sickness and in health."

His face continued to fill with light with every word she muttered and finally, it was as if he could restrain himself no more. With a yelp of glee, he wrapped her in his arms and squeezed her tight. She struggled gently against him, trying to draw breath.

"It's all right, Zane. You can let go of me now. I'm not going anywhere."

He laughed and slowly released her. He stared into her eyes. "Do you really mean it? Do you really want to give this a go and see where it leads?"

She nodded and smiled, her heart swelling with tenderness. "Yes, I really mean it. It scares me almost as much as it scares you, but I'm not going anywhere."

With another *whoop* of excitement, he enfolded her in his embrace. His lips found hers and they shared the sweetest kiss. Meghan snuggled against him and despite everything that had happened, she was more content than she'd ever been in her life.

Their breathing was quiet in the silence as Zane idly stroked her hair. She closed her eyes and enjoyed the sensations.

"What happened with Sarah?" he asked awhile later. "Why did she move out?"

Meghan's lips tightened on a sad grimace. "I thought it would be okay, asking her to move in with me," she said, "but to tell you the truth, it was awful. Sarah and I are so different. Even though we're related, we have nothing in common. We shared the same house for many years, but we weren't exactly cohabitating. She was in her wing and Cody and I were in ours. Sometimes we'd go days, even weeks without seeing her."

Zane nodded. "It's not quite the same as sharing a small space, is it?"

She glanced up at him, relieved he understood. "You're right. I should have known it wouldn't work out."

"What happened?"

She told him about the nasty argument and how her half-sister had stormed out of the apartment.

"Even though I knew it was for the best," she continued, "it still upset me. I hate thinking that she left on such awful terms. I don't want to fight with her. We're family. We should love each other. That's what family does. I hate that we're at odds."

Zane's arm tightened around her in a reassuring hug. "You're right. Family's important. Take it from me who has had no one."

She came up on one elbow and pressed a soft kiss against his lips. "You have me."

Zane's answering smile lit up every inch of his face. "You don't know how lucky I feel. Until this moment, I never thought I'd find anyone like you. Growing up the way I did, it does something to you, way down deep inside. It's tough to realize no one wants you, loves you, treats you like they do their own kids. Even my parents didn't want me.

"So you do what any kid in that situation would do; you harden your heart. You build a shell around you so impenetrable, nobody can get inside. And that's the way it has to be. The only way you can survive. And even as an adult, when you're older and you look back and you see things through an adult's eyes, it doesn't change a thing. You still feel unloved, unwanted, unneeded."

Meghan seethed with helpless anger at all that Zane had endured. Some people didn't deserve to be parents and the poor kids like Zane sure as hell didn't deserve to be treated like that. She vowed to do everything she could to turn his life around, to make him feel more wanted, more loved than he'd ever felt in his life.

"You're a special man, Zane Sullivan and don't ever let anyone tell you different. You might not have been given all the privileges I was, but you're a wonderful man, and you've built yourself a life and a career you can be proud of. I know I'm proud of you."

Tears welled up in his eyes. Her heart clenched with emotion. She stared at him fiercely. "I've got your back, Zane. I'm here for you. I'll never abandon you. Ever. I swear."

Chapter 20

Zane woke up with a start. The room was dim with only the light from the moon seeping through the curtains. He stared at the unfamiliar picture that hung on the wall across from him and for a moment wondered where he was. Then he turned over and spied Meghan lying on her side with her back to him, her legs twisted in the sheets.

Immediately, he was overcome with contentment. He still couldn't believe she wanted to be with him, to be in a relationship, to see where it would lead. Meghan Chifley! The woman with the whole world at her feet! He wanted to pinch himself, to make sure this was real, but then she rolled over and kissed him and it was as real as it could get.

"What time is it?" she asked sleepily.

He glanced at the clock on her nightstand. "A little after eight."

She gave him a wry grin. "I must have fallen asleep."

He smiled back. "Me, too."

His stomach took that moment to rumble noisily and he remembered he'd skipped lunch and it was well past dinner time.

Meghan giggled. "How about we go and get something to eat?"

He nodded. "Sounds great, but first, I want a kiss." Pulling her to him, he kissed her slowly on the mouth, savoring the softness of her lips, the sweetness of her taste. Finally he pulled away from her.

"Later," he promised.

She laughed. "I'm going to hold you to that."

Together, they climbed out of bed and pulled on their clothes and soon were heading out the door.

"Do you like Thai food?" Zane asked.

She smiled. "I love Thai food. And I know just where to get the best Thai food in Sydney!"

She winked at him and he smacked her saucily on the bottom. Strolling arm in arm, they turned away from Meghan's apartment building and walked off down the street.

Sarah seethed in silence from her familiar spot in the shadows. The anger that had been on the backburner since Meghan had kicked her out now erupted into flames. Any moment, it felt like she might combust.

So, her little sister was getting it on with the lead detective...

Sarah had guessed as much. She'd sensed a closeness between the two of them when she'd arrived to find him in Meghan's condo and this had just confirmed it. They'd strode away from Meghan's building, kissing and canoodling, as if they didn't have a care in the world. Well, she'd show them. Nobody crossed Sarah Chifley and got away with it.

Stealing a glance over her shoulder to check the way was clear, she hightailed it across the road. Pulling her hat down low over her face, she keyed the code to Meghan's condo into the security pad. The quiet click of the gate opening was music to her ears. Glancing once again behind her, she let herself into the complex.

Aware of the CCTV camera perched in the far right corner of the foyer, she once again kept her face averted and pressed the button for the elevator. It arrived a few minutes later and to her relief it was empty. She'd spent enough time in her sister's place for most of the neighbors to be familiar with her face. The last thing she wanted was to be recognized.

The journey to her sister's door was uneventful. The corridor was empty of occupants. As quickly as she could, she keyed in another code and slipped inside. The apartment was pretty much the way she'd left it, except her fastidious sister had cleaned up the food scraps, the cigarette butts, the empty plates...

Sarah sneered. They couldn't all be perfect like Princess Meghan. But enough of that. She needed to get busy before the happy couple got back. If she had time she'd even have a smoke inside and snuff it out on the leather sofa…

With that thought in mind, she set about trashing the place. She picked up chairs and tossed them at the floor-to-ceiling glass. They bounced back without damaging the thick panes, but the chairs didn't remain unscathed. She chuckled at the sight of their broken legs. There'd be no more sitting in those.

Next she went to the fridge. Once again, it was ordered and tidy and clean. Leftovers were in separate dishes, easily accessible and arranged in neat stacks. With a cackle of delight, she tore off lids and opened packets and tossed food all about. By the time she'd finished, the kitchen looked like a pigsty.

Pulling a large knife out of a block on the kitchen counter, she approached the soft white leather couch. As she slashed and tore at the expensive fabric, she was filled with jubilation. No doubt Daddy had paid for the couch, like he paid for everything in the twins' lives. Until Cody overstepped the mark by becoming a drug addict. No, that wasn't something Daddy couldn't tolerate, or fund.

But Princess Meghan never put a foot wrong. She was the perfect child. Sweet and obedient, smart and beautiful. She was everything Sarah wished she could be, but wasn't. It infuriated her when she was a lonely teenager with a face full of acne and carrying too much weight, and it still infuriated her all these years later when her daddy compared her to his princess once again and once again, he found Sarah lacking.

She still felt bad about her daddy's murder. She hadn't gone there to kill him. But he was already in a mood when she arrived. She found him in his bedroom, getting ready for bed, but he was a long way from sleeping. Apparently Cody had been there before her, asking him for money. He assumed she was there for the same reason and he'd had enough.

'Get out, you fat, lazy, stupid cow,' he'd screamed at her. 'You disgust me! You can't hold down a job—you've never had a job. You're as lazy as your mother. The best day of my life was when I divorced her. I should have done it years ago. My only regret was that I didn't let her take you with her when she left.'

His vicious words had ripped her to shreds. She'd stood rooted to the spot in shock. But his ugly words had kept coming and finally she'd spun on her heel and tore out of the room, sobbing hysterically all the way down the stairs.

She'd been shocked and furious and baying for blood. She wanted to make her father pay. He had no right to treat her like that! She was his daughter! Just like Meghan was.

She found herself in the kitchen. It was quiet and dark and she remembered Mrs Abbott was away. Her gaze fell on the knife block and all of a sudden the noise in her head receded and she felt incredibly calm. She reached for the largest knife and held it down along her side. It was time her father learned a lesson. He wasn't going to treat her like that again.

On the way back to the staircase, she passed by her father's study. It was a room he spent a lot of time in. His office, his den, his sanctuary. She flipped on the light switch and gazed around at the wall of bookshelves, the priceless works of art. She wanted to take the knife to every single piece of it, everything he held so dear.

Her gaze landed on the heavy glass paperweight Meghan had given him when she was a child. It was a favorite piece—of course it was—and had taken pride of place on his wide carved desk ever since. She'd picked it up and tested its weight in her hand. With no firm plan of action in mind, she turned and headed for the exit. On the way out, she flipped off the lights and made her way up the staircase using her memory and the slimmest shaft of moonlight to aid her way.

Her daddy didn't hear her come in. He thought she was long gone. Crying in her handkerchief, like she'd done so many times before.

Not this time…

She caught him unawares and with one blow of the paperweight, brought him to the ground. He fell heavily, but the soft carpet cushioned his fall. He stared up at her in shock. When she produced the knife she'd hidden beneath the folds of her voluminous skirt, his eyes grew wide with fear.

The sight of him groveling before her had filled her with a sense of righteousness and glee such as she'd never felt before. For once, *she* was the one in control. *She* was the one setting the rules. And right now, there were none.

With a feral shout of triumph, she'd swung her hand high in the air and landed the first blow. The knife was sharp and slid through his flesh with only a hint of resistance. Over and over, she plunged in the blade until her hand was slick with blood and all she could think of was how she'd finally get her hands on his money—at least her share of it.

And then she'd slipped and cut her hand and it hurt like hell. By then her father lay motionless and silent. She stabbed him a couple more times, just for good measure. And then, exhausted and slowly coming off her bloodthirsty high, she sank to the carpet and stared at him.

And then she had started to cry... Hot tears of pain and sadness.

She'd been distraught over what she'd done. For all his faults and failings, he was her father and he was the only father she'd had. It took a long time before she managed to haul him into her arms and carry him to the bath. With tender strokes, she'd washed his wounds until a casual observer might think he was merely asleep in the tub.

The guilt had set in and she couldn't bear to have him stare at her like that, his eyes fixed and lifeless. So she rinsed out the washcloth for the final time and spread it across his face. She'd collected his torn and bloody pajamas and stuffed them in a garbage bag she found under the kitchen sink. She washed the knife thoroughly and returned it to the block. She'd also grabbed an armful of cleaning products and set about slowly and methodically washing the blood off the walls. She attempted to remove the large stain that marked the carpet, but it was beyond her capabilities. It was during her second time past the study that she spied the rug lying on the floor.

She'd known just what to do with it and she'd hauled it up the stairs. After covering the large blood stain, she'd taken a moment to survey the room. Everything looked neat and tidy. Nothing was out of place. That was good. She then returned for the final time to the bathroom and stared down at the corpse.

'Why did you have to be so mean, Daddy? It wasn't nice of you. It hurt me, Daddy. It hurt me a lot. You turned me into a thief. I was forced to steal your money. A few measly hundred dollars off your dresser. That's what you reduced me to. A common thief. Desperate. Without a conscience. Why couldn't you love me like you loved Meghan?'

Meghan.

The perfect child. The perfect woman. The perfect daughter for Grant Chifley. It was all Meghan's fault that Sarah had been driven to murder. It was Meghan's fault their father lay dead in his bathtub.

Meghan should pay for what Sarah had done. It was Meghan's fault Sarah had gotten so mad. She'd been sick of being compared to her perfect little sister, never quite measuring up.

Sarah stumbled down the corridor of Meghan's condo and found herself in her sister's room. The sheets were mussed, like they'd only recently been slept in. And no doubt they had. From the way she'd seen Meghan and the detective nuzzling each other, it was no surprise they'd recently shared a bed.

Sarah's lip curled in disgust. If only their father could see his perfect little princess now. Sleeping with a police officer, like a common slut. She could have chosen one of those bigwig lawyers who populated her firm. That would have made Daddy proud. But no, she'd spread her legs for a commoner, a cop. Well, she hoped her sister had enjoyed her little liaison because if Sarah had her way, it was all about to stop. Forever.

———————

Meghan keyed in some numbers on the pad outside the door of her condo and then turned the knob. Zane nuzzled her neck from behind. They'd enjoyed a sumptuous Thai dinner and had decided to head home for dessert. From the feel of Zane's erection pressing against her ass and the way his hands came around to fondle her breasts, she was almost certain what dessert would be and she couldn't wait.

Reaching for the light switch, she flicked it on and gasped. "Oh, my God! I've been burgled!"

Zane immediately went into cop mode. His gaze narrowed as he looked around. Then he told her to stay put while he searched through every room. Finally, he gave the all clear and she collapsed against the wall she'd been leaning on.

"Who could have done this? How did they get in?" They were questions for which she had no answers. She looked at Zane, foolishly hoping he might have some answers.

"I don't know. They sure made a mess. Can you tell if anything's been stolen?"

Her gaze went to the wide flat screen TV and sophisticated sound equipment Cody had given her before his life went down the drain. It was still in place. Her laptop lay on the kitchen table where she'd left it.

Heading down the hallway, she cried out to see some of her artworks had been slashed. Only some of them were expensive, but all of them she held dear. A couple of family portraits had been knocked off their hooks and lay broken on the floor. She picked her way carefully through the glass.

She walked into her bedroom and gasped at the sight of her bedsheets cut into strips. A cloud of feathers covered the floor, presumably resulting from the slashes and tears sustained by her pillows. It was like a madman had been set loose in her apartment and had been told to inflict as much damage as he could. She still didn't have a clue who might be responsible.

And then she remembered the late night phone call she'd received from Cody. It felt like a lifetime ago—

"Has anything been taken?"

She turned and saw Zane enter the room. Crossing over to her nightstand, she bent and opened the bottom door, revealing a safe. Punching in the code, the safe opened. She riffled through the papers and jewelry she stored there. Nothing appeared to be missing.

She stood and met Zane's concerned stare. "No, I don't think so. But someone went out of their way to be destructive."

"You're right. This doesn't look like a robbery. This looks personal. This looks like revenge."

She frowned, startled. "You can't think this was Sarah's doing?"

Zane shrugged. "Do you have any other ideas?"

She paused. "Do you remember when I told you about the phone call Cody made to me late the night my father was murdered?"

He looked at her warily. "Yes."

"And do you remember how upset you were that he'd given my security code to one of his friends?"

Zane's expression hardened. "Of course I do."

"What if it was him—Cody's friend?"

Zane's lips compressed into a grim line. "You mean his bagman?"

Meghan shrugged. "What difference does it make? If it was this…this…bagman, it proves Cody was telling the truth. He's innocent, Zane! You said yourself you had doubts about his guilt. He didn't murder our father! He met with his dealer that night, just like he said he did, and struck a bargain with him about getting him his money. The dealer's finally made good on the deal. He broke in looking for cash, or something he could steal."

Zane looked unconvinced. "You said nothing was taken."

She nodded, deflated. "True."

"Still," Zane continued thoughtfully, "your theory does have merit. I seem to recall you telling me the dealer's name was Gordo."

"Yes! Gordo! That's it! Cody called him Gordo."

"No surname?"

"No. He only said Gordo."

Zane pursed his lips. "Well, that's better than nothing. I'll call the station and get someone sent over. They might be able to lift some prints. I'll also talk to Cody. If he knows this might let him off the hook for good, he might be more forthcoming with information. I'm still not ruling Sarah out, but we need to make sure it isn't this Gordo."

Meghan looked around the mess and sighed. "It's late and I'm tired. Do we have to get the police over here tonight? Will it make any difference?"

Zane moved closer and took her in his arms. He pressed a kiss on the top of her head. She leaned into him, taking comfort from his strength.

"No, I guess not," he replied.

She sighed again and tilted her head up for another kiss. Despite everything, she was very glad he was there. She could get used to having Zane Sullivan in her life. There was no doubt about it.

"We probably should go to a hotel tonight," Meghan suggested. "I'm not up to cleaning up this mess tonight."

"You're right. And we best not touch anything until forensics have done their thing." Zane tilted his head. "We could always spend the night at my place. It's not much, but it's home."

A wealth of emotion passed over his face. He

looked at her with a mixture of uncertainty and hope. Meghan's heart flooded with tenderness. She hurried to reassure him a night spent with him anywhere would be enough.

"I'd love to see your place."

A flash of relief was quickly followed by a grin. "Really?"

She smiled. "Yes. Really."

"It's not swish like yours. I mean, it's a small terrace in Newtown. A long way from the beach."

"Newtown? Not so far from the city."

"Maybe, but definitely no water views. Are you sure you're up for this?"

Meghan strode toward him and draped her arms around his neck. "You bet. Besides, water views are so overrated."

With that, she kissed him.

Zane woke to the smell of percolating coffee. The space in the bed beside him was empty. He forced aside a stab of disappointment and climbed out. Pulling on his underwear, he made his way to the kitchen. Meghan sat at the counter, already dressed for the day in the spare clothes she'd taken from her apartment. A mug of coffee sat near her elbow.

He grinned. "I see you've made yourself at home." He pointed toward the mug.

She blushed and his heart flipped over. "I'm sorry. I hope you don't mind. I woke up early and couldn't get back to sleep. Too much on my mind. Would you like a cup?"

Zane nodded. "That would be great."

"Strong and black, right?" She climbed off the stool and poured him a cup. He took a seat next to hers at the counter.

"*Mm*, that's good. Just the thing," he murmured. He could get used to waking up and finding Meghan in his kitchen. Or he in hers. He wasn't fussed over the details. He wanted to be where she was. Period.

Oh, man, he was falling hard...

The knowledge should have sent him into a panic, but all he did was smile. He'd been doing a lot of that lately and it was all because of Meghan. He wondered if it was too soon for her to consider spending the rest of her life with him.

You don't want to scare her off. He silently admonished himself. Okay, so she'd made mention that she believed in forever and she'd told him she wanted to be with him, but everything was so new and fresh between them. They were still getting used to the idea of each other, feeling their way. He needed the time as much as she did to see if this was going to work.

"I had a call from the morgue," she said, interrupting his thoughts.

He came alert. "Oh? What did they say?"

"They're ready to release my father's body. They said I can make arrangements with the funeral home to come and collect him."

He eyed her carefully. "That's good news. Are you...okay with that?"

She nodded slowly. "Yes. It will be a relief to finally be able to lay him to rest. Did you know he had a brain tumor? Apparently he only had a matter of weeks to live. No wonder he'd become so aggressive with Cody and Sarah." She shook her head sadly and then added, "I'll call Cody and Sarah and see if they want to help plan the service."

At the mention of Cody, Zane remembered his intention to call the man and ask him about Gordo. He wondered if Cody's memory had returned enough for him to recall the late-night conversation he'd had with his sister. With the fingerprint belonging to neither Cody nor Blackwell, it seemed more and more likely Cody wasn't the perp after all.

He glanced at Meghan. She calmly sipped at her coffee. He needed to apprise her of the status of his investigation, in particular, that he was now almost certain her brother was innocent, as she'd claimed all along. He cleared his throat in an effort to stave off a sudden case of the nerves. His gaze locked with hers. He drew in a deep breath. Though she already knew he'd developed some reservations about Cody's guilt, what he said next would change everything.

As if becoming aware of the tension that held him in its grip, she frowned. "What is it, Zane? You look...strange."

He drew in a breath and eased it out, all the while he continued to regard her steadily. "I don't think Cody is the killer."

Her mouth gaped in shock. "Oh, my God! Thank God! What changed your mind?"

He told her about Arnold Blackwell and how his prints weren't on the paperweight. "I was running with the theory your brother had an accomplice, but now I'm almost certain there was only one person involved and if my theory's correct, it wasn't Cody."

She cried out in joy and relief and then threw herself into his arms.

"Oh, Zane! You don't know how much that means to me! I never wanted to believe Cody was guilty, but I'm ashamed to admit as time went on, I began to doubt his innocence."

He stroked her soft cheek. "Hey, it's not your fault. I doubted him, too. You were his staunchest supporter. He's lucky to have you."

"I need to call him, tell him the good news," she cried.

Zane nodded. "That's fine, but do you mind if I call him first? I'm the reason he has a murder charge hanging over his head. I also want to ask him about Gordo."

"So you think Gordo could be responsible for the break-in at my apartment?"

Zane shrugged. "It's possible. Especially if your brother was telling the truth the night he called you. He admitted he argued with your father that night. He could have met with his dealer afterwards, like he told you. He didn't have the money to pay his debt, so he gave the asshole your security code. Then he got an attack of guilt and called you to warn you. It stands to reason a germ like Gordo might have followed through on his threat."

Meghan sighed heavily. "I can't believe Cody got himself tied up in so much strife. He used to live such a perfect life. He went to work, went to the gym, and spent time with his family. It seems like a lifetime ago that things fell so completely apart." She paused and then added, "He told me he was willing to go to rehab. He wants to do everything he can to get his life back on course. I told him I'll support him every way I can."

Zane stared at her and his heart filled with tenderness. "You're a good woman, Meghan Chifley. You know the true meaning of family. The true meaning of unconditional love. Your father would be proud."

Tears glinted in her eyes and she blinked hard to remain in control. He pulled her into his arms and held her close, pressing kisses against her soft curls.

"Th-thank you," she stammered, her voice muffled against his chest. "That really means a lot."

The words "I love you" were on the tip of his tongue, but something held him back. It was too soon to feel this strongly about a woman he'd only just met. With his lifetime of avoiding commitment, did he really want to say something he might regret? Best to leave things as they were...at least for now.

Slowly he set her away and then reached up and gently wiped away one of her tears. "I need to call in the burglary. The sooner forensics do their thing, the sooner we can identify the culprit. I don't want you staying there while the person responsible is still on the loose."

"It's fine," she protested. "There's no sign of forced entry, so it was someone who knew the codes. We both think the perpetrator is more than likely Gordo, but even if it was Sarah, she's not going to come back. She's had her petty act of revenge. She'll be fine, now."

Zane frowned and then forced a smile, his old insecurities coming to the fore. "Don't you like my place?"

"Of course I do!" she responded enthusiastically. "Your place is great. I love the cute little courtyard out back. Did you plant those geraniums?"

He gave an embarrassed nod. She took his face in both of her hands and planted a kiss on his lips. "They're beautiful. And I love the color." Her expression turned serious. "I'd be happy to live anywhere with you, Zane. Being with you makes me happy. But I'm not going to be forced out of my home by my sister or my brother's drug dealer. We'll get the police to do their job and hopefully find who's responsible. In the meantime, I'll change my security codes."

Zane nodded, relieved her decision to return to her apartment had nothing to do with him.

"Okay, I understand," he said. "But at least let me come with you and help you with the cleanup."

She grinned and held out her hand. "Deal."

Chapter 21

Zane hung up the phone and looked across at Willie. "That was reception. Cody Chifley and his lawyer are waiting downstairs. Do you want to sit in on this?"

Willie nodded. "Sure. It's not every day we drop murder charges. Besides, I'd like another opportunity to quiz him on who *he* thinks might have murdered his father. Even though he's been out on bail, a few days in the lockup might have given him some quiet time to reflect."

Zane pushed away from his desk and stood. He'd come into the station late after spending the morning helping Meghan at her condo, but he was keen to meet with Cody and get the answers he needed.

The two detectives made their way to the exit. Cody stood when they entered the waiting room. He introduced his lawyer as Maxwell Heard. The man looked like he was in his fifties and had a no-nonsense attitude Zane liked. They followed him and Willie into the interview room.

"Thanks for coming in," Zane said as they seated themselves.

Cody merely nodded. "What's this about, Detective?"

"It appears you're no longer a suspect in your father's murder," he continued. "I'll inform the prosecutor right away and he'll set about informing the court."

Cody's eyes widened in surprise. "I'm free to go?"

"Yes. We're dropping the charges against you. New evidence has come to light exonerating you."

"What new evidence?"

Zane cleared his throat. "We discovered a fingerprint on a weapon left at the scene. It didn't belong to you."

"So you finally believe me?"

"Yes, but if you don't mind, we have a few more questions. Who do *you* think murdered your father?" Willie asked.

Cody frowned. "I've been over this so many times in my head. I don't *know*! I wish I did! I don't know of anyone who hated him that much. He was a good guy, the best. We didn't always see eye to eye, but if I was in his shoes, I'd probably feel the same way about refusing to fund my son's drug habit. It was tough love, and I needed it."

He paused and then added, "Looking back, I realize he did what he had to do because he loved me. He offered to pay for rehab—Meghan did, too. I just didn't want to listen, was terrified of giving up the stuff. I've been drug free for the past eight days and... I'm not going to pretend it hasn't been hell. I've been going out of my mind.

But I also feel good that I've been able to do it. To get through a day, two, then another without a hit. I think I'm going to be okay."

"Good," Zane replied. "I'm glad. Your sister's going to be so happy."

"You're right. Meghan hated it just as much as Dad. She's been so good to me."

"She's a good person," Zane agreed. "Did you know she invited Sarah to move in with her? Unfortunately, things didn't work out."

Cody stared at Zane in surprise. "Sarah? Wow! I can believe Meg was sweet enough to make the offer, but I can't believe Sarah took her up on it. She's always held a grudge against the two of us."

"Because you stole away her father?"

"Yeah, that and other things. Let's just say she made it clear we were interlopers and that we didn't belong. She hated that our father loved us as much as he did."

"Do you know a man by the name of Gordo?" Zane asked.

Cody's lips tightened. "Yeah. Gordo Ivanov. He's my bagman. At least, he used to be. I haven't seen him since I stopped using and paid him back everything I owed."

Zane started in surprise. He glanced at Willie, who looked equally startled. "So you don't owe any money to Gordo?"

"Not anymore."

"When did you pay him?"

"Three days ago. I called a good friend—an old work colleague. He loaned me the money. I'm done with the drugs. I'm determined to get my life back on track. I want to be with my wife and kids. I want to be able to hold my head up, contribute again to society, instead of being a burden and another sad and wasted addict."

Zane looked at him with admiration. "Good on you, Cody. It takes some guts walking away from the shit. I wish you all the best."

Cody stared at him, his expression full of gratitude. "Thank you. That means a lot."

"Just out of interest," Zane added, "did you give Gordo the security codes to Meghan's apartment?"

Cody flushed with embarrassment. He hung his head in shame. "Yeah. I was totally high on crystal meth when I did that. I'm not proud of it. Not one little bit. It was a low act. But I confessed to her about it. I told her everything. I'm sure she's changed her codes by now."

"Do you know where we can find Gordo?" Zane asked, ignoring the statement.

Cody offered a wry smile and slowly shook his head. "Yeah. He's in the lockup. Got busted two nights ago for drug trafficking. Or so I heard."

Once again, Zane shot Willie a look. Zane had already brought his partner up to speed on Meghan's break-in and on Gordo Ivanov. Willie nodded in understanding and then pushed away from the table. Zane stood, too.

"Thanks for coming in, Cody," Zane said. "We need to follow up on a few things and see where they lead. Rest assured, we're doing all we can to find the person responsible for your father's murder."

He shook Cody's hand and did the same to the lawyer who'd remained silent throughout the exchange.

"I'll get the paperwork to the prosecutor first thing," Zane told the man.

Heard nodded. "Thanks, Detective. I appreciate that. I'll stay in touch with their office."

With that, Willie showed the men out and then the detectives returned to their desks. Zane pulled his keyboard toward him and made a few keystrokes that got him into the police database. He typed in Gordon Ivanov's name and got a hit straight away.

"Cody was right. Gordon Ivanov was arrested two nights ago for possession and supplying a commercial quantity of methamphetamine. Our boy's been refused bail. He's been behind bars since then. He couldn't have broken into Meghan's apartment."

Zane blew out his breath on a sigh of frustration and raked his hands through his hair.

"What were your first instincts when you surveyed the evidence of the break-in?" Willie asked. "You said nothing was taken, so robbery wasn't the motive. What was your gut reaction when you came on the scene?"

Zane frowned and misgivings stirred in his gut. He wasn't sure if his instincts were way off the mark, but he needed to put it out there, just in case.

"To tell you the truth, my first thought was that Meghan's half-sister had done it as a petty act of revenge. Meghan had asked Sarah to leave. They argued. Sarah left in a huff. There were no signs of forced entry. It was done by someone who knew the security codes, both for the front gate and the door to Meghan's apartment."

"That's why you also thought of Gordon Ivanov."

"Yes. But now it's obvious Gordo's not our man."

"So we're back to Sarah Chifley," Willie finished.

Zane compressed his lips, feeling grim. It gave him no pleasure to have to consider Meghan's half-sister as a serious contender for Grant Chifley's murder, but the more he thought about their victim's oldest daughter and her lies, the more convinced he became that she could very well be the one responsible.

"Let's go through what we know," he muttered. "First, she's right-handed and she had a cut on her right hand."

"I asked her about that again when I went to see her yesterday," Willie clarified. "She gave me the same answer. Cutting vegetables. But she wouldn't give me any details. I asked her about Arnold Blackwell and why she lied about him being friends with her brother. Again, she wouldn't give me a straight answer. She did admit to smoking pot every now and then. When I put pressure on about her flat-out lie about how long she'd been fending for herself, she got angry. I could tell my questions were getting under her skin. She refused to answer any more questions and asked me to leave. I had no grounds to arrest her, so I did as she asked."

Zane nodded grimly. His instincts were telling him Sarah was the one. They just had to prove it. "I'm going to call around the emergency departments and see if any of them have a record of her attending on the night of the murder. It might be a bit more than the scratch she claims it to be."

On the second call, Zane hit pay dirt. The Nepean Hospital confirmed Sarah Chifley had been treated in the emergency ward in the early hours of the morning of October fifteenth, the night her father had been murdered. According to the nurse, Sarah had suffered a significant knife wound that had required several stitches. She'd been sent home later the same morning with a prescription for antibiotics and a direction to keep the wound clean and dry for at least ten days.

Zane ended the call and tried to get a hold on his burgeoning excitement. He looked up to Willie where his partner leaned against Zane's desk.

"It's her."

Willie nodded, having heard every word of Zane's end of the conversation. His eyes were wide anticipation. "Let's go and pick her up."

Meghan took a sip from her coffee cup, stared out at the ocean and sighed. With Zane by her side, she'd answered the questions from the officers there to investigate the break-in and had then spent the rest of the time cleaning up the mess. Zane had helped for as long as he could, but eventually had left for work. She understood and was grateful for the time he'd given her. She hoped his day was going well.

By now, he must have broken the news to Cody about his release. She should call her brother and congratulate him and talk to him about their father's funeral arrangements. Which reminded her... She needed to speak to Sarah, too. She felt bad about the way they'd parted. Though she still felt justified in her actions, she wished it hadn't come to that. Sarah was probably still feeling hard done by and annoyed, but Meghan hoped that since her sister had had some time to calm down, she might be ready to concede she'd overreacted.

Meghan didn't expect Sarah to apologize. That was one thing she'd never seen her sister do, but as long as they could be civil to one another, that would suffice. Family was so important. They needed to stick together, no matter what.

And then she had another idea: She could invite both of her siblings over to dinner. And maybe Zane could come, too. If he wasn't too busy. Or at work. Already he'd become an important part of her life. She couldn't see any harm in introducing him properly to her brother and sister—as her boyfriend, not as the detective investigating their father's murder.

She was sure the news would take her siblings a little adjusting to, but she was equally certain they'd be pleased for her, as she would be for them in the same situation. With her mind made up, she pulled out her phone and dialed Sarah's number.

———————

Sarah ended her call from Meghan and couldn't hold back a malicious grin. She couldn't have planned things better if she'd tried. Her unsuspecting, perfect sister had invited her back into her precious condo. Probably hired someone to clean up, too.

It was priceless. She obviously didn't have a clue it was Sarah who'd taken a knife to the place. Or that it was Sarah who'd flown into a rage at their father and had stabbed him to death in a frenzied attack. She was as stupidly innocent as she'd been all those years ago when she was just a child. She always saw the best in people. She refused to believe everyone didn't have some goodness inside them, even people like Sarah.

Sarah ought to feel guilty for even thinking about hurting Meghan, but she'd had enough of Little Miss Perfect. It was time Meghan found out what it was like to be dead. Just like their father. Perhaps, wherever they went when they died, they could swap stories about the oldest daughter who'd gone wrong. That would be a laugh, for sure. What they didn't know was that she'd be the one to have the last laugh—and boy, she'd laugh the loudest of all of them.

As a plan came together, excitement began to build. The police were looking firmly at Cody. They'd already charged him with murder. It was a stroke of luck that he'd been released on bail. The cops would just think he'd gone on yet another drug-induced rampage, this time against his sister.

Sarah had made sure no record existed of her arrival at the mansion the night of the murder. It had taken a matter of moments to find the CCTV file on the computer in her father's basement and erase it. And when the bodies were discovered, she planned to be suitably horrified when they told her Cody had struck again.

The younger cop had paid her another visit only the day before, but she'd appeased him with vague answers and half-truths. In the end, he'd gotten a little too close to the bone. Especially when he'd accused her of lying about how long she'd lived at Macquarie Fields and about Cody's relationship with Arnold. She should have gotten to Arnold sooner, keyed him up about what to say. A couple bags of high grade pot should have made him hers.

But she hadn't gotten around to visiting him before the cops did and he'd denied knowing Cody at all. It damaged her credibility and since he'd found that out, the detective was sniffing around for more. So she'd refused to answer any more questions and told the cop to leave. And that was that.

Now she was heading over to Meghan's for a reconciliation dinner. Things didn't get any better than that. Pulling out a lethal-looking knife from its hiding place under her bed, she stared in delight at its shiny blade. She'd always been fascinated with knives and though she hadn't come armed with one the night she murdered her father, it had been a natural choice of weapon. She also retrieved the knife she'd taken from Meghan's condo and then stashed both knives in a backpack.

She sighed with pleasure. Armed and dangerous, that's what she was. She chuckled. This was going to be even better than the last time. Of that she had no doubt. They'd totally underestimated her. A grave mistake.

———

Zane and Willie made their way up Sarah's cracked and stained concrete path. The wooden boards creaked under their feet as they strode across the porch. Zane rapped on the front door. The house remained silent. Willie moved to look through the dirty front window and shook his head.

"Nothing."

Zane knocked louder and called out Sarah's name. He tried the doorknob. It was locked. "Let's go around the back," he said.

Willie nodded and the two of them split up, each doing a turn around the house until they met at the back steps. The back yard was as unkempt and untidy as the front.

"Anything?" Zane asked.

Willie shook his head. "Nothing. I looked into a bedroom and the kitchen through the outside windows. It doesn't look like she's home."

"Yeah, nothing my way, either."

"What do you want to do?" Willie asked.

"I'll put out an APB. In the meantime, I'll call Meghan. She might know where her sister is. Besides, I want to give her the heads-up that

Sarah might be dangerous. I'm sure she wouldn't be so brazen to murder another family member, but we don't want to take any chances."

With that, he pulled out his phone and dialed Meghan's number. The call went straight to voicemail. He cursed under his breath and left a message.

"Hi, it's Zane. Call me as soon as you get this."

He ended the call and climbed into the squad car and, with a niggling sense of dread, headed back to the city.

Meghan rinsed the shampoo out of her hair and then started shaving her legs. The thought of seeing Zane again filled her with excitement. She wondered how Cody and Sarah would react when they discovered she and the lead detective were seeing each other but then decided the opinions of her siblings didn't matter. As much as she loved them both, she made her own decisions about her life and that included matters of the heart.

She suddenly remembered she hadn't actually called Zane or Cody. Neither of them even knew about the dinner she had planned. *Dammit! How could she have forgotten?* She shook her head and smiled at her forgetfulness.

Turning off the water, she stepped out and toweled herself dry. She padded out of the bathroom and into her bedroom where she'd left her phone. She picked it up and noticed she'd missed a call. Her heart skipped a beat. It had been from Zane.

Disappointed, she listened to her voicemail. Zane's message was short and concise. She wondered at his somber tone. Without hesitation, she called him back.

"You've reached Detective Sergeant Zane Sullivan of the City of Sydney Police. Leave a message."

The phone beeped in her ear and she did as he asked, disappointed again to have missed him. Rallying, she left a message inviting him to dinner at her place.

"Sarah's coming and hopefully Cody will, too. It's going to be a kind of celebration dinner and also...I thought we might be able to tell them about us."

The last she'd added in a rush and when she finished, her heart thumped. Whether from the exertion or the sudden nerves that assailed her. She wondered what Zane might think.

Would he be uncomfortable about going public with their relationship so soon? It wasn't like they were teenagers still needing permission from their parents—or their siblings. It was true, things had happened fast, but they were adults. Still, all of a sudden she was beset with doubts.

In an effort to distract herself, she called Cody. She smiled in relief when he answered.

"Hi, Meggie."

"Cody! I heard the good news! I'm so glad the police have dropped the charges!"

"Thanks, I'm glad, too. I just hope the police find the real killer."

They talked about the case a bit more and then Meghan invited him to dinner. "Oh, by the way, Detective Sullivan might be joining us. Is that all right?"

Her question was met with silence and then Cody replied, surprise clearly in his tone, "The detective on Dad's case? The one I met with earlier who told me I was no longer a suspect?"

"Yes. His name's Zane Sullivan."

"I know his name. What I don't understand is why you'd invite him for dinner?"

She bit her lip and all of a sudden, she wished she hadn't tried to rush things. She should have just kept things quiet about Zane until the murder investigation was over and Cody had been given time to get over the fact he'd been the police's main suspect. But it was too late now.

Quietly, she explained.

"You're kidding!" Cody exploded.

"No, Cody. I'm not. We've...been seeing each other. We like each other a lot. I hope you can accept that. I've invited him and Sarah over for dinner. I want us all to be together again, like a real family. I know it's what Daddy would want."

Cody remained unconvinced her dating the detective was a good idea, but they ended the phone call on good terms with Cody promising to come over for dinner. She smiled, relieved that he wasn't too upset. She assured him she looked forward to catching up with him soon.

The sound of her front door buzzer caught her attention. She frowned. It was too early for her dinner guests. Throwing on some underwear and a sundress, she padded out to the intercom. Sarah's face filled the screen. Meghan started in surprise.

"Hi, Sarah. I wasn't expecting you so soon."

"I hope you don't mind me coming over a little early. The truth is, I was in the neighborhood and had nothing else to do."

"It's fine," Meghan hastened to assure her.

The last thing she wanted was to start the evening with them at odds once again. This was a chance to smooth over the rocky waters, to reconnect and share as a family. It had been a long time since they'd had a peaceful time with one another.

She pressed the button that released the gate and waited for Sarah's arrival. She wished she'd been given a little more time to get ready... To blow dry her hair, put on some makeup, just in case Zane made it over for dinner.

She sighed. With Sarah already on her way up, the opportunity for Meghan to put on her glad rags was gone. They'd just have to take her as she was.

CHAPTER 22

Zane listened to Meghan's message and his blood ran cold. He had no proof Sarah held deadly intentions toward her half-sister, but the misgiving that had started in his gut was spreading through his veins. He couldn't shake the feeling that the woman he cared for was in danger and that she'd invited that danger inside her home.

He punched in Meghan's number and prayed she'd pick up. He was still at least half an hour away from her place, stuck in rush hour traffic. When the call went through to voicemail, he cursed long and loudly and hurriedly left a message.

"Meghan, it's Zane. Listen to me. I'm concerned about you there with Sarah. I think she might have... I think she might have murdered your father. As soon as you get this, call me. I'll be there in thirty minutes."

Zane ended the call and tossed his phone back in his pocket. He glanced at Willie who sat beside him.

"We could call the station, explain the situation. They could send someone over. They might get there quicker than us."

Zane compressed his lips, feeling grim. "You don't think I'm overreacting?"

Willie shook his head. "No. It all fits. And if you're wrong and you end up looking stupid...? Who cares? At least Meghan will be safe."

Zane shot Willie a grateful look. "Thanks, mate. I appreciate your candor." He paused and then came to a decision. "I'm going to do it. Let's call it in."

With that, Willie picked up the handpiece and talked to dispatch. Zane half listened to the conversation, his mind focused on the road and the snarl of traffic in front of him. Willie replaced the handpiece and turned to look at him.

"I'm not sure how much of that you heard. A couple of officers have called in sick. They're going to do what they can to find someone to do a drive by, but that's all they can promise for now."

"Shit!" Zane thumped the steering wheel and let out a few more curses. At the same time, he switched on the lights and siren. He'd argue later with anyone who wanted to know whether or not he was enroute to a legitimate emergency.

Twenty-six minutes later, his phone had remained stubbornly silent, but he pulled up outside Meghan's complex. The street was calm, but he knew better than anyone how deceptive a quiet street could be. Without waiting for Willie, he leaped out of the car. Racing over to Meghan's gate, he pressed the buzzer.

"Did you hear the good news?" Meghan asked.

She'd been doing her best to engage in pleasant conversation with her sister, but Sarah wasn't making it easy. Her sister had been churlish since her arrival, despite Meghan's efforts to draw her out and talk about pleasant things, like the beautiful spring weather they'd been experiencing and Cody's recent release.

"What good news?"

"The police have dropped the charges against Cody. Isn't that great?"

Meghan expected Sarah to be pleased about the announcement, but her sister merely frowned and then narrowed her eyes at her.

"Are you sure?" she demanded.

Meghan blinked in surprise. "Yes. Of course I'm sure. I heard it from the lead detective."

"Oh, you mean the lead detective you're fucking?"

Meghan froze in shock, not only at her sister's coarse language, but also at what she'd said.

How did Sarah know what Meghan had been doing with Zane?

To her consternation, her cheeks burned hot. She grimaced, annoyed with herself. She was an adult. She could sleep with anyone she wanted. She didn't need Sarah's permission. It wasn't like she'd done anything wrong.

With an effort, she kept control of her temper and plastered a smile on her face. "Can I get you a glass of wine? Or perhaps you'd like a beer? I have Corona—your favorite."

Sarah sneered at her. "Ever the perfect hostess, aren't you? Don't you get tired of that bullshit?"

Meghan gaped at her in surprise. She was trying so hard to be nice and Sarah was throwing her efforts back in her face. All of a sudden, she regretted issuing the dinner invitation to her sister.

"I-I'm…" Meghan stammered—at a loss.

"You were always his favorite. Little Miss Princess Perfect. All smiles and sunshine. You could do no wrong. Do you know how much I despised you? How much I *still* despise you?"

The anger and bitterness in Sarah's face took Meghan aback. A tiny frisson of fear shivered down her spine. She risked a glance toward the front door. She wondered where Zane was.

"Don't worry, I made sure to tell Dad how I felt about you, how it sickened me to watch him fawn over you. He didn't even try and hide the fact he loved you more than me."

"Sarah!" she gasped. "How can you talk about Daddy like that? How can you say such things, knowing how much he did for all of us and how he suffered before he died? It isn't right."

Sarah merely chuckled. "Oh, yeah. I know exactly how much he suffered. I don't know how many times I stabbed him, but it was a lot."

Shock held Meghan rigid. She stared at her sister, almost unable to comprehend what the woman had said. A light of madness glittered in Sarah's eyes, filling Meghan with terror. She looked around her once again, seeking a means of escape. Once again, she came up empty.

Her mind went into survival mode. She had to find a way to get Sarah out of her apartment before her sister turned on her. *Please, Zane, get here quickly.* She'd even be happy to see Cody at this point. Anyone to help protect her from the madwoman who stood mere feet away.

The sound of her front door buzzer momentarily distracted both of them. Realizing what it meant, Meghan spun on her heel and raced for the intercom pad. Not even waiting to see who it was, she pressed the button to let them in. Sarah stared at her with venom in her eyes.

"You shouldn't have done that, little sister."

The malice in Sarah's voice chilled Meghan to the bone. She turned to see her sister right behind her, brandishing an evil-looking knife. The long blade winked under the overhead lights. Meghan's legs turned to water. She put her hands out, imploring her sister.

"Sarah, what are you doing?"

"I'm going to kill you, just like I did our father."

Meghan stared at her in horror, still unable to believe the atrocity Sarah had committed. She shook her head in helpless disbelief.

"Why, Sarah? *Why?*" Her voice cracked under the strain.

Sarah cackled. "I told you why. He loved you and hated me. He threw me out of the house! He called me fat and lazy! He cut off my allowance! He treated me abominably! Why do you think I did it?"

All of a sudden, Sarah lunged at her with the knife. Meghan screamed at the same time her visitor pounded on the door. She knew her only chance of escape was if she had someone to help her. Dashing past her sister, she gripped the knob and flung open the door.

Zane filled the opening. Behind him, she glimpsed his partner. Both of them had their guns drawn. She almost collapsed with relief.

"Zane! Thank God!" she gasped.

In one swift movement, he pushed past her and when he saw Sarah brandishing a weapon, he thrust Meghan behind him.

"Put down the knife!" he shouted, training his gun on the woman who laughed at him in glee.

"Oh, it's the knight in shining armor! How lucky for Meghan! Too bad you're not going to be of any use to her."

With that, Sarah lunged at him.

Meghan's scream of terror rang in Zane's ears. Years of training forced him to block the noise and concentrate exclusively on the mad woman in front of him. Willie stood behind him, also armed and hopefully keeping Meghan safe.

Ordinarily, Zane would have fired his weapon toward the very real threat Sarah represented, ensuring her death and his safety. But this was Meghan's sister. He knew how important her family was to her. She'd already lost her father.

Could he be the one responsible for her losing another family member?

Though everything inside him screamed for him to pull the trigger, he hesitated.

Sensing his indecision, Sarah lunged at him again.

Searing pain burned through Zane's chest. Pain like he'd never known before. He looked down in surprise at the blood that stained his shirt.

"Zane!" Meghan screamed.

From the corner of his eye, he saw her running for him. He tried to put out a hand to stop her, but his legs crumbled. Holding on to his side, he fell to the floor. Meghan grabbed a heavy iron skillet that was on the kitchen counter and swung it wildly at Sarah's head. By some stroke of luck, it connected at the same time a shot rang out.

Sarah's mouth opened in a gurgling gasp. Her eyes went wide in shock. She crumpled to the ground. The wailing of police sirens in the distance were the last sounds Zane heard before everything faded to black...

EPILOGUE

It felt like there was a truck sitting on top of Zane's chest. Every breath he took was agony. He thought the pain had been bad when Sarah had knifed him, but it was nothing compared to the way he felt now. Forcing his eyes open, he turned his head, seeking help. Instead, he found Meghan.

Immediately his panic subsided. He drew in a shallow breath and tried not to wince against the pain.

"Zane! You're awake! Oh, thank God! You're awake!"

The relief in her voice was palpable. It made him realize there might have been a time they thought he might not wake up. He tried for a smile, but it was beyond him. Instead, he opened his mouth.

"Hurt," he croaked.

She nodded and leaned over and pressed a soft kiss on his cheek. "I know it hurts. The doctor said you're going to be in a lot of pain for the next few days, until you start to heal. He gave you something for the pain not too long ago. I can call the nurse and see when you're due for another dose."

He nodded and then winced again as the movement pulled against his wound. Cautiously, he looked down and saw the wide white swath of bandage swaddling his chest. He remembered Sarah lunging at him and the burning pain as the knife sliced through his flesh. He remembered feeling surprised at the dark red blood that bloomed on his shirt. It was like it all had happened in slow motion.

He saw Meghan move away and press the buzzer. A few moments later, a nurse came in.

"Oh, good. You're awake," she said in a cheery voice. "I'm Erin. What can I do for you?"

"He's in a lot of pain," Meghan answered for him. "Is there something else you can give him?"

The nurse picked up his chart from the end of the bed and flipped through the pages. After a moment, she nodded. "Doctor's written up a few things here. I'm sure I can find something that will help. I'll be back in a minute."

She closed the door quietly behind her. Zane tried to lift his hand, needing Meghan close. He barely raised it an inch off the mattress, but she seemed to sense his need. She moved closer and took his hand and brought it up to her lips. She pressed a kiss against his knuckles, just like he'd once done to hers. That seemed like a lifetime ago.

"So sorry," he rasped.

"You have nothing to be sorry for."

"Sarah...?"

"She died at the scene."

Tears burned behind his eyes. Despite everything, she'd lost another family member. Though he wasn't directly responsible, it pained him just the same. He remembered Sarah lunging at him and then Meghan charging in with the skillet. Everything happened so fast...

"She was your sister."

Meghan's eyes darkened with emotion. "She was so troubled. I had no idea. She made her choices, just like I did."

"You saved my life," he whispered.

Her hand tightened around his. "I chose you, Zane. I chose *you*." Her eyes darkened with an intensity that halted his breath. She leaned closer, so close her lips caressed his cheeks.

"I love you," she whispered. "I love you with everything I am. I'd die for you. Do you understand?"

She moved slightly away and captured his gaze. The tears that threatened now spilled down his cheeks. He couldn't believe she loved him! And then she moved close again and kissed the moisture away.

"I love you, too." He choked with the emotion that had clogged up his throat and stared up at her through his tears. "I never dreamed I'd find someone to love me the way you do. I don't deserve you."

"*Shh,*" she whispered. "Don't talk such nonsense. You risked your life for me. No one's ever done that.

You don't know what that means to me."

"I'd do it a thousand times over and not think twice," he rasped.

"And I'd do the same. So we're even. Okay?"

She smiled and he did his best to smile, too. The pain in his chest was unbearable, but somehow, with Meghan by his side, he knew he was going to be all right.

Squeezing her hand with all the strength he could muster, he grinned. "Better than okay."

Note To Readers

I do hope you have enjoyed reading Zane and Meghan's story. If you've enjoyed this book, I would appreciate it if you could leave a review for A Toxic Inheritance at Goodreads and your favorite digital retailer. Every review increases visibility and helps other readers to find books they enjoy.

Malicious Love is the next book in The Sydney Legal Series.

Here's a sneak peek:

Successful family law attorney Mallory Patterson has worked hard to put the tragedy of her childhood behind her. She was only ten years old when her mother abandoned her and her father, leaving her marriage and daughter behind to return to her life in her native Argentina. Mallory has keenly felt her absence every day since she left, but she's managed to push the hurt away and make something of her life. She's proud of what she's achieved and her position in Sydney Legal. Even better, she gets to work in the same firm as her beloved father.

Then a body is discovered buried deep inside a cave and Mallory is suddenly filled with questions. When the police identify the body as belonging to her mother, everything Mallory once believed as the truth is suddenly turned on its head.

Is the body in the cave her mother, or have the detectives made a mistake?

PROLOGUE

Joey Fielder's breath came fast. His shoulders ached from the weight of his backpack and he had blisters on both his heels. His mom had warned him about bushwalking in his new joggers, but he'd refused to listen. At the time, he'd been too excited at the thought of exploring with his best friend, Carver Lewis.

They'd been friends since pre-school. At twelve, there wasn't anything they didn't know about each other. They spent all their free time together and now it was the beginning of summer break. Christmas was just around the corner. They had six glorious weeks before they had to return to school and they were determined to make the most of it.

Today, Carver had suggested they explore the walking tracks around West Head, a popular part of the Ku-ring-gai Chase National Park, north of Sydney. He'd sweetened the deal by mentioning to Joey that there were caves in this part of the park.

"Caves?" Joey had asked, his attention now fully on his friend.

"Yeah. Plenty of 'em. There might even be glow worms."

Joey had at once been keen. He loved everything there was about caves. His mom chided him over it, but he didn't care. There was something fascinating about them. Crawling around in the dark, damp spaces made him feel like he was an explorer from another time. Any moment he could discover a lost treasure, hidden for centuries. He'd be famous. And rich.

But they'd been walking for more than two hours and his feet were sore. Carver was getting further and further in front.

"Hey! Wait up!" he called.

Carver turned momentarily. "Come on, slow coach. We haven't got all day"

"How much further is the cave?" Joey panted, tugging his T-shirt down to cover his protruding belly.

"Not far. Come on. Keep going. It'll be worth it. I promise." Carver shot him a wide grin and then turned away, his athletic body and nimble grace making the rough track look easy.

Joey swallowed a sigh and concentrated on putting one foot in front of the other. He couldn't wait to get to the cave so they could take a break. He just hoped the pain was worth it, like Carver assured him.

"There it is!"

Carver's yelp of excitement spurred Joey on. Ignoring the discomfort in his shoulders and the pain in his heels, he picked up his pace and climbed the steep incline that apparently led to the mouth of the cave. Carver stood at the top, peering down at something. Joey hurried the final few steps, his breath coming fast.

"Where is it?" he panted.

"There!"

Carver pointed toward a clump of rocks mostly concealed behind tall grass. Joey frowned.

"I don't see anything." He didn't bother to hide his disappointment.

"It's just there," Carver replied, a hint of impatience in his voice. "Beyond those rocks. See that dark patch? That's the opening."

Joey squinted against the morning sunshine and looked again. At last, he saw it. He was filled with a surge of excitement.

"I see it! You're right! It's the mouth of a cave!"

Carver grinned. "See? I told you, didn't I?"

Joey nodded. Carver had discovered the cave a few weeks earlier. He'd come to school full of excitement about his discovery. Joey had been busy with end of term stuff and hadn't been able to come out here—until now. He let out a *whoop* of excitement.

"Let's go!" he yelled and took off at a run, his blisters and aching shoulders now forgotten.

Carver laughed. "Hey! Wait for me!"

The two boys ran toward the cave entrance. Tugging out flashlights from their backpacks, they made their way inside. The cave's opening was wide enough for them to walk through. It was dank and dark and scary enough to set Joey's heart thumping. He looked across at his friend in the dimness and smiled. Carver's eyes beamed with excitement.

In silence, they made their way further into the cave. The pitch blackness was broken only by the thin beam of their flashlights. Joey put his hand against one wall. The stone was cold and damp. Rough, but soft in the places where moss grew, tickling his fingers.

"Do you think anyone lived here?" Carver whispered. "Like, a million years ago?"

Joey shrugged. "Maybe. It's not real big, but big enough, I guess. Maybe Neanderthal?"

Carver chuckled and Joey grinned. He was being silly, but it felt good. The cave opened up into a kind of room. It was at least two arms' span across and his fingertips could barely graze the roof. He moved his flashlight around the walls, hoping for a glimpse of glowworms.

"Hey! Get over here! I found something!"

The excitement in Carver's voice interrupted Joey's search. He hurried over to where his friend kneeled on the ground, digging at the loose earth with his fingers.

Joey dropped to the ground beside him. "What is it?"

"I don't know. It feels like some kind of blanket."

Joey ran his flashlight over the area. There was definitely some kind of raised area on the ground. Carver kept digging and finally pulled on the edge of what looked like a piece of carpet.

Joey kept the light stead. Each tug Carver gave revealed more of the rug. It was like it had been rolled up and left there. It had been there a long time by the look of it.

"Oh, my God!"

Carver's cry was filled with alarm. Joey stared down. Bones the color of chalk gleamed in the dimness. Ribs, finger bones, a skull...

"Shit!"

The curse word fell from Joey's lips as he scrambled backwards. He was glad his mom wasn't there. She'd ground him if she'd heard. Twelve-year-old boys were not supposed to curse.

"What the hell is it?" he asked, his heart still thumping.

Carver looked as scared as he felt. "I don't know. It looks like a skeleton."

Joey nodded grimly, keeping his distance. "Yeah, that's what I thought, too."

"Who do you think it is?" Carver whispered, his eyes wide in the dimness.

"I don't know. But whoever it is has been here a long time."

Malicious Love will be released on
30 April, 2019 and is available for pre-order
from your favorite digital retailer.

About the Author

Chris Taylor grew up on a farm in north-west New South Wales, Australia. She always had a thirst for stories and recalls writing her first book at the ripe old age of eight. Always a lover of romance and happily-ever-afters, a career in criminal law sparked her interest in intrigue and suspense. For Chris to be able to combine romance with suspense in her books is a dream come true.

Chris is married to Linden and is the mother of five children. If not behind her computer, you can find her doing the school run, taxiing children to swimming lessons, football, ballet and cricket. In her spare time, Chris loves to read her favorite authors who include Richard North Patterson, Sandra Brown, Kathleen E Woodiwiss and Jude Devereaux.

You can find out more about Chris and sign up for her newsletter at her website:

http://www.christaylorauthor.com.au

* 9 7 8 1 9 2 5 1 1 9 6 0 2 *